DEADLY GAMES

A Jamie Austen Thriller

TERRY TOLER

Deadly Games

Published by: BeHoldings, LLC

Copyright ©2022, **BeHoldings, LLC**
Terry Toler
All Rights Reserved

All rights reserved. No part of this publication may be reproduced, stored in a retrieval system, or transmitted in any form, or by any means – electronic, mechanical, photocopying, recording or otherwise – without prior written permission.

Book Cover: BeHoldings Publishing
Editor: Donna Toler

For information email: terry@terrytoler.com.

Our books can be purchased in bulk for promotional, educational, and business use. Please contact your bookseller or the BeHoldings Publishing Sales department at: *sales@terrytoler.com*

For booking information email: booking@terrytoler.com.
First U.S. Edition: July 2022
Printed in the United States of America

ISBN 978-1-954710-14-6

This is a work of fiction. All of the characters, organizations, and events portrayed in this novel are either products of the author's imagination or are used fictitiously. Any resemblance to actual persons, living or dead is entirely coincidental.

OTHER BOOKS BY TERRY TOLER

Fiction

The Longest Day
The Reformation of Mars
The Late, Great Planet Jupiter
The Great Wall of Ven-Us
Saturn: The Eden Experiment
The Mercury Protocols
Save The Girls
The Ingenue
Saving Sara
Save The Queen
No Girl Left Behind
The Launch
The Blue Rose
Body Count
Save Me Twice
Cliff Hangers: Anna
Cliff Hangers: Mr. & Mrs. Platt
Cliff Hangers: The Quarterback
Cliff Hangers: Macy
Cliff Hangers: The Book Club
Triggers

Non-Fiction

How to Make More Than a Million Dollars
The Heart Attacked
Seven Years of Promise
Mission Possible
Marriage Made in Heaven
21 Days to Physical Healing
21 Days to Spiritual Fitness
21 Days to Divine Health
21 Days to a Great Marriage
21 Days to Financial Freedom
21 Days to Sharing Your Faith

21 Days to Mission Possible
7 Days to Emotional Freedom
Uncommon Finances
Uncommon Health
Uncommon Marriage
The Jesus Diet
Suddenly Free
Feeling Free

For more information on these books and other resources visit terrytoler.com.

Thank you for purchasing this novel from best-selling author Terry Toler. As an additional thank you, Terry wants to give you a free gift.

Sign up for:

Updates
New Releases
Announcements

At terrytoler.com

We'll send you a copy of *The Book Club*, a Cliff Hangers mystery, free of charge.

1

Somewhere over Turkey

Running a spy mission at 41,000 feet wasn't something I'd ever done before or ever wanted to do again.

On paper, in the comfort of an air-conditioned secured conference room at Mossad headquarters in Tel Aviv, it seemed like a good idea. The targets, two Turkish oligarchs, along with their six heavily armed bodyguards, would be in a confined space. A corporate jet. With nowhere to run or hide.

In reality, it wasn't such a good idea. The six heavily armed bodyguards were in a confined space with nowhere to run or hide. Same for me. That's what made it problematic.

Kill or be killed were the only two options. Like gladiators in an arena. The octagon being the fuselage of an airplane.

A few minutes from now, when the shootout happened, I had to kill all six bodyguards before they fired a shot. If they somehow managed to get a shot off, one of two things would happen. Neither of them good. The bullet would either hit me or miss me.

Either way, I was likely screwed.

If a bullet hit me, it's not hard to figure out why that was bad. If it missed, stray bullets on an airplane were never a good thing.

Any number of things could happen to that bullet. It could hit a window and blow it out. That's a big problem. The plane would depressurize within seconds. All the oxygen in the room, so to speak, would be sucked into oblivion. Anything not tied down would be pulled violently in that direction and forced out of the aircraft into the earth's atmosphere.

A person sitting next to the window, even though ten to twenty times the size of the nine by twelve-inch window hole, would be sucked through it and sent for the ride of his life, if not strapped in.

Who wears a seat belt on a corporate jet?

Nobody.

Also, assuming the bolts of the seat attached to the floor hold.

All the possible scenarios bounced around my head like a pinball in an arcade machine. Or ping pong balls flying around in the glass container about to reveal the numbers for this week's Powerball.

If I wasn't sucked out of the plane, I had far more worries. The cabin would lose all pressure. Oxygen masks would drop. I had less than a minute to get one of those masks over my nose and mouth, or I'd become disoriented from the lack of oxygen. Three minutes before I was dead.

Hard to shoot a gun while trying to fiddle with an oxygen mask. There were no inflight instructions for such a scenario. I made up my own.

If you're traveling with someone who's trying to kill you, put your oxygen mask on first, then kill them. Once the mask is on your face, breathe normally.

Yeah right!

I had six armed goons trying to kill me. I wouldn't be breathing normally until ten minutes after all of them were dead.

If you don't have enough time to put your mask on, Jamie, then don't worry about it. You'll die either way.

I tried to tamp down the smile on my face. The thoughts in my head were cracking me up. Releasing the tension if nothing else. I couldn't let the other bodyguards see it. They'd know I was up to something.

I turned my mind back to the more dire thoughts.

Even if I did manage to kill the six bodyguards and get the oxygen mask over my face, the pilots would have to gain control over a depressurized airplane. Not always easy to do. If they couldn't, then I'd be better off without the oxygen mask. All it did was prolong the inevitable and make the last few minutes of my life shear torture as we plunged out of the sky and crashed to the ground.

How was that better than taking a bullet and getting it over with immediately?

It wasn't.

Of course, the bullet might not hit a window. Probably wouldn't. At least, those were the odds.

If a stray bullet punched a small hole in the aluminum skin of the airplane, it might cause a minor leak, but the aircraft was designed to compensate for it. Even a few small holes would have no effect. That meant I had more time to kill the six bad guys.

But then there's the wiring.

The hydraulics. They ran from the back of the plane to the front. If a bullet damaged them all kinds of things might occur.

It could damage the entertainment system wiring. No big deal. We wouldn't be able to watch an inflight movie. *Die Hard* was playing on the televisions at that moment. I hoped that wasn't an omen.

The biggest worry. The stray bullet could damage the hydraulics. Then we'd all die. Come crashing down to the earth. The laws of gravity would override survival instincts.

Not my worst fear, but close.

My mission would be a failure.

Not an option.

Why was I even taking this great a risk? For the four girls up there with me. I wasn't there to kill a few bodyguards or Turkish oligarchs. I was there for the flight attendants.

The sex slaves. Human trafficking victims.

I wished they knew who I was. Jamie Austen. Highly trained operative. A spy. I can take care of them. I was there to save them from their plight.

To them I was a bad guy. One of the tormentors. The bodyguard of an oligarch who was going to make them have sex with him sometime during the flight. Actually a Mossad agent, also there to rescue them.

How could they possibly know I was risking my life to save them?

Hard to believe they were sex slaves by looking at them. Beautiful. Well dressed. Educated. Israeli citizens. Fresh out of college. Which was why Mossad was involved. Mossad was the intelligence arm of the Israeli military. The equivalent of our CIA.

I worked for them.

Another thing hard to believe. Jamie Austen, the CIA's most valuable spook for more than ten years was no longer in their employ. I ran more missions for them than I can count.

For years, I was the deadliest female assassin on the planet. Still was. But the CIA wouldn't touch me with a ten-foot pole. Even though I was trained by them. At the Farm. By Curly.

Now, I'm *persona non grata* to the CIA. Too hot to handle. After the fiasco with CIA Director Fuller, no one in the executive branch of my government wanted to touch me or my husband, Alex Halee. Who happened to be the foremost computer hacker in the world and the second best assassin on the planet.

Although, he'd argue that last point. He'd say he's the best. No way to prove it without one of us killing the other. Since we were married, that could happen someday.

Anyway. I digress. The US government's loss was Mossad's gain. Alex and I agreed to run this operation for them. One of two missions we agreed to do on their behalf.

I was dreading mission number two just as much as this one. But, at the moment, I didn't have time to think about it. If I didn't live through the next five minutes, there wouldn't be a second mission.

Back to the girls.

Several months ago, someone ran ads in a Tel Aviv newspaper advertising for flight attendants to serve private functions on corporate jets. Above average pay. Only thin, beautiful women needed to apply. More than seven hundred did. They interviewed at a local hotel. One hundred were accepted.

They showed up for training and were never heard from again. They disappeared faster than a cloud in the sky. Without a trace.

Alex and I were called in to find them. It didn't take long. The girls were being trafficked. Instead of flight attendants, they were put on flights with Middle Eastern oligarchs and flown to various destinations. Expected to provide sexual favors to the clientele. The flights went from one private airstrip to another, and the girls were always under armed guard. Escape was impossible.

Rescuing them was my job. With Alex's help, we tracked them to Jordan. Not so bad. I expected them to be in Iran or Russia. That didn't make it any less dangerous, just easier to operate in Jordan than in a closed country where I could be arrested and could easily disappear never to be heard from again.

We infiltrated the organization. While we didn't find their main headquarters of operation, we did manage to make contact with them. Mossad had a man who was able to pass himself off as a Turkish oligarch and got me on one of the planes. Traveling as his bodyguard.

When we arrived at the private airstrip at the appointed time, the other bodyguards mocked me.

"She's a woman," one of the men said. Laughing.

I pushed up my sleeves and balled my fists. I got in his face. "Give me all of ten seconds and I'll show you what a woman can do."

The Mossad agent separated me from the man. That didn't stop the chatter. I gave as much as I took. But that's how I got on the plane with a gun. It was good that they underestimated me.

Once we boarded the flight, a truce ensued, and he hadn't looked at me since. I'd looked at him. I couldn't wait to put a bullet between his eyes.

The problem was that he wasn't the only threat. Each oligarch had two bodyguards and two more were assigned to guard the girls.

I was outnumbered. Six to one. Not good odds.

That meant I had to draw my gun, fire six shots, and kill all of them before any of them got off a shot. It also meant I couldn't miss.

No problem. I hadn't missed what I was aiming at in years. Curly taught me that. Don't fire unless you're sure you're going to hit something. *A bullet is a terrible thing to waste,* he used to say.

May he rest in peace. I missed my mentor and best friend other than Alex. Although Curly would tell me I was a fool for taking on this mission.

Missing wasn't the problem. Getting the shots off in time was the issue.

Curly was probably right. I was well trained, but I didn't know about the six bodyguards. If they were well trained, they'd get off a shot and wouldn't miss, and I'd be dead. If they weren't well trained, they'd get off a shot and miss and we might all die.

Which brought me back to my biggest worry. The stray bullet doesn't hit the window or the hydraulics. It hits the fuel tank.

The whole plane blows up.

I can't let that happen. The only control I had was not to miss. Six bullets had to hit their marks in a little over six seconds.

Not impossible. Not likely either.

I had to live through this. For the girls.

Four girls were on the plane, but I had ninety-six more to rescue after I saved these four.

I took in a deep breath.

Here goes.

I made eye contact with the Mossad agent. Signaling him that I was about to act. His eyes shifted back and forth. I couldn't tell if he was ready or nervous. Or both. Regardless, once the bullets started flying there was no turning back.

Nowhere to run. Nowhere to hide.

Forty-one thousand feet in the air.

Not a good idea, Curly said in my head.

Too late now.

2

Celerina Olympia Bobrun
St. Moritz, Switzerland

Alex Halee had done a lot of stupid things over the years while running missions for the CIA, but this felt like the dumbest thing he'd ever done.

A few years before, he snuck across the Demilitarized Zone into North Korea and let himself be captured, tortured, and thrown into prison. All so he could infiltrate a cyberwarfare lab run by the notorious Pok. As if that wasn't dangerous enough, he broke out of prison and went on the run with a young Korean girl, Bae Hwa, who had stolen nuclear codes from Iranian terrorists.

Dumb.

This was dumber.

Alex once commandeered a helicopter carrying a dirty bomb in London. He killed the terrorists who were determined to explode the bomb in downtown London on the Queen's birthday. With the timer ticking away, he flew the bomb out of the city and into a remote area where it detonated. He barely escaped with his life but saved tens of thousands of lives. For his efforts, he was granted knighthood by the Queen.

He was more scared now than he had been then.

Why was he so nervous? Those who knew him thought he had ice running through his veins. Curly trained him not to be afraid of anything.

Alex thought he wasn't. He'd been shot at more times than he could count and that never bothered him. In most circles, he was considered the foremost assassin and spy operative in the world.

His wife, Jamie was second. She'd argue the point. She thought she was better, but she was wrong. He was.

No way to prove it though.

Alex took a deep breath. The cold air felt like sharp needles in his lungs. The sun had been in hiding since they arrived two days ago. Snow fell lightly from the sky in a powdery mist wetting his helmet and visor. Overnight brought almost a foot of fresh snow.

Also part of the problem. Alex hated the cold. The shivering contributed to the anxiety.

He needed to find a way to warm his body and tamp down the fear.

He talked to Jamie about it the night before even though it hurt his claim of being the best operative in the world. She thought he was being a wuss. Not supportive at all. She practically mocked him.

"You're going sledding tomorrow," she had said. "I'm getting on a plane with six terrorists carrying guns."

"I'll gladly trade with you."

"Be careful not to get hurt in a snowball fight either," she said. Her words dripped with sarcasm.

He wanted to ignore the snarky comment, but couldn't help but push back.

"It's not a sled," Alex argued. "It's a bobsled. They are extremely dangerous. Seventeen people have died bobsledding."

"Forty-three people a day die from falling in the shower," Jamie quipped. "Be careful when you wash your hair tomorrow. If you fall, you might not even make it to the winter playdate with your friends."

"Forty-three people don't die every day in the shower," Alex said. "You're making that up."

"It's true. Look it up."

Turned out, it was true. He did look it up. Something like fifteen thousand people a year died while getting in or out of the shower. Alex didn't know how Jamie knew that piece of worthless information, but she did.

Anyway, she could mock him all she wanted. This was a dangerous mission. He wasn't going to let her downplay it.

He also wasn't going to argue with her anymore. He didn't want her mad at him.

That thought brought a smile to his face.

If Jamie were angry at him, he'd be more frightened than he was now. Making her mad would be dumber than what he was doing at that moment. A lot of men had done that over the years and paid a serious price for their stupidity. Most of them weren't breathing anymore.

Knowing Jamie, those six terrorists were dead or would be shortly. He almost felt guilty. She was right. He was fretting about riding a sled.

When he looked at it that way, he felt better. Momentarily.

Until he realized they were next in line. The five-hundred-pound, state-of-the-art bobsled, purchased by the Israeli Olympic Committee, was being placed into position at the starting line.

John Keller, the team leader and driver of the bobsled, suddenly had a sense of urgency in his voice which shocked Alex back into reality. "Let's go over your instructions again," he said to Alex.

"I've got them," Alex replied. "Run like a banshee for five seconds. Jump on the bobsled. Hang on and lean into turns. Simple."

"It wasn't simple when we practiced it," John said. "You were having a hard time running on the ice."

Who is good at running on ice? If God had intended us to run on ice, we'd have feet like polar bears or penguins.

Alex didn't say what he was thinking. Instead, he just made an excuse. "I need longer spikes."

"You can't have longer spikes. They'll get caught in the ice and you'll trip. You could fall at the start. The last thing you want is to slide down half the course before anyone can get to you. Trust me. You don't want to go on that nightmare ride."

John knew what he was talking about. The man had more than ten years experience in the sport of bobsledding. He was the epitome of perseverance. Israel had never won a medal at the Winter Olympics. John was determined to change that.

Ten years ago, with no experience whatsoever, he decided to start an Israeli bobsledding team. Not so easy to do in the middle of a desert.

He got no support. No money from the Olympic Committee. No sponsors. He also didn't have a clue about how to drive a bobsled.

After running into too many obstacles to overcome, John decided to learn how to skeleton. Another form of bobsledding. An individual sport. John joked that they called it skeleton, because you risked breaking every bone in your body.

The skeleton was more dangerous than the bobsled. One person plummeted headfirst on the frozen track, lying on a small sled, reaching speeds of eighty miles an hour. Alex would rather try to climb Mount Everest.

John actually made the Olympics in that sport but didn't medal. It made him a national hero though. He never gave up on his dream to build a bobsled team. A year ago, he finally secured a sponsor.

What he did to get the bobsled team qualified in that short of time was nothing short of a miracle. He persevered and pulled a team together and they worked their tails off. When they qualified by .02 tenths of a second, their spot at the Olympics was secured.

That's when Mossad intervened and put Alex on the team.

John was livid. He didn't understand. The team was gelling. Why disrupt the chemistry? How was he supposed to choose which member to kick off? To make matters worse, Alex had zero experience. John would have to train Alex from scratch. They only had three months. It made no sense.

John had no idea Alex was on a top-secret mission. He thought Alex was being forced on him by the powers that be as some kind of political favor. Maybe Alex was the son of a powerful man.

He let his disdain for Alex be known at every opportunity.

For the last four weeks, they'd been training in Tel Aviv. Training consisted of wind sprints. High intensity interval training. Thirty second sprints. A minute of rest. Repeat. For hours at a time.

Alex thought he was going to die before he ever made it to the bobsled track. Every muscle in his body ached like he'd been tortured in a prison. It did get him in shape though. The best shape of his life since he had been put through the ringer at The Farm, by Curly.

While they could work on conditioning in Israel, Alex couldn't actually learn bobsledding. That's why they were in St. Moritz, Switzerland. To train on an actual track. With their new top-of-the-line bobsled. No expense was spared to make sure this team made a good showing at the Olympics. Not for the competition but for the ruse.

Alex and Jamie were to find the terrorists and kill them. Mossad would spare no expense to make that happen.

John at least appreciated the new sled and realized they wouldn't have the new ride if not for Alex, so he accepted it, and was trying to make the best of it.

"Are you good?" John asked Alex as they neared their turn at the starting line. "The team is only as good as its weakest link."

That meant the team wasn't very good and John knew it. Any hope of a medal was gone. The best they could hope for was not to embarrass themselves.

"Don't worry about me," Alex said. "I'll be fine."

His words were said with more confidence than he was feeling.

"We're not worried about our time today," John said to the entire team who were gathered around him. "It's all about getting down the course without killing ourselves."

"I'm all for that," Alex said.

John forced a grin although his eyes betrayed him. He was concerned as he looked away from Alex and down the hill at the winding bobsled course. Fifteen curves. 1772 meters. 130 meters drop in elevation. They'd reach speeds of ninety miles an hour.

What sled goes ninety miles an hour, Jamie?

This would be their first bobsled run as a team. On the oldest bobsled course in the world. And the most famous. St. Moritz. Where bobsledding was invented. Courses were few and far between. Sixteen total in the world. Alex was supposed to be in awe of the opportunity.

He'd rather be in a dentist's chair.

Only ten such courses existed in Europe. Two in the U.S. One in Canada. This was the only one made from natural snow and ice. Covering concrete. That's what made it special. All the other courses used artificial ice and snow.

Teams came from all over the world to train there. Getting on the course was equivalent to playing the Masters golf course in America.

John and the other members of the team were clearly excited. *Good for them.*

The view at the top was stunning. Alex would give them that. Except that the goal was to be at the bottom within a few seconds and without crashing.

Stupid.

"Don't forget to check your chin strap," Mark said.

Mark "Handy" Handelman was a second team member. He handled the braking. On every four-man team was a driver, a braker, and two pushers. John drove, Handy braked, and Matthew and Alex pushed.

And hung on for dear life.

Why was he there?

Because someone in Mossad, Saul Geller to be more precise, got the not-so-bright idea to run a mission at the Olympics. Apparently, Mossad had good intelligence that terrorists intended to launch an attack on Israeli Olympic athletes during the upcoming Winter Olympics in Bavaria, Germany. The same country where terrorists killed eleven Israeli athletes at the Munich games in 1972.

Alex and Jamie were to pose as Olympic athletes, find the terrorist cell, and take it out. Alex had no problem posing. Pretending to be an athlete. This went beyond that. He was expected to compete. Make it believable.

He didn't even believe it himself. How was he going to make others believe he was really a bobsledder?

He was given three months to become a real Olympic athlete. People trained their whole lives for this opportunity. How was he supposed to do it in three months?

And why did it have to be the bobsled? Why couldn't it have been curling? That didn't look dangerous at all.

The only consolation was that he wasn't asked to be a ski jumper. At least, on the bobsled, he was in a vehicle that remained on the ground for 130 meters. The ski jumper flew the 130 meters in the air!

Alex could see the ski jumping training facility off in the distance.

No thank you.

Jamie was luckier. She got to be a biathlete. Meaning she got to flit around on cross country skis and shoot a rifle at targets. No danger in that. Some people were saying Jamie was really good at it. Alex figured she would be.

How hard could it be?

Saul said they weren't expected to win. Just compete. Jamie wasn't wired that way. She wanted to win a gold medal. That was her competitive nature. Alex was competitive as well, but he'd be satisfied if he didn't die.

He was focused on the real mission. Protecting the athletes. Nine of them. Four skaters. The bobsled team. And Jamie.

The nervousness returned with a vengeance when the last team before them cleared the course. They were up next. Alex felt his heart begin to race.

Handy motioned to Alex to check his chin strap again. Not necessary. The strap was so tight, it cut into Alex's chin. After what happened to Handy, Alex wasn't taking any chances.

Handy was paralyzed from the waist down.

Several years ago, in a bobsled competition, Handy's chinstrap was too loose on his helmet. During a competition run, the visor dropped below his eyes, and he couldn't see. He didn't brake at the right time and the bobsled smashed into the wall at the end. He broke his back in several places and would never walk again.

Handy was already sitting in the bobsled. An obscure rule allowed for a member to start from inside the bobsled. Not ideal, for any number of reasons. The start, the first five seconds of the run, were the most important. At least that's where the race could be lost. All four members of the team were generally outside the bobsled to give it a running start. An all-out sprint for five seconds.

The disadvantage was they'd only have three pushing. Alex was bigger and stronger than Handy, so if he could get up to speed, it might even out.

All morning, they'd practiced the start over and over again. Alex wasn't good at running on ice. He wasn't as fast as the other, more experienced sledders. He also wasn't good at getting into the moving sled. Once the five seconds was up, Alex had only a few precious seconds to get in position. A challenge in and of itself. At the right moment, the team members had to do what they called "load."

While the sled was still moving, they had to jump into the bobsled one at a time. With precision. Careful not to bump or impede the other team members which would cost them valuable time.

Sounded easier than it was. Alex brought up the rear and had yet to do it right in practice.

Curly would think Alex was crazy to even try it.

Actually, if he saw Alex right now, he'd die laughing. Alex would never hear the end of it. He was wearing a skintight aerodynamic suit, designed for bobsledders. So skin tight, Alex felt like he was naked. He kept wanting to put his hands over his private parts.

Underneath was what was called a burn suit.

A burn suit?

To protect from burns on the ice. Should he be ejected out of the bobsled or fall at the start.

Please God, don't let that happen.

It was time.

Alex could hear his heartbeat in his ears. Alex's hands gripped the bar attached to the bobsled. They rocked it back and forth to gain momentum.

The countdown started. Ten seconds. 9. 8. 7. 6.

It felt like a NASA countdown.

Alex felt the sudden urge to check his chinstrap again.

He let out the breath he was holding.

The buzzer sounded. He took off sprinting as fast as he could.

So fast, Alex struggled to keep up. The other men were faster than him.

The five seconds passed in a blur.

Alex prepared to load.

As he did, he felt his foot begin to slide. He couldn't gain traction to push off.

The other two pushers were in the bobsled. Alex was hanging on to the bar.

He wasn't going to make it. The bobsled was traveling too fast.

He had to let go.

He landed headfirst. Hard.

His face splattered on the ice. The visor shattered but was the only thing that saved him.

He suddenly remembered the words. "Don't fall at the start. You might slide down half the course before anyone can get to you. You don't want to go on that nightmare ride."

Alex felt his body picking up speed heading for the edge which was right before him. Like Niagara Falls. He couldn't see the drop coming. He could see the bobsled speeding away without him.

Why did I agree to do this?

Stupid.

3

Murphy's law can rear its ugly head at 41,000 feet as easily as it does on the ground.

How could everything go wrong all at once?

I'd been worried about three things. Four actually. A bullet hitting me. That didn't happen. A stray bullet hitting the fuel tank. That didn't either since the plane was still in the air.

The other two biggest fears did come to pass. A bullet blew out a window. A huge hole in the side of the aircraft to be more precise. A bullet also hit the hydraulics. Apparent, because of the sudden serpentine of the aircraft which rocked back and forth like a baby in a cradle.

Hopefully, the four girls were safe. Earlier, they'd gone into the back of the plane to prepare to do what they were brought there for. To be sex slaves for the oligarchs who paid big money for the opportunity.

Their choices were to service the men or die. Each of the two oligarchs would take their turn with the girls. They could choose one or all four at once. In any order. A decision up to them.

The Mossad agent, Geli, was there to participate as well. He told the other two oligarchs that he'd go last. Although, no one was going back in that room.

I'd die before I let that happen.

"So, you don't mind being the last horse at the trough," one of the oligarchs said to Geli, disgustingly.

I wanted to slap him to the other side of the universe if that were even possible.

When the girls went in the back and were still alone, that's when I decided to act. Their two guards stood in front of the door that led to the bedroom. The men had their hands crossed in front of them and their eyes semi alert. The armed thugs probably weren't expecting trouble but were more on the ball than the other four bodyguards who were sitting in their chairs to my left.

One slept, two skimmed through magazines, and one stared out the window. I sat in a seat to the right of the plane riding backwards. Next to Geli. The two Turkish oligarchs were in the lounge area near the bar. One right next to the window.

Both looked like a couple of horny teenagers at a prom.

Revolting.

I wanted to wipe those lustful looks off their faces by putting a bullet in the bridge of their noses.

But my focus had to be on the six bodyguards. The Mossad agent was presumably ready to take out the two oligarchs.

When we were ready, I stood to my feet and stretched. With a plan in place. It seemed prudent to take out the two guards in the back who were best prepared to get a shot off at me. I wore black leggings and a tight form fitting black shirt, covered by a black leather jacket. The jacket concealed my weapon, although everyone on the plane knew I had one.

After I bent down and touched my toes, I straightened and put my hand in my jacket, but didn't touch my gun. Instead, I pretended to scratch an itch. The two bodyguards in the back flinched at the sudden movement, but then relaxed. Which was what I wanted. When I reached a second time, they'd just think I was scratching again.

By the time they saw the weapon in my hand, it was too late for them.

Tap. Tap.

Two shots. Above each nose. Efficient. One barely had time to move his hand toward his gun. The other simply stood there stunned for about a second. Not knowing what hit him.

Gunfire sounded strange on a plane. It's the first time I'd ever fired a weapon inside an airplane. Hopefully, it'd be the last.

Ideally, I would've shot each of them twice, but I had to fire six rounds within seconds. Dead was dead. One shot above the bridge of the nose would be sufficient.

That's when everything went to hell in a handbasket. Although, I wasn't sure exactly what that term meant. Curly hated it and said to never use it. A handbasket was for carrying bread. Like Hansel and Gretel.

Curly used a different four-letter word to describe what I was facing at that moment.

It wasn't my fault.

Things were going as planned from my perspective. I spun toward the four remaining bodyguards with the element of surprise on my side. I began to kill them in the proper order and with precision. The one sleeping would be last for obvious reasons. Right after the two holding the magazines. First to die was the one looking out the window. He was distracted but his hands were free.

When window guy heard the first two gunshots, he looked my way. Perfect. I swept my gun toward him and put a bullet between his eyes. His brain didn't even have time to process what was happening or reach for his weapon.

First magazine guy was dead two seconds later.

What happened next was a blur. Because I didn't see what happened, I could only speculate.

A shot rang out behind me. The Mossad agent no doubt. Out of the corner of my eye, I saw one of the oligarchs slumped in his chair. The next thing I knew, a bullet struck a window next to where the other oligarch was sitting and blew it out.

Along with the entire seat. Jerked right out of the floor and through the skin of the aircraft with such force it sounded like a crane had fallen inside the cabin.

I almost didn't believe it.

The airplane jerked.

The rushing wind sounded like a freight train was barreling down on us.

The sudden movement caused me to lose my balance and prevented me from firing the last two shots. The back of one of the seats was nearby and I reached out to steady myself.

I needed a breath and tried to take one. All I could do was gasp in panic.

All the oxygen had literally been sucked out of the cabin. The yellow oxygen masks deployed, but I still had the two threats to contend with and couldn't take the time to put one over my nose and mouth.

Tap. One of the threats went down quickly. The bullet hit him in the side of his head. As I prepared to fire another shot the plane suddenly lurched violently to the right, throwing me toward the open hole.

I fell to the floor of the plane. Probably the only thing that saved me. I was able to reach out and grab the metal legs of the seat where I'd been sitting and hung on for dear life.

The plane bounced me up and down, but I maintained my grip. Praying that the bolts and brackets of the seat would hold. My body was stretched out like a flag flapping in the breeze on a flagpole.

The pressure on my head and ears was intense. Like a huge vacuum cleaner was sucking me toward the blue sky and white clouds I could see through the hole in the side of the plane.

Then I saw a flash of light.

Geli had fired wildly. I assume that's what hit the hydraulic wiring. The plane then lost all control. It dropped several thousand feet at once.

My stomach felt like it was in my throat. My ears were popping. I lost my grip on the seat and was suddenly at the top of the aircraft where I banged hard against the ceiling. Pinned there for several seconds by the G forces.

At least, it took away the threat of me flying out the open hole. Curly always said to find the bright side in every situation. Even the bad ones.

It didn't get any worse than this.

The plane dipped like the waves in a wave pool. I dropped like a dead weight to the floor. So hard it would've knocked the breath out of me if I had any in my lungs.

I desperately needed to get to an oxygen mask.

But the final threat still faced me. He had the advantage. He was still in his seat and on the opposite side of the aircraft from the massive hole which seemed to be getting bigger.

I wondered if the aircraft was going to break in two.

Somehow, the gun was still in my hand.

Two forces were working against each other. The hole in the plane tried to pull me toward it. With a powerful suction motion. The loss of hydraulics caused unseen forces to pull me in the opposite direction. It felt like my body was going to snap in two like a twig in a tornado.

For whatever reason, I thought of Alex riding the sled down the hill and his comment that he preferred to be doing what I was doing. I doubt he'd feel that way now.

If I didn't do something soon, I'd never see him again.

The plane stabilized momentarily allowing me to regain my feet. That gave the bodyguard the chance to get his bearings as well. His gun was now pointed in my direction.

He fired several shots.

The sound of the rushing wind was so loud, I actually didn't hear the gunshots. But I saw the flashes of light and instinctively ducked and felt the bullets whiz by. Either by my imagination or I actually felt them.

I dove behind a seat. A lot of good that would do me. A bullet would go through the seat cushions like a knife through butter.

So, I got low to the ground and looked for anything that might make a better shield.

The television on the wall was my first thought. Held on by a bracket which had broken and was hanging by its wires. The back wall that led into the cockpit was behind me. Interestingly enough, the wiring for the entertainment system still worked. *Die Hard* still played on the screen.

Don't remind me.

In movies, the main guy got shot at hundreds of times and always got out of his predicaments. This was real life. My fate wasn't written into a script that everyone had to follow.

I was going to die hard if I didn't do something.

Even if I managed to kill the remaining threat, we were likely going to die anyway. We had a big hole in the side of the plane and no hydraulics. The plane continued to descend rapidly. Crashing in the ground seemed inevitable.

As long as I was alive, I'd keep fighting. Curly drilled that in me.

The plane kept changing speeds. Going faster, then slowing down. Like the pilots were trying everything they could to stabilize the aircraft. The instability of the plane helped me as much as it hurt me. The G forces had pulled the gunman back into his seat.

The plane rocked back and forth again. Like a drunken man trying to walk a straight line. Wobbling. Dipping up and down. Then side to side. I could only imagine what the pilots were thinking or doing to try and stop it.

The gunman fired again, but he missed badly. I raised my weapon and steadied my hand.

Thank you, Curly.

I could shoot with the plane lurching. Curly had made me practice it. He sat me in an office chair and spun it around in a circle expecting me to hit the targets. If I didn't, I had to continue practicing until I did.

The last bodyguard didn't seem to have that skill. He fired wildly several more times. He must've realized he was getting low on ammunition, because he stopped firing and waited for an opportunity to aim and fire.

Not finding one, he became resourceful. He grabbed the dead man sitting in the seat next to him and used him as a shield. I held my fire. No use filling the dead man with more bullets. I had thirteen left. More than enough.

Curly taught me to count my number of bullets. So I'd always know how many I had left.

The bodyguard still had the advantage. He was in his seat. The oxygen mask was within reach. I had to give up my position to reach one. The gunman pulled it down over his face and took in a deep breath.

I'd been holding my breath for at least a minute and was starting to feel my lungs burn. Smoke from the engine also filled the cabin, giving me a new worry. Because of the heightened adrenaline, my body screamed at me to find air. Every last bit of oxygen inside of me had been scarfed up by the panic going on inside.

When bullets start flying, the body fills itself with a rush of hormones to give you the adrenaline to face the threat. Normally, you start breathing faster. Panting almost.

I couldn't. I had to function without oxygen. Soon, I'd start to border on delirium.

Curly taught me how to respond to that adversity as well. He made me fire at targets while he stood behind me with his hands over my nose and mouth for more than a minute. He deprived me of oxygen. Then forced me to make good decisions and clean shots until I nearly passed out.

Geli had an oxygen mask over his face but was too far away to help me with mine. He fired several shots at the remaining assailant, but the bullet struck the man he was using as a shield.

Don't do that.

I didn't want any more stray bullets. The aircraft was probably going to crash anyway, but why make things worse by hitting the fuel tank. Or blowing another hole in the other side.

Then the idea hit me. Why not blow out another window?

What would it hurt?

I fired a shot before thinking it through. The bullet went through the window directly behind the bodyguard. It exploded. He was pulled toward it. He struggled to grab something. I was no longer his main worry.

He released his grip on the man shielding him and fought to grab anything to keep himself from being sucked out the window. His chest was exposed. I steadied my aim. Blinked several times and shook my head from side to side to keep from losing consciousness.

It worked and my focus returned. Having my bearings helped me time the rocking which was more uniform and predictable.

Tap. Tap. Tap.

Three shots. Two above the bridge of the gunman's nose. One on the forehead.

Alex would say I was showing off.

Just in time. I stood to my feet and struggled to stand. Staggered like a punch-drunk fighter.

The yellow lifeline was within reach. I put it over my nose and mouth and sucked in the precious oxygen. The air was cold in my throat and lungs. It felt good.

All the threats were dead.

Geli was next to me now. I took the mask off and shouted to him, "Go check on the girls."

I pointed to the back.

"Where are you going?" he shouted back.

"To the cockpit. To see if we're going to crash."

4

The two pilots were fighting the controls. At least, they had their oxygen masks on and appeared to be calm. I donned a mask and put on a headset so we could communicate.

"What happened?" they asked me.

"There was a traitor on board," I said. "One of the bodyguards tried to kill my client. I took him out. He shot two holes in the cabin."

"Our hydraulic pressure is falling fast," the pilot said. He might've been calm, but I could sense the panic in his voice. He sat forward in his seat and his arms were taut as he wrestled the steering wheel of the plane.

"Can you get us on the ground?" I asked.

"That's where we're headed either way."

His eyes flitted back and forth between me, the controls, and the horizon. We were still above the clouds, but the controls on the dashboard read we were below twenty-thousand feet and descending fast.

At least we hadn't fallen out of the sky like an out-of-control meteor.

The copilot said, "We're in communication with air traffic control. The nearest airport is twenty minutes away. I told them to prepare for a crash landing."

"At the rate we're losing altitude, we'll be on the ground in fifteen," the pilot said.

The plane suddenly lurched to the right. If I hadn't been sitting down, I would've gone flying against the side of the wall.

"You should go back to your seat and buckle in," he said. "Tell everyone it's going to be a rough landing."

He had no idea the only ones left were the four girls, Geli, and me. Presumably, the Mossad agent was getting the ladies situated at that moment. I'm sure they already knew how dire our predicament was.

"What are our odds?" I asked.

"Less than twenty percent. More like ten," the pilot said. "If we can find a safe place to land. I've notified my boss to come looking for us. I've given them our transponder number so they can track us, although they already had it."

The pilot didn't know how desperate I was to find out who his boss was. First, I had an idea. A way Alex could help.

I stepped out of the cockpit and back in the main cabin but far enough away from the hole in the side that I was safe. Geli was still in the back with the girls because I didn't see him.

The hole didn't seem to be any bigger, but the power of the suction had decimated the cabin. A couple of the dead men were no longer there. More than likely sucked out the hole. I pulled the other four toward the center of the fuselage, relieved them of their ID's, then gave them a little shove and sent them skydiving without a parachute. Hopefully, those bodies would never be found.

Even if we did survive the crash landing, it'd take the pilot's headquarters time to piece this all together. I wanted to make it harder for them. I took out my phone and confirmed a signal then called Alex.

He answered on the first ring.

"You won't beeeliiieeve what happened to me," he said.

"Alex, I need you to"

"We were training for the bobsled. You know. I told you about it. Anyway, We were making our first run. I slipped on the ice and smashed my chin. I've got a big gash in it. Blood was all over the ice. I told you it was dangerous."

I tried to interrupt him several times, but he was talking so fast and the cabin was so noisy, he didn't hear me. Or he wasn't listening. Probably the latter.

"Alex, It's Jamie. I needyou to track our plane"

"This German punk made fun of me," Alex said. At the cafeteria. I wanted to smash his face into a table. But I'm not allowed. No one's supposed to know I'm anything other than a bobsledder."

"Alex!"

"This jerk is the favorite to win the gold. A smug son of a gun. I'd like to break both his legs so he can't run. Can you believe he wanted to pick a fight with me? I could twist him into a pretzel."

The plane lurched again, or I would've said something sarcastic. I was about to die, and Alex was talking about falling on the ice and being bullied by some German.

The nose dropped.

The pilots overcorrected. I let out a muted scream. It's a good thing I hadn't eaten anything since early that morning.

If Alex heard my scream, he didn't acknowledge it.

The plane seemed to be descending faster than the pilot had anticipated. I wasn't sure how much longer we were going to be in the air. From the looks of things, we'd crash land within five to ten minutes. Not nearly enough time for me to do what needed to be done.

Especially since Alex was wasting valuable time prattling on about his stupid bobsled training run.

"AlexI'm in troublehere"

He kept talking over me. If I could slap him through the phone I would.

Things were made worse by the roar of the wind creating a massive wind tunnel through the hole in the fuselage. I also had to speak through my oxygen mask.

"I slid halfway down the bobsled run," Alex said. "Can you believe it? I was finally able to stop on one of the curves. I was soooo scared."

I lost it.

"Alex," I shouted at the top of my lungs.

"What?" he asked.

"Our plane is about to crash."

Silence for several seconds.

"Why didn't you say so?"

"You wouldn't let me."

"What happened?"

"No time to explain. The nearest airport is twenty minutes away. The bird won't be in the air longer than ten. We have a huge hole in the side of the plane."

"That's not good."

"Tell me about it. I need your help."

"You got it."

"I need you to find our plane on radar. Use our transponder. I want you to make it seem like we smashed into the side of a mountain. Find out where we end up and send help."

Silence.

"Alex. Can you hear me?"

Nothing.

"Alex."

The line was dead. Did he hear any of it?

I tried calling him again but couldn't get through. We were carrying satellite phones that were supposed to work anywhere. One of an operative's worst fears was equipment not working properly in the field.

"Shoot," I said, then slapped the wall.

The back bedroom door opened, and Geli appeared. Carrying two parachutes. He carefully made his way through the cabin, mindful to stay as far away from the hole as possible.

"How are the girls?" I asked, after he'd slipped an oxygen mask over his face. We had to shout in each other's ears to hear anything.

"They are scared, but safe. I got some intel as to where they've been. Their flight to Jordan took a little over an hour. I suspect Turkey. Maybe Syria. The other girls are being held in a building with prison bars. Probably an abandoned prison."

"That's good information. Maybe I can get more info from the pilots."

"What did you find out?"

"That this plane is going down. We aren't going to make it to the nearest airport. Hopefully, we can stay up long enough to find a pasture to land in somewhere. I'm afraid the plane's going to break up even if we land on a runway. I figure the back is the safest place."

Geli lifted the two parachutes in the air.

"Luckily, I found these."

"That's only two parachutes. There are six of us. Are there more?"

"No. This is all I found. These were for the two oligarchs. I assume. Put one on and let's get out of here."

"I'm not going. I have to stay with the girls."

"You can't stay, Jamie. You're too valuable an asset. You need to complete the mission."

"The girls are the mission."

"This isn't a suicide mission. There are ninety-six more girls who need rescuing."

"No girl left behind."

"That's stupid. You need to save yourself."

"You can go if you want."

"I am going. You're going with me."

Gili handed me the parachute. Then began strapping on his own.

I handed him mine.

"Give this to one of the girls. At least you can save one of them."

He shook his head. "The girls don't know how to operate a parachute. You know how risky a jump is in these conditions. It's going to be tricky for us to clear the plane and get the chutes deployed in time as it is. We also have no idea where we're going to land. We'll have to fly by the seat of my pants. No pun intended."

He smiled nervously when he said it.

"Do you have a harness?" I asked. "Take one of the girls with you on a tandem jump."

"No. This is all that's on the plane. It's too late to rig something."

I let out a huge sigh.

Leaving the girls went against every principle I'd ever stood for.

"Jamie, you have to come with me," Geli said with more emphasis. "You're no good to us dead. What about Alex? What about the terrorists at the Olympics. I get it that you want to help the girls. But there's nothing you can do for them. Sometimes we have to make hard decisions. You can't save everybody."

"I'm not going. I'll be okay. I've been in worse situations."

Although I couldn't remember when.

He grimaced.

Shook his head from side to side like he thought I was crazy. I probably was. His chute was on now. He gave me a hug and offered me his gun. Not sure what good that would do me, so I told him to hang on to it. I wasn't sure where we were. He could easily parachute into a swarm of soldiers. Things might not be safer on the ground.

He looked back one more time, gave me a salute, then disappeared out the side of the aircraft.

The feeling wasn't regret, but a realization that I was probably making a mistake.

The parachute needed to be secured so it wouldn't get sucked out of the plane. Satisfied, I went back into the cockpit and donned the mask and headset.

"What's your plan?" I asked. According to the controls, we were a little over ten thousand feet and falling fast.

If I were going to parachute out, it'd have to be soon. I wasn't even considering it. Curly was surprisingly silent in my head. Normally, he'd be screaming at me not to be such a fool.

"We don't have one," the pilot said. "Other than keep the nose up. If we can keep it up slightly, we might buy some time and can glide to the ground. Maybe get lucky and get the wind behind us and make it all the way to the airport. We'll try, but more than likely we're going to end up landing wherever we can."

"If the nose goes down, we only have a couple of minutes," the copilot added.

The pilot continued to struggle with the plane but seemed to have it under control. His back was bowed as he was obviously trying to force the nose to stay up.

All kinds of warning lights were going off in the cockpit, but they were mostly ignoring them.

A plane had recently crashed with the nose down. I'd seen the news reports. It made a huge crater in the earth. It penetrated so deep, the ground around it swallowed it up. When first responders arrived, they couldn't even see the plane. The recovery operation took weeks.

The reality of the situation was that the pilots were likely going to die no matter what. I intended to go in the back and prepare the girls as best I could for a crash landing. If the nose went down first, we'd all die. If we somehow landed, my intuition told me the aircraft would break up upon impact.

The back was the safest place to be. The pilots would likely go tumbling and be smashed to bits. If we survived, I wanted Alex to make it look like we didn't. So the pilot's bosses assumed everyone was killed in the crash. So no one would come looking for us. Then I could question the pilots and get valuable intelligence.

But I hadn't gotten to talk to Alex. I don't know how much of the last part of the conversation he heard before we were cut off.

Geli was right. Ninety-six more girls needed rescuing. That meant finding out where they were being held prisoner. That's where the headquarters were. The pilots had to know. Otherwise, how did they get the girls on the plane? Where did they pick them up?

The questioning would have to happen now. Did I have enough time?

"Where are we?" I asked.

"We're over Romania."

"Where were we headed before all this happened?"

"Croatia."

"Where did the plane originate?"

The pilot hesitated.

"Where did the plane leave from?" I asked again, more roughly.

"I'm not allowed to divulge that information."

I could feel the anger building inside of me. We didn't have time for games.

"Who do you work for?" I asked.

"What difference does it make?" the pilot said.

"How long have you been flying these flights?" I demanded.

"Two years," the co-pilot said.

"Shut up." The pilot glared at the copilot. That told me the pilot did have valuable intel.

My anger was focused on the pilot. "Did you know why these girls are on this flight?"

I saw a smirk come on his face.

He knew.

Now I didn't care if he lived or died.

I pulled out my gun and held it to his head. He started to raise his hands, but the steering column lurched, the nose dipped, and he quickly put his hands back on it to make the correction.

"We picked you up in Jordan," the pilot said.

"I know where you picked me up. Where are you based? Where did you come from before you came to Jordan?"

He hesitated.

I pressed the gun into his head. "Do you want to die?"

"What are you doing?" he asked, straining his head away from the gun. I kept it pressed against him.

"I need to know who hired you," I said.

"Are you crazy? We're about to crash here."

"I am crazy. I don't care about that. I care about who hired you."

His eyes widened. "Are you the one who caused all this?"

"Yeah, and I'm about to kill you."

"Then who will fly the plane."

"He will." I waved the gun toward the copilot. "Don't make me ask again. Who hired you?"

"I don't know."

I smacked him on the side of the head with the gun. Hard enough to stun him.

"Where did this plane originate from?" I said. "I'm not going to ask again."

The plan had been to hijack the plane, eliminate the threats, rescue the girls, and then Alex was going to track the plane. Find out where it originated in the flight plan. That way we could find the headquarters and where they were keeping the other girls.

I had to know. I might not live to get that information to anyone, but the pilot was going to answer my question.

I acted like I was about to hit him again.

"Pull up your flight plan." I said, moving the gun to the copilot's head. He fumbled around. Then gave it to me.

It originated in Germany.

What?

"Wer hat Sie eingestellt?" I asked who hired them in German.

The pilot looked at the copilot. I saw recognition in their eyes. They knew what I asked, telling me everything I needed to know.

The gun was back at the pilot's head.

I asked again.

"What's the man's name who hired you?"

I raised the gun like I was going to hit him again.

"Herman Hoffman," the copilot said.

The pilot glared at him, telling me all I needed to know.

My heart skipped a beat.

I knew that name from my days at the CIA.

This was worse than I thought.

5

"You're part of the BGS?" I asked, hardly believing what I'd just heard. The copilot told me Herman Hoffman was behind the sex trafficking.

Hoffman ran the Brown-Green Syndicate.

The pilot was still uncooperative and sneered at me defiantly. If looks could kill, the copilot would be dead from the glare the pilot had given him.

I wasn't sure who the copilot was more scared of. Me or his buddy. Probably both. The man sitting in the right seat of the cockpit was shaking like a dog who'd just had a bath.

Herman Hoffman. What a shocker.

Out of all my years in the CIA working with the sex trafficking division, I'd never seen Hoffman's name or the BGS linked to sex trafficking. They were into everything else nefarious. Arms. Drugs. Funding terrorism. Destabilization of governments was what they mostly trafficked in.

With one main goal. The annihilation of Israel. Starting with the expulsion of all Jews from Europe and the Middle East. It seemed like sex trafficking would be a distraction. An unnecessary risk. Maybe the two Turkish oligarchs were helping the organization, and the girls were Hoffman's way of thanking them.

That made the most sense. Profit wasn't the motive. Although, Mossad had paid a pretty penny to get their agent and me on that plane.

It's always been amazing to me how the most fundamental right-wing groups with such strict moral codes actually lived such depraved lives. Kidnapping women. Selling them as sex slaves. To godless men.

When they purported to be the keepers of the truth. The only true Christians.

The disgust was probably written all over my face.

I pointed at the flight plan which was now in one hand. My gun in the other.

"Does Hoffman live in Germany as well?" I asked, even though I thought I knew the answer.

It didn't seem possible. While he was a fascist nationalist and believed himself to be the second coming of Hitler, Germany wasn't a place where he could easily hide.

The pilot refused to look at me. He simply stared straight ahead. Flying the plane. At the moment, the plane was stable.

"If not, where is he?" I asked in a stronger, more demanding tone.

Nobody answered my question.

Somewhere on that flight manifest I presumed.

The CIA had been looking for Hoffman for years. As had Mossad. I wanted them to answer, but the flight plan told me a lot. The information in my hand was more valuable to Mossad than all the gold in the world.

The gun was back at the copilot's head. He began to shake nervously. Squirmed in his seat. He might've soiled his pants for all I knew. That's how nervous he was. I was breathing out of an oxygen mask and not aware of any smells in the cockpit if there were any. Thankfully.

"Don't kill me," the copilot said. "I'll tell you what you want to know."

"Shut up!" the pilot shouted. "You're a traitor. You're not worthy to call yourself a freedom fighter."

Another irony. They were holding four girls in the back of the plane as sex slaves but considered themselves freedom fighters. The BGS, the Brown-Green Syndicate, was a loosely formed alliance of Fascists and Islamists. Brown being the color of the German nationalists and green being the color of Islam.

The group was made up of the fringe of both ideologies. The word extremists didn't even describe them properly. They were so out of the mainstream, the worst hate mongers in the United States paled in comparison.

"You'd better start talking and fast," I said.

I felt a sudden sense of urgency. For more than one reason. The plane was under ten thousand feet now. Before long, we'd all know if this conversation was meaningless anyway. Intelligence was useless if it were unactionable. As in, I was dead and the information died with me.

"We're just pilots," the copilot said. "Don't kill us."

"Somebody had better tell me everything you did today, or I'll kill you both."

The pilot laughed. "Who's going to fly the plane? You need us."

"I'll fly it."

I didn't actually know how to fly the plane, but they didn't know that. It actually was an option. I'd considered killing both of them and calling A-Rad. He was my pilot for AJAX, back when I was running missions for the CIA. He could talk me through what to do.

I wish A-Rad were here at the moment. If the plane could be landed without crashing, he was the only person in the world I knew who could do it. Maybe the Colonel who also worked for Alex and me. He'd be harder to reach but was an option.

I was mostly bluffing. A-Rad's phone could be off. I also remembered my dropped call with Alex. The odds were, calling A-Rad wasn't an option.

So, I needed to keep one of these two low-lifes alive. Easy to know which one. They'd made the decision for me.

"You're weak and pathetic," the pilot said. "Heil Hoffman." He took his hand off the steering wheel long enough to raise it in the air in a recognizable fascist gesture. "General Hoffman will know of your insubordination and will deal with you accordingly."

I'd heard enough. When I heard the word "heil" anger erupted inside of me like gasoline on a fire pit.

I swerved the gun to my left and fired one bullet into the pilot's head. Pointing it downward, so it'd go through his head and into his shoulder. I didn't want a bullet exiting his brain and blasting out the cockpit window. If that happened, I might as well turn the gun on all of us. We weren't making it out of this alive.

The pilot slumped to his seat, deader than a tree stump lying on the ground. I quickly grabbed him by the shirt collar, so he wouldn't fall onto the steering column and affect the flight.

With the pilot out of the way, I put the gun on the copilot's head. He was sweating profusely, even though the cabin wasn't hot at all. Fear consumed his entire face.

"Tell me what you know," I said to him. "And I'll let you live."

"I'll tell you everything I know. Please don't shoot me."

"Answer my questions, and we all might make it out of here alive."

I had to hurry. The plane was down to an altitude of under seventy-five hundred feet. We weren't going to be in the air for very long. The copilot kept nervously looking at the altitude as well. Probably even more terrified since he'd have to land the plane by himself now.

He couldn't possibly know what was churning inside of me. I had an excruciating decision to make. Before I made it, I had to get all the intel I could.

"Where is Hoffman holding the girls?" I asked, with the gun still at his head. Although it was hard to steady it. At the lower altitude, the plane bounced around like a pickup truck on a road full of potholes.

"In Syria."

I leaned forward to see his face. I was trained to know if someone was lying. He was telling the truth.

It made sense. The girls couldn't be held in a civilized country like Jordan or Germany. Not easily anyway.

"Is Hoffman in Germany?"

He hesitated.

I pushed the gun against his head.

"Don't mess with me," I said. "I'll kill you and fly the plane myself."

"How do I know you're not going to kill me anyway?"

"You have my word."

"How do I know I can trust it?"

"You don't. That's a chance you'll have to take. The alternative is you're a dead man for sure."

He shook his head. "No. We live in Germany. That's where General Hoffman keeps his airplanes. A private airport south of Munich."

"Where does Hoffman live?"

"I don't know for sure. But I think he's in Hungary. Just across the border from Germany. I don't know the town. He lives on a mountain. I understand it's hard to get to."

"Go on."

"Like I said, the girls are in Syria. You've got the information on the manifest."

"And you were taking us to Croatia?"

"Yes. We fly there. Land and refuel and then fly you back to Jordan after we drop the men off in Turkey. Then we take the girls back to Syria and fly home."

"Do you know these girls are being trafficked as sex slaves?"

"Yes," the copilot said. "We take turns with them on the way back to Syria. It's part of our payment."

His head slumped in shame.

"You're pathetic."

He didn't answer.

"How long have you been transporting girls like this?"

"Two years for me. He's been flying for General Hoffman for ten years." He pointed at the dead pilot when he said it.

I had no idea. How did Hoffman not get on my radar? I thought I knew all the major groups involved in sex trafficking.

I stood to my feet.

"Where are you going?" he asked.

"Good luck landing the plane," I said sincerely, as I took my mask and headset off.

I left the cockpit and went back into the main cabin and began to make sure the parachute was in order.

Tears were already streaming down my face.

The pain I felt overwhelmed me.

I had to leave the girls. At that point, I had no choice.

I looked back at the bedroom door and the tears began to flow more freely.

It wasn't my fault.

The intel changed things.

As soon as Herman Hoffman's name was mentioned, I had to do everything in my power to get this intel to Mossad. If there were ten men in the world Mossad most wanted dead, Herman Hoffman would be at the top of it.

A dangerous man with a sick ideology. Pure evil. The BGS was a small organization, but powerful. Worse than any terrorist organization in the world in that they hated everyone. Russia and the United States equally. They detested communism as much as they did capitalism.

That left them isolated, but Hoffman had somehow managed to make enemies of everyone, while still successfully evading authorities and carrying out his destructive ways all across the world.

Shock therapy as he called it. Everything he did was for maximum shock value. They were fascists in the sense that they wanted their values forced on the entire world. Far right extremism.

Ironically enough, they wanted as few government restrictions as possible. Complete freedom of behavior. World domination by a select few.

It seemed counterintuitive that BGS would be aligned with Muslim extremists. Hoffman operated under the veil of Christianity, although everything he did was against the teachings of Jesus. Hate. Fear mongering.

Sex trafficking.

The unholy alliance was formed because they had one common enemy—Israel. Hoffman called for the annihilation of Israel. So did much of the Muslim world. By whatever means necessary. Genocide even. A second holocaust so to speak. If they ever came to power, that'd be the result.

God forbid.

Which was why I couldn't stay on that airplane.

I had to get this information back to Mossad. I knew Hoffman's location. The manifest in my pocket told me everything I needed to know. Where Hoffman kept his planes. Where the girls were being held in Syria.

While I didn't know Hoffman's exact location, it wouldn't be hard to find in Hungary.

I took out my phone and tried to call Alex again, but the call didn't go through. If I could get in touch with him, I could give him the information and then stay on the plane to help the girls.

The pain I felt inside approached agony. How could I abandon the girls? I'd put them in this situation by starting the gunfight.

Alex and Curly would argue with me. As would any other sane person. Hoffman put the girls in this situation when he kidnapped them. I was only trying to help. A Good Samaritan act that went bad. The fact that six bodyguards and two oligarchs and a depraved pilot were all dead was no consolation.

Saving innocent lives was my ultimate goal.

I was powerless to do so in this instance. What if the plane crashed and I died, and the intel died with me? I couldn't risk it.

That left me with no choice. I had to parachute out.

The faces of the four girls were seared in my mind like an image on an IMAX movie screen. I felt the sudden urge to walk back to the bedroom and tell them. To explain myself. To tell them I was sorry. But if I saw their faces, I wouldn't be able to leave them.

The parachute was on my back now. I checked and double checked the straps to make sure they were secure. My eyes were blurry from the tears. I tried to fight them away, but they kept returning. One of the few times in my career I hadn't been able to control my emotions.

We were below the clouds now. I could see the ground.

No girl left behind. That had always been my motto. I risked life and limb to save those girls. I always found a way to save them. Even against the worst odds.

How did I get in this position?

The right thing to do was to jump.

The intel I had in my pocket would save countless lives. The scales tipped all the way to the side of jumping.

What were four girls in the grand scheme of things?

Four innocent ladies. At the wrong place, at the wrong time. Trying to better their lives. Start their careers. Apply for a job. Then forced into human trafficking.

"I'm sorry," I said toward the bedroom as I took up my position by the hole in the cabin.

My legs felt like they were standing in molasses.

My heart was heavier than a bag of cement.

I willed myself to jump.

The rest was a blur. I instinctively deplaned in the proper position. Avoiding any potential dangers. My chute deployed.

The tears still flowed, but the wind blew them away. I didn't have any goggles to protect my eyes.

For whatever reason, I had to watch the plane fly away. So I steered my chute so I faced that direction. And stared like a zombie. More like a gawker who had to watch a deadly pileup when he drove by the accident.

Something shook me back to reality and into operation mode. I wasn't out of the woods yet. I had the presence of mind to get my bearings. I was away from any cities. In a countryside. I landed gently in a field. With several cows and horses.

I'd corral one of the horses and ride to a safe place.

Surprisingly, I landed on my feet. Instinctively, I looked off in the horizon.

The plane was nothing more than a blip. But I could still see it. Couldn't look away.

Watched in horror. As it flew into the side of a mountain and exploded.

I collapsed to my knees and sobbed.

6

Tel Aviv, Israel,
Five days later

"They sure do things differently at Mossad," I said to Alex.

"A lot different than I'd do it," he said.

We'd just come from a tactical meeting with Mossad. Discussing what to do about Herman Hoffman. The leader of BGS. I'd gotten actionable intelligence while on the plane that they were able to confirm. We wanted to go to Hungary right away and take him out.

Mossad leaders were extremely appreciative of the intelligence. They thanked me profusely for putting my life at considerable risk to get it. But they pushed back on acting immediately.

"We'll respond at a time and place of our own choosing," Alex said, mimicking the voice of Saul Geller, the director of Mossad who had hired us for the mission.

That's what he said when we pressed him about acting now.

"What does that even mean?" I asked. "I'm not that patient. If I know where a bad guy is, I'm going to go there and take him out. Why wait?"

"It means they're being careful. I guess."

"Curly always said don't be careful. Careful gets you killed."

Alex changed lanes. He must've cut someone off because I heard a horn honking at him. He ignored them. We were in a car driving somewhere. I didn't know where and Alex didn't say, although he seemed to know exactly where we were going. He hadn't hesitated when making turns and hadn't asked me to look up directions on my phone.

"I agree with you and Curly," Alex said. "Don't be careful. Follow the mission through to the end. While it has momentum. In fighting it's called going for the jugular. In football, it's kicking them while they're down. In other words, when you have an opponent on the ropes you finish them off. Or an enemy in this instance."

Alex was the starting quarterback for the Stanford Cardinals which was where the college football analogies were coming from.

"It gives Hoffman time to regroup," I said. "We even offered to do the dirty work and take him out ourselves."

"You should be glad you don't have to get shot at."

I ignored that comment. Curly drilled into us a sense of duty. We never shied away from danger. Like a firefighter running into a burning building. A policeman chasing a man with a gun. A soldier breaking down the door of a house not knowing what was on the other side. We were geared that way. While it wasn't pleasant, it's the only way to get the job done.

It's like Mossad wanted to plan out all the risk. Not possible. At least from my experience.

"I want to at least rescue the girls in Syria," I said. "They won't even let me do that."

"They're going to send in a small army to get those girls back. I think they'll act quicker on that front. They can handle it. Like I said, at least we don't have to get shot at."

"Being shot at comes with the territory. I just don't want Hoffman to get away. He might get spooked by one of his planes crashing."

"He doesn't know why it crashed into the side of that mountain. He might suspect foul play, but he'll have no proof. Hopefully, he'll think it crashed because of a mechanical problem or pilot error."

Talking about the plane crashing sent a pain through my heart like I'd been stabbed in the chest with a dagger. The four dead girls still weighed heavily on my mind. Considering they died on my watch.

Neither of us said anything for a few seconds. It was my turn to respond, and I didn't want to, for fear my voice would crack and Alex would see that it still bothered me. We weren't supposed to show weakness. Not even to our own partners.

When the feelings got too much to control, I blurted out, "I don't know how much longer I can do this."

His right eyebrow bowed slightly. "What do you mean? Do what?"

"Seeing those girls crash into the mountain and go up in flames was tough on me. I still have nightmares about it."

"I understand why you would feel that way. That would be traumatic for you."

"Alex Halee!"

"What?"

He looked over at me with both eyebrows raised considerably, clearly concerned he'd said something wrong. He hadn't.

"That was a thoughtful thing for you to say," I said sweetly. "You were being supportive."

"Why do you sound so surprised?"

"I figured you'd pull a Curly on me."

I lowered my tone and did my best Curly imitation.

"Suck it up, Jamie. Don't go soft on me. You can't save everybody. The world is messy. Feelings will get you killed. If you can't take the heat, put out the fire."

Alex chuckled.

"You do a good Curly impression. That sounded like him."

"You didn't say any of those things and I appreciate it," I said. "You let me vent how I was feeling without trying to change them or tell me how I'm supposed to feel."

"You *are* going to have to put it behind you," Alex said. "We've got an important mission ahead of us. I need you focused."

"You couldn't leave well enough alone could you," I said sharply. "Now you're trying to handle me."

He was referring to the Olympics. Mossad told us to turn our focus to that task. In less than a week, we'd be traveling to Bavaria Germany to complete our training. Both for the Olympic events and the hunt for the terrorist's cell. If it actually existed. We didn't know for sure.

I'd turn my focus to the next mission when I was good and ready. Not a minute sooner.

"All I'm saying is, that you've always been able to move on," Alex said. "You're resilient, Jamie. We've lost people before. I've never seen it bother you like this. You haven't been yourself since you got back."

"Whatever."

"I am trying to be"

I cut him off.

"Don't worry about me. When the time comes, I'll be all in. Right now, I'm just venting. All I'm saying is that I don't know how much longer I want to do this. It's getting too hard."

My arms were crossed in front of me, and I was getting close to the line of feeling sorry for myself. I didn't want to cross that line, but I had to talk to someone about how I was feeling. Alex was right. This wasn't like me. I had to snap out of this funk or I wouldn't be at the top of my game when we got to the Olympics.

"That doesn't sound like the Jamie I know."

"Maybe it's catching up with me. When you see the things we see, I don't know how we keep our sanity."

"We never had our sanity to begin with. If we did, we wouldn't be doing what we do."

We were both silent for several minutes.

Where are we going? I still didn't know. I'd save that question for when I wanted to change the subject.

"You did the right thing," Alex said. "Jumping out of the plane."

"I know. That's what makes it hard."

"That took courage to evaluate the situation and make the right choice."

"Doesn't make it any easier."

"No. It doesn't. I'm here for you if you want to talk about it some more."

"Now you're mocking me," I said.

"I'm not mocking you. I'm serious. I'm a good listener."

"Since when."

"Maybe I'm getting in touch with my feminine side. You should try it sometime."

"I should be allowed to hate what I'm doing if I want."

"You don't hate it."

"Don't tell me how I feel."

Now I was being a brat.

The tension in the car was rising. Like a pot of boiling water. A fight was imminent if either of us didn't diffuse it.

"Answer me this," Alex said. "When you were on that plane and you thought you were about to die, what did you think about?"

"I don't know. I was in the moment. Trying to figure out how to get out of it."

"I know. But when you realized that you were probably going to die, what did you think about?"

"I thought about you."

"No, you didn't."

"Yes, I did. I called you."

He was making me mad now. I was sitting up in my seat, my arms were no longer crossed.

"You called me to tell me the intel," he said.

"What's your point?"

"You were thinking about the mission."

"So."

"So you weren't thinking about me. Or our future together. You weren't thinking about the fact that you'd never have a baby. All you could think about was how to save those girls. Not how to get home to me safely."

"That's not fair. They are one and the same. Those other things would be a distraction. Curly taught us to put distractions out of our minds."

"Don't misunderstand me. I'm not saying you don't love me. Or that you wanted to die. I'm saying that when you're on a mission, and at death's door, you think about the mission. Saving the girls. Not your own life. That's what makes you special."

The words caused conflicting emotions. What Alex said warmed my heart but made me even angrier at the same time.

He continued. "So, when you say you want to quit, I don't believe you. The day you're up on that plane or facing down someone trying to kill you and you think about me and our baby, and not killing that person or saving someone else, that's when I'd say you're ready to quit."

"That's deep, Alex." I said it half sincerely and half mockingly. "Quite philosophical. You're full of you know what though. I'll think about whatever I want to think about on a mission."

The obstinate jab was only so he knew I wasn't ceding the argument.

Alex was right. I was thinking about those four girls. Maybe at some point I thought about him and our future. But it was fleeting. If the choice had been different and I had to choose between saving the four girls or saving myself, I would've saved them.

Which was Alex's point. I put the safety of those girls ahead of Alex and my future. Ahead of having a baby. Which brought me back to my original point. I didn't want to do this anymore. That was lunacy. No sane person would make that choice.

Time to change the tone of the conversation.

"I want to grow old with you," I said with tears welling up in my eyes.

"At the rate we're going, I'm not sure that's going to happen. I almost died on that bobsled course."

His smile was wide, so I'd know he was kidding. I punched him on the arm.

We both laughed, relieving the tension somewhat.

"Where are we going?" I asked.

"It's a surprise."

"You know I don't like surprises."

"You aren't going to like this one either."

"I don't think you understand the concept of a surprise, Alex. It's supposed to be something the person likes. By definition. That's what makes it a surprise."

"Then it won't be a surprise. It'll be something else... What's the antithesis of surprise?"

"I think you mean an antonym."

"No. Antithesis is the opposite of something."

"It's the opposite of a person or thing. The opposite meaning of a word is an antonym."

"Whatever. The point is you can be surprised by something you don't like."

I reached over and hit him on the arm with a fist. Harder this time.

"Oww. What did you do that for?"

"Were you surprised I hit you?"

"Very."

"I guess you're right. Surprise does go both ways."

"You're incorrigible."

"I'm not playing that game."

A couple of years ago, Alex started looking up big words in the dictionary to surprise me with. So I'd be impressed. I wasn't in the mood at the moment. He had me thinking about the surprise I wouldn't like.

"What's the antithesis of incorrigible?" Alex asked.

"The *antonym* of incorrigible would be amenable. Curable. You're definitely not that. There's no cure for what ails you."

"What's the antithesis of ails?"

"Shut up."

We didn't say anything for several minutes. It felt good to be with him though. My thoughts were still elsewhere. Thinking about the plane crash and the girls. Alex's words had been thought provoking. Insightful. I was introspective at that moment.

Why didn't I think about him? I didn't like that revelation.

I loved Alex. He's the love of my life. I couldn't imagine my life without him. I wanted to grow old with him. Having a baby had always been in our plans. If I had a child at home, would I have still chosen the four girls over my own life?

I don't think so. In fact, we'd decided that when I got pregnant, I'd quit. Maybe that's what I was trying to say. I was ready to have a child.

Now wasn't the time to bring it up. But I would soon. We needed to have a serious discussion. I also wanted to know what Alex thought about when he was in a life-or-death situation. I had assumed he thought about me. Now I wasn't so sure.

The car began to slow. We'd long since left the main city of Tel Aviv and were in the suburbs. A fairly large crowd had gathered in one of the towns and a heavy police presence had blocked off several streets. The town was bustling with activity.

Alex maneuvered his way around it, like he knew where he was going. My curiosity was beyond piqued.

"What's all this?" I asked.

It looked like some kind of festival.

"You'll see."

I let out a noticeable sigh. Why all the secrecy? Why couldn't he tell me where we were going? That's why I didn't like surprises. Don't I have a right to decide what I do and when I want to do it?

I clearly needed to lighten up but didn't want to. It might be a good surprise. I might actually enjoy it. Although, if Alex said I wouldn't like it, I was probably going to hate it.

He pulled into a parking space next to a parking garage.

"Let's go," he said.

I didn't move. My seatbelt was still buckled. "Not until you tell me where we're going."

I didn't like being dragged around by the nose.

"We're going to meet my bobsled team. We're doing an appearance at this event for the village."

I opened the car door. "Why didn't you say so? I'd love to meet your team."

Now I was confused. Why would I hate this surprise? I walked around the car and took his hand and walked with him to the garage.

An entire level was cleared out. No cars were parked in the garage. Instead, I saw the strangest things.

Bathtubs.

Alex looked at me like he was trying to watch my reaction.

More than a dozen bathtubs. Several feet apart. They were on wheels. People milled around them.

Alex walked directly toward one particular bathtub. Two men stood around it, wearing hillbilly costumes. One was in a wheelchair in overalls and had a straw hat on his head and a quirky smile on his face.

The bathtub was a large old timey white tub sitting on a piece of metal with four wheels attached to it. It had a pipe coming out of the back and rising above the tub with a showerhead on the end.

"Fellows," Alex said. "Come meet my wife, Jamie."

I dutifully stuck out my hand to the closest person.

"This is John," Alex said. "He's the driver of the bobsled. The organizer. He's the glue that holds the team together."

John's handshake was firm. He was slightly smaller than Alex but extremely fit. Ruggedly handsome in a mountain man kind of way. Not a typical Jewish look. Scruffy beard. Thick eyebrows. Friendly smile, but more business-like than warm.

"This is Handy," Alex said, pointing to the man in the wheelchair. "He handles the brakes."

"So, you're on the team," I said. Not trying to sound too surprised so he wouldn't be offended.

"Yes Ma'am," Handy said. "I'm the one who keeps us from flying off the course at ninety miles an hour and killing ourselves."

"I appreciate you keeping my husband safe. I can see where you have an important job."

I instantly liked Handy. He was warm and friendly, and I appreciated anyone willing to compete at such a high level with a disability.

"That's Matthew over there," Alex said.

Matthew looked up and waved. He had a tool in his hand and was tinkering with the contraption.

"What's this for?" I asked, pointing at the tub.

"It's called the *Running of the Tubs*," Alex said. "It's a race."

"It's the fourteenth running," John added.

"We race other teams, running down the main street. It's part of our training. John thinks it'll help us at the Olympics. The start is similar to a bobsled start. It's also good for conditioning. Plus it's a promotion for the bobsled team."

"Sounds like fun."

Why would Alex think I wouldn't like it? Watching him run down the middle of the street pushing a bathtub and wearing an outfit was beyond amusing. I could use the pictures against him for years to come.

John was suddenly next to me trying to hand me something.

"Here's your outfit," John said.

"Outfit?" I asked. "What are you talking about?"

He held it up. In his hands was a lady's one-piece swimsuit. Clearly old and used. Brownish color. Ugly. Also in his hand was a shower cap.

I didn't take them from him, even though he shoved them my way.

"You obviously didn't tell her," John said to Alex who was fidgeting back and forth.

"Tell me what," I said roughly.

"You're going to be on our team," John said.

"I am not."

Alex had a mischievous smile on his face.

He said, "Jamie, you're going to wear this swimsuit and sit in the tub and pretend to be taking a shower while we push you down the street. In front of all those people who are here to watch the race."

"Alex Halee! You have lost your freaking mind if you think I'm going anywhere near that bathtub wearing that... that hideous bathing suit."

My arms were firmly crossed in front of me.

"Yes, you are," he said firmly.

It'd take a small army to get me in that outfit and inside that tub.

7

"Jamie, you look utterly ridiculous," I said to myself in the ladies restroom. While staring at the mirror.

I'd donned the one-piece hideous looking bathing suit and shower cap and was now drumming up the courage to go out in public dressed in it. I'd rather walk outside and fight four large men.

"I can't believe I'm doing this."

I grimaced at myself in the mirror when I said it. Alex had talked me into it. His arguments were persuasive.

"Mossad has heard chatter that the terrorist cell may have a man at this event," he had said.

"What does that have to do with me dressing up like a circus animal and making a fool of myself in that bathtub?" I asked.

"Your job is to find the man in the crowd. There's nobody better at spotting a terrorist than you."

"Then let me roam around the streets."

Alex shook his head.

"The bathtub is the best way to spot someone. This is a race from one end of main street to the other. We're going to run the full length of the crowd from one end to the other in a matter of two minutes. If the man is here, you'll see him."

Spotting terrorists was something I was good at. Terrorists had a certain look to them. I'd seen so many over the years, I knew how to spot them. It's not something I could pinpoint or necessarily explain in a training class.

Terrorists had a hardness about them. A hatred that permeated their faces. It's in the demeanor. The dress. The way they carried themselves. The way their heads were always on a swivel. I look for nervousness. Twitching. Hands in the pocket. A bulge in the clothes.

Their jaws were usually clenched. Sometimes their fists were in a ball. Their eyebrows furrowed. The *Running of the Tubs* was supposed to be a fun event. Most people had excited looks on their faces. Anticipation. A spark or twinkle.

A terrorist would be noticeably nervous. Serious. The way most people would feel if they were about to do something wrong. Or risky. Dangerous.

Mostly it was in the eyes. I had the ability to spot evil. Terrorists had the look that they were up to no good.

An operative can have the same looks. Not evil so much, but the same nervousness, twitches, and demeanor. Curly had spent days training it out of us. Warning us that the slightest inhibition could get us killed.

I looked again at myself in the mirror. I couldn't help but chuckle. What I saw was anything but a highly trained CIA operative. I looked like a stooge at a carnival.

Alex had handed me a long-handled bathroom brush. I held it up and looked at it. I almost lost it when he told me what it was for.

"While the tub is moving, you need to pretend to bathe yourself with that brush," Alex said, unable to hide his amusement. "You know. Raise your arm in the air and pretend to wash your underarms."

"Alex Halee, you have lost your mind. There's no way in you-know-what that I'm doing that in front of all those people."

"You said for better or for worse. Those were our wedding vows."

I glared at him.

"The brush has a camera in it," Alex explained in a more serious tone. "You can use it to scan the crowd. That way if you miss the person, we'll have footage to look at."

I rubbed my eyes roughly. "I'm not doing it."

"You have to. Our guns are going to be in the tub. You need to be prepared to take out the threat if it arises."

"Why can't you do it?"

"I'll be running. My focus will be on the race. I won't even be carrying my gun. Remember, no one is supposed to know we are agents. We're supposed to be Olympic athletes. We have to maintain our cover."

"You just told me to take out the threat. If I do that, everyone will know I'm with Mossad."

"I said to take out the threat if it arises. As a last resort. We'll blow our covers if we have to. If it'll save lives."

"I thought your team didn't know you were a Mossad agent. They'll know as soon as they see the guns in the bathtub."

I was grasping at any straw I could find.

"They know now," he replied. "Mossad briefed them. They had to. We decided we couldn't keep them in the dark. They should know that their lives are in danger. They're fine with it, but only because I assured them we would protect them. I need your help."

I shook my head no. Violently. From side to side.

"Nope! Not going to do it. I'll protect them from the crowd. It'll be easier for me, since I won't be moving."

Then Alex made the most persuasive argument of all. He guilt-shamed me.

"So, you'll get on an airplane and risk your life for four girls you don't even know, but you won't do this to possibly protect your own husband's life?"

I let out a huge, exaggerated moan.

At that point, he had won the argument. Nothing I could do. He was right. Alex would be running down the street with no cover. A terrorist with a halfway decent aim could pick him off like a duck on a pond. I might not see the threat in time, but I had the best chance of it.

Alex explained that there'd be Mossad agents interspersed in the crowd. We'd all have earpieces so we could communicate with each other. If the terrorist was there, it'd be a big break for us if we spotted him. We'd be able to confirm the cell actually did exist and that there really was a plan to attack Israeli athletes at the Olympics.

If we captured him, we could interrogate him and gain valuable intelligence. We might even break up the cell altogether and Alex and I wouldn't even be needed at the Olympics.

When he put it that way, what could I say?

So here I was. Standing in front of the mirror. Deeply regretting having gotten out of bed that morning.

All I could do was make the best of it.

I summoned my courage. Surprisingly, it took more than if I were going out to shoot somebody. I exited the bathroom and walked back to the garage, mindful of all the stares. People were pointing. The kids were enjoying it. The parents far too much. I tried to ignore them.

When I got back to where the team was assembled, they were noticeably ignoring me. I could see the smirks on their faces, but they kept their heads down. They weren't making eye contact with me and pretended to be hard at work preparing for the race. Alex must've read them the riot act. He knew if one of them made fun of me, they probably wouldn't be able to physically run the race.

Alex bit his lip when he saw me. I knew he wanted to burst out laughing but managed to control himself. Thankfully, our old team wasn't here. A-Rad. Colonel. Bond. They wouldn't have been so considerate. They'd been ribbing me from the moment they saw me and for years to come.

"No pictures!" I said jokingly to John and the rest of the team trying to be a good sport about it.

"I'm afraid there are going to be thousands of pictures of us on social media by tonight," John said. "Every person in the crowd has a cell phone. With a camera. That's the way it is these days. Nothing happens in public that's not captured on camera."

I let out a groan.

"I think you look cute," Alex said. He leaned in to kiss me on the lips, but I turned my mouth to the side in a frown and then my head so he could only kiss my cheek. He tried to playfully poke me in the ribs, but I pushed his hands aside.

"Let's get this show on the road," John said. "I think we're ready."

The team began rolling the tub out of the garage, down the street, and toward the starting line. Fortunately, we went through a back alley and avoided most of the people. The only consolation was that the members of the other race teams looked almost as ridiculous as I did. Almost.

They were all dressed in some kind of themed costume that matched their tubs. Some of them were highly creative. I wondered if they had a contest for best presentation. We wouldn't win it if they did.

"Ugh!" I muttered under my breath. I hadn't been that self-conscious since the day I got braces on my teeth when I was ten.

John lifted Handy out of the wheelchair and into the tub. He sat in the front. I sat in the back, so I'd be under the showerhead. The guns were between Handy and me covered by towels.

Someone should take one of those guns and put me out of my misery.

The bottom of the tub was hard on my back side. It was also slick. I wasn't sure how I was supposed to raise my arm in the air and pretend to wash my underarms with the brush and not slide right into Handy.

It felt really uncomfortable. I'd been in a lot of awkward positions on missions. Stuck in the trunk of a car for hours. One time, I spent several days in a dank, dark, moldy, leaky makeshift third world prison cell. Strapped to a chair and tortured. I parachuted out of a plane into the eye of a hurricane. Barely survived it. When the hurricane hit, the only shelter I could find was under a pier. Colonel was with me. We tied ourselves to the pier while the hurricane pummeled us for hours.

It was ridiculous to think, but I preferred those scenarios to what I was feeling at that moment. I knew deep down that wasn't true. The uncomfortableness of the present was almost always worse than the memories of the past.

I checked the guns under the towels. That made me feel better. Something about having a gun in my hand made it feel more like a mission.

If I didn't get to shoot someone, and release some of this tension, I'd be disappointed.

When we got to the starting line, the mission nerves erupted, overcoming feeling sorry for myself. A different kind of nervousness. My senses heightened. The adrenaline started flowing. I felt a sudden burst of energy.

I was in full mission mode now. We checked the radios, and everything was good. We'd keep the frequency clear unless one of us saw something. It felt strange being on a mission without my team. I wasn't used to the silence. Bond, A-Rad, and Colonel were always chattering in my ears. Cracking jokes. Making fun of each other. And me.

I missed them.

The *Running of the Tubs* did seem like a fun event for the fans. From our vantage point, we could hear the loud cheers from the crowd as the teams raced down the middle of main street to the finish line.

There was a buzz around us. The other teams were clearly into it. Someone said this was an annual event and the locals prepared for months to see who could build the best bathtub. With the most creative idea.

I was starting to get into it. I could do this. I'd played many roles over the years. Being a CIA operative was like being an actress. That's what it felt like. More like Daffy Duck or Baby Huey than Marilyn Monroe or Ginger Rogers, but for a few seconds, all eyes would be on me, and I'd be the center of attention.

As our tub was pushed up to the starting line, I could see dozens of kids sitting on the curbs. The smiles on their faces would make it worth it.

That's what I told myself anyway.

Protecting them would certainly be worth it. Protecting Alex. I could see now why this was the best plan.

We were up against a group of firefighters. They were in the right-hand lane. Their tub was in the shape of a fire engine. They wore all the gear. Black tee-shirts, yellow fire caps, beige fireman pants.

They were going to wipe us out faster than a brush fire.

Not sure if that was an appropriate pun in my mind, but they outnumbered us. They had four pushers. We only had three since Handy was in the tub with me.

Another thing that seemed strange. I was a married woman sitting in a bathtub with another man. With my husband nearby.

I felt ridiculous again.

Until the starter pistol erupted, shattering my thoughts. That and the sudden movement of the tub made me jump.

Focus Jamie.

It was harder than I thought it would be. I had to balance myself in the tub, while pretending to wash myself with the brush. Making sure the brush picked up the crowd on both sides of the road. All while trying to scan every face in the crowd. Looking for that needle in a haystack. That one person who might be there to do us harm.

He could be anywhere. On a rooftop. Inside a building. I looked for open windows with rifles sticking out of them.

The tub picked up steam. We were going faster now. The cheers of the crowd were surprisingly loud.

We were three fourths of the way through the course before I knew it. Alex, John, and Matthew were straining. I could hear their heavy breathing. The firemen were slightly ahead, but we were keeping it closer than I expected.

Then I saw him.

Wearing a brown leather jacket. Even though it was hot outside.

Dark skin. Black hair. Thick eyebrows. Tensed forehead.

I was trained to block out the unimportant. The peripheral. To notice everything important.

He had a five o'clock shadow. Scar on the side of his face. A quarter of an inch. From his right eyebrow going slightly down his cheek.

His eyes flitted from side to side. His hand was in his pocket. He was trying too hard to blend in. That made him stick out like a goiter on the side of the neck.

I alerted everyone.

"Hostile. Forty-five degrees to my right. Standing. On the move now."

We passed him so he was behind me.

I couldn't look back.

"I see him," Alex said.

"Got him in my sights," I heard one of the Mossad agents say through the com.

"Where is he?" another one said.

The chatter began ringing in my ears. Everyone was speaking at once. I wished I had a way to silence them.

We crossed the finish line at the same time as the firefighters. I wasn't sure who won. A photo finish probably. I didn't care. I grabbed the two towels that were covering the guns. I had my gun in my hand with a towel over it resting on my lap.

When the tub came to a stop, I stood and put the other towel around me. Then bolted out of the tub in a flash.

I'd kept my sneakers on and began running toward where I last saw the terrorist. Being sure to cover the gun with the towel, so I wouldn't blow my cover. Most of the crowd had their eyes on the street anxiously awaiting the next contestants to come racing by.

The terrorist was on the move. That provided more confirmation to me. He was only there to watch our race. To scope out the Olympic bobsledding team. See what he sees. Maybe to get shots off if possible.

For whatever reason, he decided now wasn't the time to act.

Where is he?

Since Alex surprised me with this whole mission, I hadn't had a chance to do my due diligence. A point I intended to make to him. Had he told me in advance, I could've studied a map of the streets. Ingress and egress points. I might've been able to anticipate where the terrorist would go to escape.

As it was, I was working blind. One wrong turn and I'd lose him altogether. Even now, I was beginning to think I wouldn't find them.

Then I saw the back of his head.

Briefly. Nothing more than a passing glance. He was moving with pace now. He hadn't seen me which gave me the advantage.

Telling the others on the com was a waste of time. I didn't even know where I was or how to tell them to find him.

I didn't need to run now, since a large crowd was around me and I didn't want to draw attention to myself. I walked at a brisk pace in the direction he was headed.

I rounded a corner. He was about fifty yards ahead. I let the towel fall to the ground.

"Hey!" I shouted.

He looked back.

Our eyes met.

He turned and faced me. I showed him my gun.

His eyes widened in surprise.

I'm sure he could hardly believe it. A woman brandishing a weapon wearing a swimsuit and shower cap.

A gun was in his hand in seconds. He raised it to aim at me. I glanced around to see if there were any innocents nearby.

He was far enough away from me that I wasn't worried about him firing the gun at me.

He thought better of it anyway.

He turned and began to run away.

I chased him. This would be our worst nightmare. If he got away, he would be able to report back that I was an operative. My cover would be blown.

I had to catch him.

It felt like I was in my birthday suit running down the street carrying a gun.

I still felt ridiculous but also resolved.

He wasn't going to get away.

I'd failed to save the girls on the plane. I couldn't have another mission failure less than a week later.

I ran faster.

8

The terrorist led me through a series of back streets. Thankfully, this area of the village was deserted. The townspeople were still at the race. All the shops were closed and no one was around to see the absurd outfit I was wearing. It also meant that if I had a chance to get a shot off, I could take it without risking hitting an innocent and also without blowing my cover.

The bad part was that the terrorist had the advantage. He knew where he was going. It made sense that he'd park his car on the outskirts of the village where he could avoid the risk of getting caught in traffic. He probably expected to breeze in, scope out the Olympic team, then whisk out without being seen.

He hadn't counted on being chased by a tall lanky blonde wearing a one-piece bathing suit and a shower cap. His mind had to be blown at that moment. He was probably amused. That'd work to my advantage.

He couldn't consider me that big a threat. At the same time, he clearly wanted to get out of there. He was moving fast, which was why I hadn't gained any ground since I first spotted him.

A problem. My cover was blown with him. This wasn't a good situation. He'd report back that I was an operative. Not an Olympic athlete. That'd give them an advantage. At that point, there'd be no reason for me to go to the Olympics and compete in the biathlon. Something I was actually looking forward to doing.

I was competitive by nature and the thought of being on the largest stage in the world competing against world class athletes was exhilarating. My Israeli trainer thought I actually had a shot to finish in the top twenty. I wanted to win a medal. Even go for the gold.

If I didn't make up some ground on this yahoo in the next thirty seconds to a minute, it wouldn't matter. He'd get away. His boss, whoever he was, would have my picture. Any chance I had of going undercover at the Olympics would be out the window.

Which was why I had to catch him. It appeared that we were getting to the outskirts of the village. I couldn't imagine him parking much further out of town.

I quickened my pace. The bathing suit had no place to hide the gun so I had to run with it in plain sight. I was fast. If I could give it my full effort, I thought I could catch him.

He was still in my sights. I was breathing harder but hadn't slowed. He had to be feeling it worse because his pace had slowed considerably. Not enough for me to get off a shot, but enough to where he had to be worried. He kept looking back to see where I was.

A rookie mistake. Curly trained that out of us. It only cost you time. You could always assume the threat was there. Curly taught us how to take one look, assess the speed of the threat behind you, then calculate how close he was at any given time. We used the turns to look back.

He made one of those turns and got a good look at me. I was closing in. I had to slow down at the corner though. I couldn't go bolting around the side of the building into an ambush. I stopped at the corner, took in a deep breath, and pressed my back against the wall. I brought my gun into position, and peered around.

The terrorist was fleeing away. Toward a parked car. He hadn't set a trap for me which now gave him a distinct advantage. He was going to get to that car and be on his way and there was nothing I could do to stop him. Maybe get close enough to shoot out one of his tires.

Maybe.

I shouted. He looked back again. Another mistake. *Ignore distractions*, Curly always said. Words won't kill you. Guns will. No reason to look back. Keep focused on getting away.

The good thing about hunting terrorists was that they weren't well trained. They focused on the unimportant. Stupid agility drills. Firing weapons in unrealistic situations. Mostly for show. I'd seen a hundred terrorist training videotapes and each one amused me. They didn't resemble real-life.

Still, he was getting away. He'd be to the car before I was close enough to get a shot off. Unless he stumbled. Or fumbled with his key fob.

I had no idea where Alex and the rest of the Mossad team were. They were supposed to be helping me. I was out of radio com, so my ear was silent. I figured we were out of range. They were probably searching for me, but they had a big area and would have no idea where I was.

I was on my own.

The man neared his car. He was getting away.

Out of nowhere came a black flash.

An SUV.

Large. Four doors with a rear cabin which probably had a third seat. The windows were darkened so I couldn't see who was driving.

Alex?

The SUV smashed into the terrorist. The front end hit him and sent him flying. At least five to seven feet in the air, where he rolled. It didn't look violent enough to kill him.

As expected, I saw him move while on the ground. He stood up and tried to limp away on the bad leg wounded by the bumper of the SUV.

The SUV was stopped now.

The doors opened.

A man got out of the driver's side. A second man from the passenger side.

Familiar faces.

I had to do a double-take.

The driver looked like A-Rad. How was that possible?

A-Rad was back in America. He didn't even know I was here. I hadn't spoken to him in weeks.

The other man was Bond. No question about it. I recognized his graying beard.

The confusion and exhilaration mixed like oil and water. It didn't make sense. Why were they here? Were they on a mission with the CIA? Tracking the same terrorists?

No. They were cut loose from the CIA, the same time as Alex and I.

Curly taught me not to waste mental energy trying to figure something out, when all I had to do was ask. They were less than fifty yards from me. I ran to where they had the terrorist on the ground. Face down. A-Rad has his knee on the man's back. Bond had retrieved the terrorist's gun which was thrown a few feet away when they hit him with the SUV.

A-Rad took some zip ties out of his pocket and secured the man's hands by the time I got to their position. Even more confusing. Why would A-Rad be carrying zip ties? Like he was in operation mode.

A-Rad jerked the man to his feet. Nodded at me when he saw me. Took the man to the back of the SUV, and deposited him in the back after securing his feet with more zip ties.

Bond looked at me with a silly smirk on his face. I knew what he was thinking.

Finally he lost his self control and burst out laughing. So hard, Bond actually bent over. With his hands on his knees.

"It's nice to see you, too, Bond," I said sarcastically.

I looked around to see if anyone was watching. No one was, so I hid my gun in the towel again.

"I think you look good," A-Rad said. Always trying to have my back. He shut the rear tailgate of the SUV and was beside me in seconds giving me a hug. It felt good to have his massive arms around me again.

I took off the shower cap and shook out my hair.

"What are you two doing here?" I asked.

"Alex said you were in a bit of a bit," Bond said, in his very British accent.

A bolt of anger rose up inside of me. Alex had called them. That's why they were here. Alex told them about the girls. The plane crash.

I was angry and felt embarrassed. Weak. Like I needed them to save me.

I made the conscious decision to lighten up. If anyone understood, it was these guys. Before they were our employees at AJAX. Now they were our friends.

I still didn't like feeling the vulnerability. Letting them see that I wasn't invincible even though they already knew it.

If I were honest, I was thrilled to see them. Everything seemed right in the world. For a moment at least. Having them there felt like old times. And they had disabled the terrorist threat. For that I was thankful, even though I didn't know how they knew to do so.

"Alex said you were in a bit of a way and told us to come and cheer you up," Bond said. "So here we are. And not a moment too soon. You're welcome, by the way. You must be slipping. Your man was about to get away."

"I had it under control."

"You're welcome, Jamie," Bond said a second time.

I should say thank you but wouldn't give him the satisfaction.

Bond was by my side before I knew it. He kissed both of my cheeks while putting his hand on my hips. In an inappropriate manner. His lips brushed against the corner of mine.

Early on in our relationship, Bond was a major flirt. At the time, I assumed he was interested in me. Now I think he did it to get a rise out of Alex. The two had almost come to blows on more than one occasion.

Bond was a former MI6 officer with British intelligence. An oxymoron, Alex used to quip. The two razzed each other nonstop. A man named Bond working for the British spy agency should expect to get a certain amount of kidding.

Bond was good at what he did though. Especially intelligence gathering. Formulating plans. Tracking down suspects. He left MI6 and came to work for AJAX. An art distributing company owned by Alex and me. Actually, a front for our CIA activities. Bond and I had shared several proverbial foxholes. If I had to go into a dangerous situation, I'd want these two by my side.

When things went south with the CIA, and AJAX was stolen from us, Bond and A-Rad were without a job. We'd paid them well enough that both didn't have to find a job right away. But spying was in their blood.

The last I'd heard, they were freelancing.

"Let's get in the car and out of sight," I said.

"Good idea."

"So why are you really here?" I asked once we filed into the SUV. A-Rad was in the driver's seat, Bond in the passenger side. The terrorist was in the back. He probably didn't speak English, but I wasn't worried about him hearing our discussion. He'd never see the light of day again.

"We told you," Bond said. We're here to save your hide."

A-Rad looked back at me and frowned. He would never make such a disparaging statement about me. He was probably this close to sticking up for me but knew I could fend for myself and wouldn't appreciate it.

"How long have you been here?" I asked, ignoring the "saving your hide" comment.

"A couple of hours," Bond said.

"Alex had us in the crowd looking for the terrorist. He briefed us," A-Rad said.

It started to make sense now. Alex called them to help us with the mission. He didn't trust Mossad. Not so much that he didn't trust them, as much as he preferred working with his own men.

"I'm surprised I didn't see you in the crowd," I said.

"You taught us well, Jamie," A-Rad said. "We stayed out of sight."

I didn't teach them. Curly did. Once they joined AJAX, they both spent three weeks at the Farm to get a crash course from Curly.

"So you saw the race," I moaned.

"Yeppers," A-Rad said.

I grimaced and waited for the snide remarks to come.

"You looked good out there. I've always wanted to watch you take a shower," Bond said. "Although, I always expected to be in there with you."

I slapped the back of his head.

"Bond, you're terrible."

"Bloody bollocks. What was that for?"

"You know what it was for."

Truthfully, it warmed my heart.

"We didn't see the terrorist until you saw him," Bond said. "It was written all over your face. I followed your eyes and saw him in the crowd. That's when we decided to help you."

"When you took off running after him, we hopped in the SUV and followed you," A-Rad said. "We wanted to have your back and be there if you needed us. You obviously did, so we decided to take him down."

"I'm glad you did. We'll turn him over to Mossad and see what he knows," I said.

"Give me ten minutes with him," A-Rad said, "and I'll make him talk."

I shook my head. "He's Mossad's problem. They're running this rodeo."

"Alex mentioned some girls in Syria," Bond said. "He said you might want to go get them. We're here to help."

"Mossad told me I couldn't."

Bond let out a chuckle. "Alex was right. You have lost it. When has that ever stopped you before?"

He had a point.

Although, storming one of Hoffman's fortresses by myself had not been something I thought was anything more than a suicide mission. Even with Alex, I didn't like our odds. With Bond and A-Rad, the odds probably shifted in our favor. Probably, since I didn't know how many armed guards there actually were at Hoffman's compound.

We'd been outnumbered many times and were still alive to talk about it.

"What now?" Bond asked.

"First things first," I said.

"What's first?" A-Rad asked.

"I've got to get out of this swimsuit."

9

The next morning
Mossad Headquarters
Tel Aviv

If you've seen one spy briefing room, you've seen them all.

The four of us, Bond, A-Rad, Alex, and I were sitting in one, in Mossad Headquarters. Waiting for Saul Geller to arrive to give us a mission assessment of the *Running of the Tubs*, which led to the capture of the terrorist who was now in Mossad custody undergoing questioning.

Enhanced interrogation we presumed. Probably involving water.

According to reports, the terrorist was spewing out information, no pun intended, faster than a broken fire hydrant.

Mossad had a way of getting prisoners to talk. Saul should have some actionable intelligence for us which was why we were there.

"What are we doing after we're done here?" Bond asked.

Alex answered, "You can do whatever you want. After the debriefing, they'll cut us loose for the rest of the week. We'll report back Saturday and head to Bavaria, Germany to begin our Olympic orientation and training. I still haven't been on an actual bobsled run."

Alex had a scab under his chin from the first attempt.

"You won the *Running of the Tubs*," I said. "That was a shocker."

Alex twisted his lips to the side. "By one tenth of a second. Barely one of your eyelashes."

"Can you imagine training all your life for the Olympics and losing a medal by one tenth of a second?" I asked.

"It happens all the time," Alex said. "Talk about regrets. I'd rather lose by ten seconds."

"The Olympics can be extremely cruel," Bond said. "I had a mate who was a runner. He was one of the favorites in the hundred meter hurdles. He fell down. He doesn't even know how. His feet got tangled up. All that work for nothing."

"I'm looking forward to going to the Olympics," A-Rad said. "I hope we have time to watch some of the events."

Bond and A-Rad weren't going with us. Mossad wouldn't let them. We hadn't told them yet. Alex and I would feel more comfortable having members of our own team with us when we tracked the terrorist cell, but Mossad wanted their men there. They couldn't get operational clearance fast enough to bring them in.

The only reason they were at this meeting was because they were technically the ones who captured the terrorist.

"How long is this meeting going to take?" Bond asked.

"I don't know," I said. "Could be ten minutes or ten hours."

"I hope it's not ten hours, I want to go to the beach," A-Rad said. "I need to check out the Israeli women."

My mouth wanted to fly open but didn't. I wasn't used to hearing A-Rad talk about checking out women. In all the time he worked for AJAX, I didn't remember one serious girlfriend.

I expected it out of Bond. He chased skirts at any opportunity, although he was more bark than bite.

Mossad headquarters were less than a mile from the beaches and I'd seen the Mediterranean when we were driving in today.

"Don't create an international incident," Alex said in a fatherly voice.

"I want to go to Hat Suck beach," A-Rad said, looking at his phone which appeared to be showing a map of Tel Aviv on the screen.

I chuckled at his pronunciation.

"It's HaTsuk, you moron," Bond said. "It's pronounced sook."

"I think it's souk?" Alex said.

I rolled my eyes at them. While I didn't know the correct pronunciation, I was sure they were all three wrong.

"Why don't you go to Hilton Beach or Stars Beach?" I asked. "Something you can pronounce."

A-Rad's eyes widened. "Will we see movie stars there?"

"Maybe," I said.

"Don't get your hopes up, mate," Bond said. "Beaches are segregated in Tel Aviv. Men and women have to be separated."

"No way," A-Rad said. "We're not going to the beach then."

"He's kidding," I said, winking at Bond.

A-Rad gave Bond a glare which only made his smirk wider.

"Do you want to come to the beach with me, Jamie?" A-Rad said. "You can be my wingman. You'll be a lot better than that bloke over there."

He pointed at Bond when he said it. "He'll try to steal my women."

"Bollocks. If I want your woman, I won't have to steal her," Bond said. "She'll choose me on her own."

"We're going to Jerusalem," I said to A-Rad. "The old city. We're going to walk where Jesus walked."

A-Rad seemed noticeably disappointed.

"I'm excited," I added. "We've got everything planned out. We're going to go to the Garden Tomb, the Church of the Holy Sepulcher, the Mount of Olives, the Temple Steps, the Western Wall, and the Garden of Gethsemane. I've been reading about these places in my Bible all my life. I can't wait to see them."

"I read where the Garden of Gethsemane has an olive tree that's more than two thousand years old," Alex said. "They think the tree was there when Jesus was in the garden."

"You should get you one of those, Jamie," Bond said with a silly smile on his face. "Finally, a plant you can't kill."

The three of them knew well my tendency to kill plants and trees. They knew not to give me one as a present. I couldn't keep them alive. They joked often that I shouldn't ever have a baby for the same reason.

"After that, we're going to float in the Dead Sea and then go to Masada," Alex said. "You should come with us."

"Does the Dead Sea have a beach?" A-Rad said. "I want to work on my tan."

"I've been there," Bond said. "It's not much of a beach. It's rocky and extremely muddy. It's hard to walk on. Also, no pretty girls there. Mostly women with kids. You don't want that."

"You don't have to come for the women. You can float on the water and not sink," Alex said. "It'll be fun."

"Sounds boring to me," A-Rad said.

"Masada is interesting," Bond said. "You have to admire the way the people of Israel held off the Romans for as long as they did. Are you going to hike up to the top or take the cable car?"

"Definitely the car," Alex said. "It's going to be over a hundred degrees outside. They say if you hike it, you should leave early in the morning to beat the heat."

"Why would you want to walk around a bunch of ruins when you can be around a bunch of pretty girls in bikinis?" A-Rad said.

The third time A-Rad had mentioned girls. Like he was back in high school. I hadn't seen him for several months, but this was a side of him I'd never seen before.

"What's happened to you, A-Rad? Why the sudden interest in girls?" I asked.

"He reached puberty," Bond said, pushing A-Rad on the shoulder playfully.

We all laughed. Everyone except A-Rad, who clearly wasn't amused. Bond was at the top of his game. He'd ripped off three funny quips in a row.

Before anyone could say anything else, the door opened, and Saul entered with a couple associates. Carrying files and a laptop. He acknowledged us, then set the laptop on the table, connected to the wireless network, to interact with a big screen on the wall.

The tone in the room immediately changed. Saul was as serious as a skill saw blade. I'd never seen him crack a smile or be one to banter.

He was all business and the joking around with my guys became a distant memory fairly quickly.

Fine by me.

I was ready to get the meeting over with and head to Jerusalem to check off some bucket list items. I only wished we had time to go to the Sea of Galilee and the River Jordan. To see where Jesus walked on the water and was baptized would be beyond thrilling. Maybe someday.

"Good work, everyone," Saul said, once his laptop was operating. "Capturing the guy at the race."

Everyone nodded because everyone deserved the credit.

"The man you captured is named Yardan Zaki," Saul said. "He's been on our radar for a while. He's talking."

"Anything actionable?" I asked.

Saul shook his head. "He's low level. He did confirm there is an Olympics plot. But he had little to no specifics."

"Is he working for Hoffman?" Alex asked.

Saul would probably get to that information, but Alex and I were both ones who liked for these meetings to be fast paced. To ask the pertinent questions and get on to a plan.

"Zaki doesn't know. Like I said, he's a grunt. But it's not hard to put two and two together. He gave us the names of his direct supervisors. With a little prodding."

I wondered if an actual cattle prod had been used.

"At least we kept him from reporting back to them," Alex said. "They'll be wondering what happened to him, though."

Saul shook his head again.

"What?" I asked.

He exhaled a deep breath. "There was a second terrorist at the bathtub race."

"A second terrorist?" I asked. "I didn't see him."

"We didn't either," Saul said. "But your camera did. Let me show you."

He typed something on the keys to his laptop. A minute or so later a video appeared on the screen.

"What's this?" I asked.

"This is the video you shot with the brush in the bathtub."

"I assumed that much. But what are we looking at? I don't see anything. It looks like my arm in front of the camera."

"That's your armpit," Saul said.

I thought I saw him crack a smile. The other three men in the room definitely did.

"You had the camera turned the wrong direction at first," he said.

My face flushed. Embarrassment came over me like a rush of water out of a faucet. On the screen was nothing but a light-colored tanned blob. In my defense, it wasn't easy pointing the camera in every direction, moving it up and down, pretending to wash myself, while keeping my eyes on the lookout for a terrorist.

"It's a good thing you shaved your armpits that day," Bond quipped.

The only one with the courage to say something rude. The others fought back a smile. Saul didn't even acknowledge the joke.

"Here it comes," Saul said. "The camera is turned the right direction now."

"It's not as easy as it looks," I said, defensively.

"Right there," Saul said.

He froze the frame and zoomed in closer. The man was not Muslim. He looked European.

"He's German," Saul said, confirming my thoughts. "Adalmar Wolf is his name. He's also on our radar. But we've never tied him to Zaki."

"It can't be a coincidence," Alex said. "They both have to be working for BGS."

Saul nodded. "Zaki confirmed as much."

"That means Hoffman is behind the kidnappings of the girls and the terrorist plot at the Olympics," I said.

"It appears so," Saul said.

"Then you have what you need to take Hoffman out," Alex said. "When do you plan on doing so?"

"I can't say," Saul said. "That operation is top secret."

"It should be soon," Alex said. "Before the Olympics. Take out his operations so you eliminate the threat on our lives."

"It's not that simple," Saul said. "Israel is a nation state. We have to act with discretion. Whatever we do will be highly scrutinized on the world stage."

"Israel has a right to defend herself," I said.

"We will act against Hoffman, at—"

"I know. A place and time of your own choosing," I said sarcastically, interrupting Saul.

"He's right, Jamie," Bond said. "It's complicated. This is a job for covert operations. Not Israeli military. Whatever is done can't be tied back to Israel. The United Nations condemns Israel every time they sneeze."

"What about the girls in Syria?" I asked. "Are you going to get them out?"

"That's complicated as well."

Not the answer I wanted to hear. I tamped down the anger. For now. The girls should've already been rescued in my mind.

"Surely recovering ninety-six kidnapped girls is within the purview of defending yourself," I said.

"I agree," Saul said. "We've looked at the operations and rejected it. Too risky."

The anger went up another notch in the thermometer of my emotions.

"You can't be serious," I said. "Are you telling me you aren't going to rescue the girls either?"

"Not at this time."

I wanted to jump out of my chair and hit the wall. "Why did you send me up in that airplane?" I said, no longer willing to mask my anger. "I risked my life. For what?"

"For the intelligence."

"My point exactly. You sent me up there to find out the location of the kidnappers and who was behind it. I did that. Why go to all that trouble to gather intel if you aren't going to act on it?"

"It's not that simple."

"If you say that one more time, I'm walking out of here."

"Think about it," Saul said. "Getting into Syria is the problem. Where the girls are being held is not that big a deal. According to satellite images, the compound only has four or five guards at any one time. It's off a main road. We know where it is and how to get to it."

"Then it's something you should do."

"Why can't special forces go in?" Bond asked. "You do these kinds of operations all the time. I imagine the Yanks and the Brits would even help you."

"It's a matter of risk reward. The international risk is too great for the reward," Saul said.

"You wouldn't say that if one of those girls was your daughter in that compound," I said as roughly as I could without causing a full-blown confrontation.

"I care about those girls, and I resent any insinuation that I don't," Saul said, almost matching my intensity.

"Doesn't sound like it."

"Mossad has greater interest in Syria to protect."

We were both sitting on the edge of our seats now.

Alex and I had to deal with these kinds of political calculations at the CIA. That's why we were freelancing. Things were so much better that way. We would've already acted and gotten those girls out if I hadn't trusted Mossad to do it.

"Why don't you let us go in and get the girls?" Bond asked what I was thinking. "We don't have any political worries. Sounds like the four of us can handle it."

Saul shook his head.

"How are you going to get into Syria?" he said. "I have no doubt you can take the compound. Then what? How are you going to get the girls out of Syria?"

"We could fly them out," A-Rad said. "Isn't there a landing strip at the compound?"

"There is, but how are you going to evade Syrian radar? They'll shoot you down before you get ten miles in. Definitely before you could get the girls out."

"We'll bring them out by ground then," I said.

"How? There are ninety-six of them."

"We'll take a bus in," I answered. "Remember what I did in Belarus. I brought fifteen hundred girls out of Russia in thirty buses."

"How are you going to get a bus through the border? You need two buses actually," Saul said.

"Saul has a point. There's no border patrol between Russia and Belarus," Bond said. "The Syrian border is tighter than my ex-wife in a pair of spandex."

I gave Bond a slight glare. At least, he cleaned it up based on what he was probably thinking.

"What?" Bond said to me. "I was going to say facelift, but I didn't want to sound sexist."

I ignored him.

So did Saul. "As I'm sure you already know, the border between Israel and Syria is closed. Going in and out is impossible. The only way in is through Lebanon by way of Jordan. Israeli citizens can't go into Syria. Americans can't get in either. Getting the girls out by bus is impossible. Border patrol will never let you. You'll be arrested on the spot."

"I'll figure out a way to get them out," I said. "We only need one bus."

Alex disagreed. "A tour bus has between forty to sixty seats. That's not enough."

"We can squeeze them in," I said. "If some girls have to stand or sit on the floor then so be it. They can take turns sitting. I don't care. That's better than where they are now. I have to get them out."

Alex nodded but continued his thought. "We'll also need supplies. Water. Food. Some of the girls might need medical attention."

"Guns," A-Rad said. "I need guns. You promised me a gunfight."

A-Rad was a nickname given to him because he was a radical. He loved action. At least when the cause was just. He felt like he'd been robbed if he didn't get to kill a bad guy on a mission. If I said we were going to storm a compound with heavy artillery, he'd ask what we were waiting for.

"We need a plan," Alex said.

"Where's the Colonel when we need him?" A-Rad said.

The Colonel worked for us at AJAX and was in charge of strategy. A retired Air Force Colonel, he ran more missions in Afghanistan than any man alive. When it came to strategy, he was one of the best. The last I heard he was flying rich people around in private planes.

"You've all identified the problem," Saul said. "As you can see, there's no good solution."

"What if I find a way around the problem?" I asked.

"You find a bus and come to me with a plan, and I'll sign off on it. As long as it can't be tied back to us."

"I'll find you that bus," I said, confidently.

Although, I had no earthly idea how.

10

The Church of the Holy Sepulcher
Jerusalem

"Did you just touch my bottom?" I asked Alex in a sharp tone. So sharp, his eyes widened noticeably.

"Yeah. So what? I'm your husband. I'm allowed."

"We're in a church," I said. "It's called the *Church of the Holy Sepulcher*. This is where Jesus was crucified and buried."

"How do they know that?"

"I know the answer. Would you like for me to enlighten you?"

He looked around disinterested, but said, "Sure."

"I was reading about it. Constantine the Great, in 312 A.D., was converted to Christianity."

"Good for him."

"His mother, Helena, was sent to Jerusalem to find out where Jesus was crucified and buried. The locals led her to this place. Ancient lore said Jesus was crucified right here."

I pointed to the display ahead of us.

"And buried down there," I added, pointing over the railing at a large structure, with hundreds of people lined up to get inside of it. Supposedly, built over Jesus's burial tomb.

"I don't know," Alex said.

"What's not to know? It's been recognized since the fourth century."

"I don't buy it."

"Most evangelical Christians don't. There's another place called the Garden Tomb. Not that far from here. It's an alternate site. We're going there next."

"I don't think Jesus was crucified upstairs and buried downstairs, thirty yards from here."

"No one really knows for sure."

"That's all I'm saying."

"I like it though. I feel close to God here."

We'd done the complete Via Dolorosa. The fourteen stations of the cross. The route Jesus likely took from his trial with Pilate to his crucifixion at Golgotha. If the lore was right, I was standing ten feet away from where Jesus was crucified.

I had my doubts. Same as Alex. That didn't mean I wasn't getting chill bumps looking at it. The solemnity of the moment had overwhelmed my emotions which was why when Alex touched my bottom again, I slapped his hand.

Even though he was joking, it seemed inappropriate.

"If you don't want me to touch you all the time, you shouldn't be so pretty," he said.

"So, you want me to be uglier?"

"No. I like that I'm married to the prettiest woman in the world."

"Flattery will get you everywhere. Keep your hands to yourself though. I'm praying."

He leaned over to kiss my lips. I turned my head away.

"Am I not allowed to kiss you either?"

"Later. At the hotel room. We're in church. This is called the *holy* sepulcher. Try to act a little bit holy. If that's possible for you."

"Have you never heard the verse in the Bible? To greet one another with a holy kiss?" Alex said. His smile was as wide as I'd ever seen it. "That's what I'm doing."

I didn't want to give him the satisfaction of laughing, but it was funny. I gave him a quick peck on the lips and continued through the line.

It was my turn.

On the wall was a large statue of Jesus on the cross. Above some rocks. Said to be *the* rocks. In front of the altar was an encasement. About waist high.

I bent down and got on my knees. My hand shook, as I put it through the hole in the glass, and was able to reach in and touch the rock. The prayer I mouthed was filled with emotion. Tears welled up in my eyes. My whole body felt a wave of peace run through it.

I prayed for the girls being held in Syria. For our safety. The success of our mission.

Alex was right. We didn't know if this was the actual spot. It didn't matter. I was near where it was. The actual location wasn't the point. The opportunity to express my thankfulness for the sacrifice was the reason I was there.

More tears blurred my vision. I slid back out, stood, and wiped them away.

Alex was next in line but followed me out. He didn't touch the rock. I asked him why.

He gave me a slight frown. "Tens of thousands of people touched it. No telling how many germs are on that rock."

That caused me to laugh out loud.

I patted my husband on the chest. More playful than anything.

Alex never ceased to surprise me. He said the most unbelievable things at the weirdest times. Which was one of the reasons I loved him so much. He was unpredictable.

He was also a bit of a germaphobe. At the hotel the night before, he had refused to lay on top of the bedspread. He said the same thing. "No telling how many germs are on that bedspread."

Alex also refused to walk barefoot on the carpet in the hotel room. I'm surprised he'd even get in the shower. He says at least it has soap cleaning it.

That's how big a baby he was about it. Although I never in a million years thought that'd keep him from touching the rock.

Clearly, this experience wasn't as meaningful to him as it was to me.

"What now?" he asked.

"Are you bored?"

"No. It's not that."

"What is it then? You seem disinterested. This is where Jesus walked. This is a once in a lifetime thrill for me. I was hoping it would be for you as well."

"I'm into it. I think it's cool."

"Cool?"

"I don't know. My relationship with the Lord is personal to me. I don't have to be in Jerusalem to feel it. I don't need an altar or a church to feel close to God. I'm glad we're here though. And I wouldn't want to be here with anyone but you."

"That's sweet. I think I understand what you mean." That caused me to lighten my tone some.

"Let's go downstairs to the stone slab," Alex said. "Remember the promise you made to the waitress this morning. To pray for her son."

Alex was paying attention. It warmed my heart.

On the first floor of the church was a stone slab. It's said to be the rock Jesus was laid upon when he died. People came from all over the world to pray at the rock and touch it. When we had breakfast that morning in Tel Aviv, we told the waitress we were coming to the church in Jerusalem. She asked us to pray for her son who had cancer. We said we would. At least, I said I would.

The stone was crowded. People waited patiently. When it was their turn we observed some kneeling and praying. Touching the stone. Some even kissed it.

"If you kiss the stone," Alex said, "I'm not kissing you for the rest of the day. Not until you wash your lips."

"That sounds like a good reason for me to kiss it," I quipped.

I didn't kiss the stone. I wasn't a germaphobe, but Alex had a point. He did kneel beside me and reached his hand out over the stone and prayed. I touched it and said a prayer for the waitress. Afterwards, we got in line for the tomb. The wait was said to be nearly an hour.

Alex wasn't sure he wanted to wait that long.

"It's going to be too late to go to the Dead Sea and Masada."

"We can go tomorrow."

"I thought we were going to Syria. To rescue the girls."

"Not until I find a tour bus."

"You haven't heard back, I guess."

"Not yet. Come on Alex. We've come this far. I want to see the tomb. When will we get another chance?"

He reluctantly agreed. I didn't like standing in line either, but didn't want to waste this opportunity. Even if it wasn't the actual tomb, I still felt something deep inside. A peace. With the nature of my job, I was constantly surrounded by evil. People who wanted to kill me. It felt good to be able to tap into my spiritual side. Even if tomorrow, we were back dealing with the dregs of the world who kidnapped girls and sold them as sex slaves.

My phone rang.

Causing me to jump.

The caller ID didn't tell me who was calling. I answered it anyway.

I was waiting on a call. Regarding securing a tour bus to rescue the girls in Syria. I'd run into a number of dead ends in Israel. Americans and Israelis weren't allowed to enter Syria. No one was allowed into Syria if they had an Israel stamp on their passport.

Renting a tour bus from Israel was out of the question. I was told to try Lebanon. A plan had been formulated in my mind. My thinking was if we could rent a tour bus, we could cross into Syria, rescue the girls, and drive them out, pretending they'd been in Syria on a tour.

Saul Geller at Mossad was actually working on getting fake passports made for the ninety-six women. So, when we brought them to the Syrian border, the authorities would let them out.

Mossad was also making Swedish passports for Alex and me. And for Bond and A-Rad. Just in case we found a bus. Something that would get us across the border safely.

I fumbled with the phone out of my pocket, but was finally able to answer it.

"You can answer a phone in a church, but I can't kiss you," Alex said. "Something's wrong with that."

"Shhh."

I pushed him away and turned my back to him. Put my finger in one ear so I could hear the person on the other line.

"Marhaban," I said. A casual Arabic greeting in case the person on the other line was calling about the tour bus. I had gone to great lengths to keep him from thinking I was American.

"This is Yousef. About the tour bus in Syria," he said back to me in Arabic.

"Do you have good news for me?" I said.

"No. Sorry. All tour buses to Syria are booked."

"We'll pay. Big money. Above the going rate."

"Sorry. No. No buses available."

I'd been warned of that. After the war, Syria opened its borders, and tourism was starting to come back. But most tour companies in Lebanon and Jordan had just started running tours again. Since Americans weren't allowed into Syria, they hadn't ramped up the number of tours. The demand wasn't that great from other countries. Not yet anyway.

The tours weren't that great anyway. A lot of the tourist spots weren't open to the public yet. You had to go through a lot of war-torn areas to get to them. Tourist dollars were better spent elsewhere. In Egypt at the pyramids. In Lebanon or Jordan. In Israel, where tourism was thriving.

"Did you try Tripoli?" I asked.

"I tried everyone I could think of."

"Did you find a guide?"

"That wasn't a problem. I've got people. No bus available."

All foreigners could only go in with a guide. Which was problematic. How were we going to attack the compound, rescue the girls, and keep the tour guide cooperating long enough to get us all through the border without getting caught?

It seemed impossible.

I hung up, unable to hide the disappointment.

Alex noticed. He'd heard my end of the conversation, so I didn't need to explain.

He gave me a reassuring hug, which didn't make me feel better, but I appreciated it, nonetheless.

It didn't help my mood though. The reason we never went on vacation. Having fun was difficult for me. I could count on one hand how many vacations Alex and I had taken over our married years.

I felt guilty when I thought about the girls and the abhorrent conditions they were subjected to. The reason I had insisted on coming to Jerusalem was because it didn't seem like a vacation. More of a spiritual pilgrimage. It had taken my mind off of the girls until the phone call. Now I was fretting again. Trying to rack my brain to come up with a plan to save them.

I was running out of options.

Maybe there weren't any options to begin with. Curly said that would happen in missions. Things didn't always work out. We just had to accept it and move on. Something difficult for me to do.

What Alex said next shocked me back into reality and out of the doldrums I was feeling.

"Do you get the sense we're being followed?" he asked, barely above a whisper.

"Now that you mention it."

"I noticed it back at the station where Jesus was tried before Pilate."

"Station one."

"The Church of the Condemnation. Then again. Where Jesus was beaten. The Church of the Flagellation."

My mouth almost flew open. Alex was paying attention after all.

"I did have this eerie feeling that we were being watched," I said.

I remembered feeling it but ignored it. Who would be watching us in Jerusalem? I thought I was being paranoid. Curly said to never ignore our instincts. A good reminder.

We both had a sixth sense about these things. Curly said he could train us how to spot a tail, but not how to feel one. That was something innate in us. A skill most people didn't have.

Alex and I both had it. It had saved both of our skins on more than one occasion.

"Do you think it's Mossad?" I asked.

"Why would they follow us?" Alex answered.

"To make sure we don't do something stupid and take off into Syria on our own."

"That's exactly what we'd do if we had the chance."

It never ceased to amaze me how Alex always had my back. We were one. Rescuing girls was my passion. But if I were going to Syria, then he was too. And he'd take ownership in it.

"I don't think it's them though," Alex said. "I feel a threat."

My arms were around Alex's neck so quickly he could barely react. I kissed him deeply. Taking his breath away.

When I stopped, my lips were still close to his. He asked, "What happened to not kissing in church? Not that I'm complaining."

I held the embrace and put my mouth by his ear.

"I saw the German," I said.

"What German?"

"Wolf. The one at the bathtub races. The second man. Hoffman's thug. I only caught a glimpse, but I'm sure it's him."

Alex looked around. Discreetly. His hand was on my bottom again. This time I didn't mind. It was part of his act. Fit with our cover.

I didn't have to tell him to be careful when he looked. He already knew it. We couldn't do anything to let the man know he'd been made. If we did, we'd lose the chance to catch him.

"He's gone," I said.

"Do you think he knows you saw him?"

"I don't know."

"What do we do now?"

"Keep acting normal. See if he resurfaces."

"We could lose him."

Alex and I were trained to lose a tail. Although, this German was apparently good at spycraft. I didn't see him at the races, and we didn't notice him until now. Losing him would not be easy. The advantage he had was all the alleyways in old Jerusalem and all the small shops. I was already mapping out a plan in my mind.

I'd memorized the map before we came. Not for mission preparedness reasons, but so I'd know where all the tourist spots were and how to get to them.

"We have to think this through," Alex said. "If we start taking evasive measures, he'll know we're onto him. I'd rather he didn't know."

"That way, we have the element of surprise."

"Exactly. Let's deal with him now," he said.

"I agree. I don't want the rest of our day ruined."

"Do you want to see the tomb first?" Alex asked.

"No. I want to go find the German and kill him."

"Is that an appropriate thing to say in a church?"

"Okay. Fine. I want to find the German and send him to hell. Is that more church-like?"

"Works for me."

We got out of the line. Alex took my hand and led us out of the church. Both of our senses were heightened. I was in full mission mode.

I also liked our kiss. The passion behind it, along with the sudden adrenaline rush from seeing the German, had sent desire through me like I'd taken a shot full of hormones.

Alex must've sensed it, too.

"Let's kill this guy, then go back to the hotel," he said.

"Works for me."

11

The Old City of Jerusalem

One of the biggest problems a spy might encounter in the field was spotting a tail and then losing him. Which was exactly what happened to us. We saw the German in the *Church of the Holy Sepulcher* and he disappeared from sight. Alex and I didn't know if he realized he was outed or if he left to set a trap for us at another location.

Either way was problematic. If he knew he was outed, he'd change his tactics and come after us differently. Or go home and regroup. Which meant we'd spend the next several hours looking over our shoulders unnecessarily. It'd put a serious kink in our sightseeing plans.

Of course, one or both of us being dead would put a bigger damper on things as well. So, we had no choice but to revert to spycraft mode.

If the German intended to set a trap for us, we had to figure out when and where. We could take evasive measures and lose him altogether, but that would only put off the inevitable. At some point, the threat had to be eliminated.

Curly taught us that. Use evasive methods to out the tail rather than lose him unless you had a strategic reason to keep him from knowing where you were going. Like you were headed for a clandestine meeting, a safehouse, or had a strategic mission objective.

We didn't have any of those. We just wanted to walk where Jesus walked and feel the deep spiritual connection that came with the experience. It wasn't lost on me that Jesus was hunted on those same streets more than two thousand years before.

Although hunted wasn't really the right word.

Jesus placed himself in the open and dared the authorities to arrest him. He came down from the Mount of Olives riding a donkey with a throng of worshipers around him. Once inside the city walls, he went directly to the temple where the most people were gathered, and where he'd be the most noticed.

As if that wouldn't draw enough attention, he overturned the moneychangers and drove them out of the temple infuriating the authorities.

We decided to do the same thing. Sort of.

The most open area in all of the Old City of Jerusalem was the Western Wall. The massive plaza held thousands of people at one time. The German had to know we would eventually make our way there. No trip to Jerusalem was complete without visiting the Western Wall.

There, we could turn the tables on him.

Become the hunter, not the hunted.

Not do something as brazen as overturn the moneychangers but let him know we were onto him. Then chase him out of the plaza and deal with the threat once and for all. The same way we did with his compatriot at the *Running of the Tubs*. Hopefully, we could take the German alive as well and turn him over to Mossad for interrogation.

He might even know more than the other lowlife. The hope being, since he was German, he might have a closer connection to Hoffman who was also from Germany.

Standing outside the Church of the Holy Sepulcher, we formulated a plan.

Alex thought if the German was going to act, he'd do so before we got to the wall. Spring an attack along the way. If he was waiting for us at the wall, he'd probably be there to reestablish the tail and was following us more for reconnaissance than to actually try and kill us.

I agreed. An attack would likely happen along the way.

But which way?

Since we didn't know, we decided to split up. The German couldn't follow both of us.

There were two directions we could go once we exited the church. To the left, took us back the direction we came. The Via Dolorosa in reverse order.

That's the direction Alex went.

He had the more dangerous route. It led him through the Muslim Quarter to the Jewish Quarter. Not that the Muslim Quarter wasn't normally safe for tourists. It was. The problem came from the many shops that lined the route and the narrow alleyways.

The German had hundreds of places to hide. He could launch an attack from inside a shop or restaurant. He could blend into a tourist group and wait for Alex to pass and then follow him. Attacking him from the rear. He could appear out of nowhere at the top of the stairs and fire down on him. He could hide among the stones of an archaeological dig and be almost impossible to see.

Alex also had the longer route. Which put him in danger longer. He'd be vulnerable the entire time until he got to the Western Wall.

Which left me with a great deal of consternation. If the German did go after Alex on the way to the Western Wall, I'd be no help to him. All I could do was pray Alex made it to the wall safely and navigate my route as quickly as I could. So I could get to the wall before Alex and make sure the German wasn't there waiting for him.

Of course, the most dangerous route was whichever one the German took. Which meant my direction wasn't safe if that's the direction the German decided to go after leaving the church. I wasn't familiar with the lay of the land on my route, but I figured from the looks of what I'd seen to that point, that it'd have many of the same dangers.

I went over the map in my mind before setting out. Trying to remember it. It was easy to take a wrong turn. That'd make me even more vulnerable if I were trying to spot a threat while trying to figure out which direction to go.

It seemed complicated. My route went from the Christian Quarter where the Church of the Holy Sepulcher was located, to the Armenian Quarter and the Jaffa Gate. Through a number of twists and turns and alleyways. All uphill.

In the German's mind, he could easily envision us going that way. It led to a number of religious spots. The Upper Room. David's Tower. Mount Zion. The area where Peter denied Christ.

I wanted to see all of those and it pained me that I wouldn't have the chance. At least not now.

Anger was building inside of me.

The German was ruining our day.

My mind shifted into full spy mode. I couldn't be distracted by what sites I was missing or blinded by rage. At that point, I didn't care if he knew I was onto him. My head would be on a swivel and my focus had to be on any potential threat. I wasn't even going to try and hide my abilities.

He probably already knew who I was anyway.

My feet still hadn't moved. Curly always said not to act until you were ready unless you had no other choice. I wanted to think through what I might be getting into. That'd help me react more efficiently if the need arose.

There'd be less people on my route. That was a good thing. Most of the tours ended at the Church of the Holy Sepulcher then backtracked to the Western Wall, where they boarded a tour bus and went to the next stop on the tour.

That'd make it easier for me to act. In a public place, the bad guy always had an advantage. They didn't care if innocents were caught up in the fire. I did. The German could fire wildly with no concern about loss of life. My shots had to be restrained and strategic.

I instinctively looked to my left. Alex had disappeared from sight. Knowing him, he was halfway to the Western Wall by now. He'd throw caution to the wind and go after the German like a lion goes after an overmatched prey.

Another thing which told me Alex was in a much better frame of mind than I was. Doubts were creeping into the inner recesses of my soul. Curly said it'd eventually happen. That I'd know when to quit. If I were like most, I'd wait too long. Like a prizefighter who kept coming out of retirement to fight that next fight because he couldn't give it up.

In my line of work, staying too long meant I was probably dead.

Better to leave too early, than too late, Curly said on more than one occasion.

I took in a deep breath. Touched the gun on my hip for reassurance. Mentally checked my heartbeat and emotions to see if they were in check. Now wasn't the time to entertain doubts about the future. Curly said if you're thinking about the future on a mission, you won't have one.

My pulse remained at an even pace, even though the adrenaline surged inside of me like an underground volcano ready to explode. I let out a deep breath, to steady the heartbeat even further.

To my right were a set of steep stairs. I took them two at a time. Easily. Once I started moving, it was usually with a purpose.

I hated stairs.

I had nightmares about running up a set of stairs and a bad guy was at the top with a gun. I'd see a flash of light, then wake up. Always before the outcome of the gunfight was decided.

Tactically speaking, a gunman at the top of the step had every advantage. The high ground usually tilted the odds in your favor.

It made me think of Masada and how the Jews held off the Romans for months. I hoped the German wasn't going to ruin that outing as well. We were planning on going tomorrow.

The steps took several turns which made it even more concerning. The German could be behind each turn. I didn't have time to stop and clear them before throwing caution to the wind and bolting around them. What was I going to do anyway? Lead with my gun. Like a Chicago cop. Scare some unsuspecting tourists out of their wits by shoving a weapon in their faces.

All I could do was round the corners at full speed and hope for the best.

If I were the German, I wouldn't spring an attack on the stairs. Not in an enclosed space. There were too many other ideal locations along the way.

A thought that made me shudder.

So many negative thoughts were going through my mind. I tried to control them, but they were unusually strong.

The girls in Syria.

I still had no good solution for getting them out of there.

The Olympic terrorist threat.

How was that going to play out?

The biathlon.

I wasn't prepared to compete on the world stage. I was suddenly afraid of embarrassing myself.

Was I going to live long enough to have a baby?

Why can't I get my mind right?

Curly would shoot me himself, if he knew I didn't have my full focus on the only thing I could control at the moment. I mentally slapped myself to get back to the task at hand. If the German did act, I would only have a split second to respond. If I were thinking about the girls in Syria at the time, the Olympics, or a baby I didn't have, that split second could cost me my life.

I don't want to do this much longer.

The last thing I should be thinking about at that moment.

At the top of the stairs was a long walkway. Completely covered. Without the sunlight to brighten it, the area was dark and moody.

My senses erupted.

This seemed like the type of place I'd launch an attack if I were the German.

That got my focus back. Every part of my being wanted to pull my gun, but I resisted the urge.

I wonder how Alex is doing?

Another distraction out of my control.

I couldn't get out of that tunnel fast enough. It was surprisingly empty. When I exited, I let out a breath I didn't realize I was holding. It took a second to get my bearings. I was near the Jaffa Gate and the Tower of David.

What now?

A plan popped into my mind when I saw the gigantic walls of the city.

The Ramparts Walk.

The city of Jerusalem was surrounded by fortified walls. Tourists could actually walk on those walls. They were roughly forty feet high and two to eight feet wide. The types of walls you'd see at an old castle in England minus the moat. They allowed movement from one side of the city to the other and had been around for fifteen hundred years. Destroyed and rebuilt numerous times.

Warfare today was much different than when the walls were first built. It caused me to smile. The United States could shoot a cruise missile through a living room window from thousands of miles away and kill someone sitting in a chair. I could see soldiers on the ground trying to hoist ladders to breach the walls and men at the top fighting them off.

It took a second to get my sense of direction.

The northern walk to the right led back to the Christian Quarter. I didn't want to go that way. If I remembered correctly, the southern walk led to the Western Wall. It'd get me there faster.

Did the German know that as well?

Of course, he did.

If I met up with him on the wall, we'd be in a confined space. Nowhere to run or hide.

I liked my chances.

Even if the German wasn't on the wall, it gave me a decisive advantage. The high ground. The purpose of the walls to begin with. Once I got to the plaza, it'd also give me a view over the Western Wall. Looking down, I could scan the area for the German.

The Dung Gate was at that location. The name of the gate caused me to chuckle. I needed to research it and see how it got that name. Seemed appropriate since I was searching for human excrement at that moment. A term Alex often used to describe the rats we searched the world for.

How is Alex doing?

If I hurried, I could find out.

Seeing the walls put me in a fighting spirit. I'd studied some of the battles for the city of old Jerusalem. Probably the most fought after city in the history of the world.

In 1967, Israel won the Six Day War when they gained control of the walls. Legend had it that the Jordanians set up fortified positions on the wall. Israeli officers had little to no information as to where they were hiding. So, they had a beautiful young Jewish girl stand on a balcony in the Mamilla neighborhood and remove her clothing in a slow and provocative manner. According to rumors, the Jordanian soldiers rushed to the edge of the walls to look at her, revealing their positions and numbers.

No one knew if that story was true or false, but it sounded plausible. Thinking of her reminded me of the girls in Syria.

It caused a pang to shoot through my heart.

I went into one of the shops and bought a ticket for the Ramparts Walk and got a map. It confirmed what I already knew. I could run on the wall without being seen by others. It allowed me to get to the Western Wall in no time.

I entered the wall by David's Tower and ran as fast as I could, careful not to trip on the uneven stones. No sign of the German.

I exited the wall at the Dung Gate and quickly made my way to the square overlooking the Western Wall Plaza. To get into the plaza required going through metal detectors. The German wouldn't risk trying to go inside the plaza carrying a weapon. Alex had his Mossad credentials, so he was able to take his weapons inside with him.

When I arrived, Alex was already there.

How was that possible?

Was I that slow?

I was really losing it. Too much thinking.

Standing in line to buy a ticket had slowed me down.

Alex was standing at the wall, facing it. I watched him write something on a piece of paper and then place it in the wall.

From the square, I could see the plaza from every angle. The German was nowhere to be seen.

Satisfied, I went through the metal detectors and met up with Alex. He had to exit first. Men and women were separated. They wouldn't let me in.

"Any sign of the German?" I asked.

"Not a hide nor hair."

"What should we do?"

"Let's enjoy the rest of our day. We'll keep an eye out for him. What else can we do?"

"Where to?"

"Garden of Gethsemane. Then the Garden Tomb."

A dozen tour buses were lined up outside the Dung Gate.

It broke my heart.

What I wouldn't give for one of those buses. It only reminded me of the girls in Syria and how I was failing them.

* * *

The next morning

We went to Masada. There we spotted a tail.

Not ours.

Someone else's.

12

Masada

Alex saw the terrorists first.

From the top of Masada, we could see for miles in every direction. At eleven hundred feet high, we looked down on the hills to the west and the Dead Sea to the east. A cloud was nowhere to be seen. The sun was bright and hot, though a haze hovered over the horizon making the deep blue waters we'd seen driving over appear to be powder blue from that vantage point.

"Jamie, do you see that tour bus?" Alex said.

He pointed to the north.

"Yeah. I see it," I said. "Do you think we could rent it?"

What I wouldn't give for a tour bus. Soon we'd be leaving for Germany and the Olympics, and I'd be unable to do anything about the girls in Syria.

"Do you see that Jeep behind it?" Alex said.

"Yeah. What about it?"

We were standing on the edge of the mesa facing east. The ruins of Masada were behind us as was our tour guide. We had abandoned the tour almost from the beginning. Not that he wasn't good, it's just our attention span was shorter than a five-year old's. In our defense, we were trained to react in a split second to gunfire.

Even on vacation, Alex and I were always higher strung than we should be and focusing for an extended period of time wasn't our strong suits.

"What's wrong with that picture?" he asked.

I didn't answer right away. Pondered the question.

Flat and straight road. Two laned. Tour bus traveling fifty to sixty miles an hour. Headed south. No oncoming traffic. The Jeep was two hundred yards behind. The Dead Sea on the driver's left side.

"The Jeep isn't passing the tour bus," I finally answered.

"Bingo, bongo. You win the grand prize. Two tickets to a gunfight with a group of terrorists."

"What do you mean by a gunfight? And bingo, bongo? Where did that come from? I've never heard those words come out of your mouth before."

"Trying to shake things up. I don't want you to get bored with me."

"I could use a little boring about now."

"I don't think you're going to get it. That Jeep is up to no good. I think they're tailing the bus."

"That's a little bit of a stretch, don't you think? You have tails on your mind."

Alex got a silly grin on his face.

"Don't even say it," I said. "Does everything have to turn into a sex joke with you? Didn't you get that out of your system last night?"

"Never. You'd better get used to it. You've got fifty more years of it. At least."

"Don't remind me. Curly always said to take things one day at a time. That's all I'm trying to do."

Alex put his foot up on the knee high wall that surrounded the fortification. He continued to stare at the bus.

The Jeep's behavior was strange. It maintained a distance behind the tour bus. Slowed when the bus slowed. Speeded up when it sped up.

I let out a sigh.

"Can't we have one day for a vacation? Is that too much to ask?"

"Doesn't look like it," Alex said. "If that Jeep turns into the parking lot, then we'll know."

The bus turned into the Masada entrance. The Jeep held back, then entered a minute or so later.

Strange.

The bus pulled into a parking space near the entrance where all the other tour buses were parked. The Jeep parked by the exit. One man got out. Loitered. Fidgeted.

My pulse suddenly revved like a sports car engine turned on for the first time in the morning. The man looked like a terrorist to me.

"Bad guys go on vacation sometimes. Maybe they're just here to see the sights," I said trying to convince myself of something I knew wasn't true.

"There are four men in that Jeep," Alex said. "Only one got out."

"The one who did get out has his eyes peeled on the tour bus," I said.

"Maybe they're going to steal it."

"Not if I steal it first."

The bus began to unload. The occupants spilled out into the parking lot. Several looked up in the sun, stretched. Others fumbled with hats, sunscreen, sunglasses, and gathering their belongings. The normal things people do on a tour. They looked Asian.

All four of the men in the Jeep were out of the car now as well. Milling around. Looking over at the tour bus. One of them started walking toward the bus. The other three lagged behind.

Both Alex and I noticeably tensed. Stood straight up. I instinctively touched my gun. Alex did the same.

"What are you going to do?" I asked. "Shoot him from up here?"

"I could get lucky."

A bullet fired from the mesa would travel all the way to the ground. The law of gravity would take over. The chances of it hitting the man were slim to none, though. With a sniper rifle, it'd be an easy shot for someone of Alex's skills. Not with a handgun.

I pointed over to the cable car. It'd just left the station and was going down the mesa to the main building. If I remembered right, it'd take it ten minutes to come back again. By the time it unloaded, then loaded the next set of people whatever happened on the ground would happen and it'd be too late for us to do anything about it.

"How do you want to play this?" I asked.

"I don't know," Alex said. "They haven't done anything yet."

The tour bus driver had his group organized and led them to the entrance and into the building. The terrorist followed them in.

His friends were still by the car.

"Who goes to a tourist stop and stays with the car?" Alex said.

"Maybe their friend is buying all the tickets."

"And maybe it's not hot outside."

The sun was beating down on us. It reminded me to wipe the sweat off my brow which was increasing because of the tense situation unfolding in front of my eyes.

The three men still made no effort to go inside. Instead, they lit up cigarettes and casually hung around the vehicle.

"Is that a bulge I see," I said.

"Yes. I'm happy to see you," Alex quipped, with a sly grin on a smug face.

I grimaced.

"Is that all you think about?" I asked.

"No. Sometimes I think about... Who am I kidding? That's all I think about."

I was as bad as Alex when it came to kidding around and off-colored jokes. As soon as the word bulge came out of my mouth, I knew one of us was going to jump on it. If we didn't have that banter, I'd think something was wrong with us.

So we did it often. At least with each other. Neither of us talked that way around other people. At least I didn't. I didn't know what Alex was like when he was with the guys and I wasn't around, although I suspected he participated some. It certainly didn't bother me if he did. Alex liked to joke around, but he was never crude.

"So much for this being a day of relaxation," I said. Disheartened. A confrontation with terrorists was the last thing I wanted to do today.

Unless it was in Syria. *Not going to happen.* I was getting close to having to accept it.

Alex grunted his agreement.

It wasn't noon yet and the day had been anything but relaxing. When we left the hotel, we spent thirty minutes taking evasive measures to lose the German. We didn't actually know if he was there, but we threw the entire spycraft book at him if he were intent on following us today.

We refused to spend the day looking over our shoulders. So we didn't even try to hide the fact we were skilled and trying to lose him. If he had followed us, he was better than I thought he was.

He couldn't possibly know we were coming to the Dead Sea and Masada. Both an hour away from Jerusalem.

I hoped he was looking for us and wasted his entire day scouring the old city. Better yet, I hoped he left the city and went into the countryside looking for us. We could be anywhere. Nazareth. Bethlehem. Caesarea. The Sea of Galilee. The sight of the Transfiguration. Where Jesus fed the five thousand. Magdala. The River Jordan.

Armageddon. That's where Alex wanted to go.

"There's nothing there." I had argued. "It's a big valley. A flat area between the mountains."

"I think it'd be cool to see where the final war to end all wars is going to take place. I hope I'm alive when it happens."

The statement caused me to laugh out loud. "Are you crazy? Have you read the book of Revelation? That's the last place I'd want to be."

"I've read Revelations."

"It's Revelation. No "s" on the end."

"Whatever. If there's going to be a final battle, I want in on it."

"I want to be raptured."

"Not me. I want in on the action."

"Something's wrong with you."

Alex grabbed my shoulder bringing my thoughts back to the present potential impending battle.

"Look," he said pointing down at the men. "They definitely have guns. I saw glint."

Glint was when the sun reflected off a gun. Soldiers looked for it on a battlefield. As a way to identify enemy positions. Curly taught us how to spot it and to avoid doing it.

"I can see the bulge in their shirts and the sun reflecting off the guns," Alex said.

"The guy who came inside doesn't have a gun. Not if he's coming up here."

To come to the top of the mountain, you had to go through metal detectors. We used our Mossad credentials to bring our weapons through security.

"We should tell someone," I said. "Let the authorities handle the threat."

"What's wrong with you?" Alex said. "Since when are you afraid of a fight?"

"I'm not afraid. It's not our fight."

"What did Curly always say about fighting?"

"A masterly retreat is a victory."

"Not that one."

"Part of the happiness in life is not winning battles. It's avoiding them."

"That's not it either."

"If you win a fight with your wife, you lose."

Alex chuckled. "That's true, but that's not the one I was thinking of either."

"Never quit fighting for those who can't fight for themselves," I said with resignation dripping from my voice.

"That's it."

I rubbed my eyes roughly. "Why does trouble always follow us?"

"Because we can do something about it. The people in the tour bus are lucky to have us."

I let out a moan.

"Oh, come on," Alex said. "It'll be fun. You won't even break a sweat."

"I'm already sweating!"

Another loud sigh.

"All right. Let's do this," I said, even though I didn't want to.

* * *

Alex rode the cable car down to the main gift shop and to our car where he could keep an eye on the three men in the Jeep. I stayed on top of the mountain and blended in with the tour so I could stay close to the man who followed the group to the top of Masada.

My job wasn't to confront him, but only observe.

Creepy guy and I followed the tour which was actually enjoyable. The guide spoke Mandarin which I understood and was able to pick up most of what she said. My senses were heightened, so I was able to concentrate on the tour guide but also keep one eye on the bad guy who was always close by.

By that point, it was clear he was following the group.

The tour of the ruins of Masada started at the Western Palace, then moved to the Byzantine church. The makeshift baths were interesting. Nine hundred and sixty people barricaded themselves on the mesa thousands of years ago. I wondered how so many people shared such meager quarters. Things like sanitation, growing food, and lack of medical care were all issues they had to overcome, while fending off the Romans for several months.

Creepy guy looked bored. I doubt he spoke Mandarin.

We viewed the ruins of the barracks, the cistern, and where the royal family lived. I didn't realize King Herod actually used Masada as a vacation spot.

The guide spoke of the courage of the Jewish people who died on that mesa. Masada had become a symbol of Jewish heroism. A source of national pride. I could feel it. Even though the guide wasn't a Jew, she conveyed the sentiment beautifully.

It caused me to bow my back. Stiffen my neck. Touch my gun. I wanted to take the low life scum out right then and there. Alex was right. We had an obligation to protect these good people.

Then the vermin left.

Without notice.

Yawned. Stretched and headed for the exit. I watched as he boarded the cable car and rode it down to the gift shop. I hurried over to the edge of the wall where I could see the parking lot. He exited the building and walked over to the Jeep where the other three men were still hanging out.

The four men got in the vehicle and left.

A wave of disappointment came over me. I was getting psyched up to kill them.

Then relief washed over me. It was better this way.

Alex got out of our vehicle and we watched them drive away. He looked up at me. I shrugged my shoulders and put out my hands in his direction then motioned for him to come back up. I wanted to finish the tour with a guide. Masada was interesting.

Alex hit the fob on our car and rode the cable car back to the top.

No harm, no foul. We'd wasted an hour, but nothing like an adrenaline rush to shake us out of any possible doldrums.

"Why did he leave? Did they make you?" Alex asked. Meaning did creepy guy realize I was on to him.

"I don't think so. I pretty much followed the tour. He hung around but got bored and left."

"So much for that. I guess we don't have to kill anyone today after all," he said.

"The day's not over yet," I said. "You might still make me mad."

He laughed, then took me in his arms and kissed me deeply. A hot and sweaty kiss. It lasted a little too long considering the dry and dusty conditions. My mouth was as dry as a camel's back and felt just as cruddy.

I grabbed Alex's hand and took him around to all the places I'd seen on the tour. Alex wasn't particularly interested in the ruins. He wanted to see the west side, where the Romans built the ramp.

"There's not much to see over here," I said, when we got to the overlook.

Alex was deep in thought. Scanning the horizon.

"What are you thinking about, honey?" I asked.

"Strategy. I wouldn't have let the Romans build that ramp."

"How would you stop them?"

Alex put his finger in the air like a pistol and began to fire in several directions.

"I would've picked them off."

"First of all," I said, adding a chuckle to the words, "they didn't have guns in those days."

"Whatever. Spears. Bow and arrows. Rocks. I would've used whatever I had to kill the people building the ramp."

"The Romans used Jewish slaves to build them."

I remembered the guide saying as much.

"Ooh. That makes sense. Brilliant. Those Romans were smart. That's why they ruled the world."

"Not that smart. Otherwise, they'd still be ruling it. World domination is not possible. Not for any extended period of time."

"Not until the Antichrist comes. Armageddon. I want to be there, so I can take him out."

A bolt of anxiety flashed through me. I searched my soul to figure out why.

We'd gotten distracted.

"Where's the tour group?" I said, my voice conveying the nervousness I was feeling.

We had been keeping an eye on them even though it appeared the threat was gone.

"They were here a minute ago," he said.

"They must've left."

We walked back to the west side of the mesa. Quickly, and it didn't take long. One side to the other was not that far.

What I saw was horrifying.

I even let out a shriek.

The members of the tour were on the bus. The Jeep was parked in front of it. Blocking it in. The man who'd been with me on the tour was now at the door of the bus. Wielding an assault rifle.

I wanted to scream at the top of my lungs to warn the people inside. Wouldn't matter. They couldn't hear me and the gunman was on board now.

The doors closed behind him.

The tour bus began to move.

It exited the parking lot. Instead of turning left, it went to the right. The Jeep pulled in behind it and followed.

"No! No! No!" I practically shouted.

Alex and I took off running at the same time. We flashed our badges to the cable car operator. Fortunately, we didn't have to wait for the car. It was already at the top. We squeezed in before the doors closed.

When we exited the cable car, we ran through the gift shop and into the parking lot to our car.

I drove.

I was better at driving at high speeds. Alex was better at shooting from a moving vehicle.

Too late.

When I pulled onto the main road, the bus was already out of sight.

13

"What's up ahead?" I asked Alex with as much sense of urgency as I could put behind my words.

We were on Highway 90, speeding south, away from Masada chasing the tour bus and the terrorists who had commandeered it. The road was flat and I was reaching speeds of a hundred ten miles per hour. I was panicked because we should've already caught up to the bus. My fear was the terrorists had forced the driver to turn somewhere and we'd missed it.

"Mount Parsa is to the right," Alex said. "Yeelim Stream is just ahead. Rahas Ascent on the right. We passed that. Midbar Yehuda Nature Preserve is coming up."

Alex was butchering the names.

"Funtasy Island is dead ahead," he said. Almost comically. I thought maybe he was kidding. Now was not the time. I was expending all my emotional fumes on the chase and what we were going to do to kill the terrorists once we found them.

"Are you kidding?" I asked.

"Nope. It's a real place. Funtasy Island. Sounds like fun."

Hard to keep my eyes on the road and roll them at Alex at the same time.

"What is it?"

I was convinced he had pronounced it wrong.

"It's an island. Where they have fun."

"Is that a real place?

"Looks like it. Ahead on the left. Five miles or so."

"It must be an amusement park?"

I had no idea why we were wasting our time talking about it.

"We're in the middle of the desert," Alex said. "It must be some kind of beach on the Dead Sea. No wait... It's a movie theater."

"Come on Alex." I was practically shouting at him. "I don't think the terrorists are taking those people to the movies by gunpoint."

The adrenaline pulsed through my veins like I had downed a dozen energy drinks at one time. I tried not to let my frustrations show. I'd been in the passenger seat more times than I could count. With Alex yelling at me to give him directions.

"You're right," he said. "Sorry. This road will take us to Beer Meruha."

"Beer?"

He must be getting that pronunciation wrong as well. Then I remembered Beersheba in the Bible. A number of towns started with Beer in its name.

"That's what it says," Alex said.

"Look at the map."

"I'm looking at it."

"Where do you think they're taking these people? Think about it. If we lose that bus, those people are dead."

Alex knew the gravity of the situation as much as I did. He was better at controlling his emotions.

"You watch the road," Alex said nervously. I'd come dangerously close to flipping us over on the first curve we had encountered for several miles.

"I got it under control."

"All right... Let's see. Where should we go?"

Alex was so calm he could be looking up a good place for lunch. I admired that about him, but it was getting on my nerves at the moment.

He said, "From Beer, however you pronounce it, they could go right toward Egypt. If they go left, it'll take them to Jordan. My guess is they'll go west. Toward Sinai, Egypt. Saul Geller said they've had a lot of problems with Egyptians kidnapping tourists and holding them for ransom. If they get across the border of Egypt they can disappear until somebody pays money to get the tourists back."

I looked down at the speedometer.

"How far until the turnoff?"

"Twenty miles."

"I'm going 120. There's no way they can get to Egypt before I catch them. Not unless they turned off somewhere before then."

"There's no place to turn until that Beer place."

"Why haven't we already caught up to them? They must've turned off somewhere."

Alex's head was buried in his phone again.

"We didn't pass any main roads. There aren't really any side roads. I don't see a place for them to turn."

"They turned off somewhere. Should I turn around?"

Alex looked down the road. We were on a straightaway and could see for several miles. He was making the same calculations I was making in my head. From Masada, the bus had a ten-minute head start. Roughly. Probably not traveling faster than sixty miles per hour. I did a quick calculation. I was going nearly twice as fast. Not the entire time though.

Still... I should've caught them within ten minutes.

Had it been that long?

I didn't think to look at the clock when we started the chase. In the heat of the moment, time takes on a new dimension. Ten minutes was a long time in the fog of war. We could also see approximately five minutes down the road. If I turned around, and they were ahead of us, they'd be gone for good.

If they were behind us and had pulled off the road, the people in the bus were in grave danger as well.

The decision was excruciating. Life and death. The welfare of those people might very well rest on me making the right decision.

Both hands gripped the wheel so hard my knuckles were white.

What to do? What to do?

Indecision when a decision has to be made immediately is always the wrong decision, Curly said.

"Go back," Alex said.

"I agree."

That confirmed it.

It suddenly seemed like the right thing to do. I slammed on the brakes and slid to a stop facing the opposite way. Screeching the tires. I could smell the rubber.

We faced north. Toward Masada. Back in the direction we came. Barely hesitating, I floored it, screeching the tires a second time.

"Keep an eye out for a side road," I practically shouted. "It has to be there."

The Dead Sea was now on our right. On the passenger side. In Israel, you drive on the right side of the road. Same as in the US. That meant the side road would be on my left. On my side of the car. I slowed down so we wouldn't miss it.

Alex was still buried in his phone which was why he probably missed the turn off to begin with.

"There's nothing on the map," he said, with frustration mounting in his voice as well.

"Forget the map," I said. "Keep your eyes peeled for some kind of side road."

"There," Alex said. Pointing. "Stop."

I slammed on the brakes. The car fishtailed. I turned into the slide to correct it. I'd had plenty of driving courses and knew how to keep the car on the road. Although, I was thankful no traffic was coming from the other direction. The rental car was being pushed to the limit. The metal groaned from the abuse. Fortunately, I didn't blow out a tire.

A dirt road went over a slight hill. I could see why Alex had missed it. I pulled off to the side and stopped the car. We got out and looked at what were obvious tire tracks. Thick tire tracks like what a tour bus would leave.

"Those are bus tracks," Alex said. "They go several inches into the dirt. Something heavier made those tracks. Like a bus."

Shouting erupted in the distance, giving us more confirmation.

A woman screamed.

Men shouted. Some in Arabic. Others in broken English.

The words were threatening. "Tamat. Rama. Qatal." *You die. I shoot. Kill.*

Alex and I pulled our weapons and ducked our heads down and made our way to the edge of the berm. Careful not to be seen. I peered over and immediately saw the bus and the men surrounding the tourists who were out of the bus now.

Alex and I fell flat on the ground at the exact same time and scooted forward until we could see them, but they couldn't see us.

The scene was horrific. Like out of a movie. The four gunmen brandished assault weapons. The tourists were huddled together. The men aimed the weapons at them and shouted more words in Arabic.

The Asians had no clue what the men were saying, but the intention was clear from the terrorists' demeanor causing the Asians to cower in fear.

One man, the bus driver, tried to calm the situation. His hands were out in front of him, and he pleaded in Arabic for the men not to harm his passengers.

The apparent leader of the band of thugs, raised his rifle and struck the bus driver with the butt of the gun, sending him to his knees. Then pointed the gun at the driver's head. Causing me to prepare to act.

"Cooperate or you die," the leader said. "Tell them to take out all their valuables and put them on the ground. Phones. Watches. Wallets. Purses. Tell them to empty their pockets and take off all their jewelry. Rings. Bracelets. Necklaces. Earrings. Everything."

The driver staggered to his feet. The gash on his head bled. His instructions to the passengers were in Mandarin. Some started to slowly comply. The thugs got more aggressive with them when they weren't moving fast enough.

Several let out screams as the men manhandled some of the passengers. Some were pushed to the ground. They grabbed hair. Pushed one man to the ground then kicked him.

The rage was rising inside of me but it was controlled so I wouldn't do anything rash.

"Open the luggage compartments," the leader said. "I want all the luggage taken out."

We maintained our cover. No reason to act too soon. The passengers weren't in immediate danger. The gunmen might intend to kill them but would wait until all the loot was accessible. Rummaging through a bunch of dead bodies in that heat would not be pleasant.

"How are we going to play this?" Alex asked.

"Straight up."

Assault weapons were good and bad from our perspective. Bad because they could fire thirty rounds within seconds. Good for the same reason. Terrorists didn't show restraint when it came to guns. They were taught to empty their weapons at whatever threat came upon them. We needed to figure out a way to get them to do so without getting struck by one of those bullets.

We couldn't win a gunfight. Four men, thirty rounds, meant a hundred and twenty shots could be fired at us within a few seconds. Even the most unskilled shooter could kill us with an assault rifle. Certainly before we could gun down all four. Even with the element of surprise.

We couldn't shoot at the men even if we wanted to. The problem was the configuration.

From our vantage point, the gunmen were between us and the tourists. That meant if we fired and missed, we could hit one of the innocents. If we circled and came in from the other side of the bus, the tourists would be between us and the gunmen. No way to shoot around them.

I had an idea.

A surprisingly good one.

Alex was usually better at logistics when it came to gunfights. I was better at executing them. Only slightly better, but I had the ability to fire my weapon with precision in the face of overwhelming odds. Alex could too. But he also had the ability to know the best way to take them out.

"I have an idea," I whispered to him.

"That's good, because I got nothing," he said.

"Do you see the Jeep?"

Of course, he did. It was right in front of us. The tour bus was on the dirt road facing west toward the mountains. The passengers and men were gathered to the right of the bus. The Jeep was off the road, a distance away. The doors were open, and the engine was still running. The terrorists had obviously exited it quickly.

"This won't be much fun," I said.

"For you or for me."

"For you."

"I thought that was what you were going to say. Not many of your ideas are fun for me. No offense."

"It was my idea to make love last night," I said, with a smug grin I could feel form on my face. I'd made him pretty happy the night before at the hotel.

"Okay. Not all of your ideas are bad. Although, why are you bringing that up now?"

I wasn't sure why. It's something we did to release the tension. Some of our best banter was in the heat of the moment. When the bullets were flying or about to. As was the case now.

"Can you make it to that Jeep without them seeing you?" I asked.

He raised his head and gave it a quick glance, then ducked back down. The sounds coming from the passengers were getting more panicky. The men's shouting, more threatening.

We probably didn't have a lot of time left.

"I think so," Alex said. "The men have their backs to us. If I sprint, I can probably get to it before they notice me."

"The driver's side door is open. The vehicle is running."

"What do I do when I get to the Jeep?" he asked.

"Hightail it out of there. The men will come running after you. Towards me. I'll be right here and take them out."

"It'll be four against one. They have assault rifles. You have a handgun."

I rolled my eyes.

Then his eyes widened in recognition. He knew what I was thinking. As soon as the men saw the Jeep driving away, they'd unload their weapons. Within seconds, their guns would be empty. It'd take them some time to eject the magazines and load new ones. About the amount of time I needed to shoot each of them between the eyes. Or in the chest. Whichever I chose.

It did mean Alex would take the brunt of the shots. Couldn't be helped. My hope was that the men would fire wildly and most of the bullets would miss the vehicle. Those that did find their marks would be absorbed by the vehicle and Alex would be safe inside.

"That's a dumb idea," he said.

"Do you have a better plan?"

"No. And I think it'll work."

I nodded.

"Three. Two. One," Alex said, and jumped to his feet to sprint toward the Jeep.

Something I expected.

When Alex had a Band-Aid on his body, he ripped it off. I tore it off slowly. He reacted impulsively to things. Before he had time to talk himself out of it.

I was ready.

Alex made it to the Jeep without being seen by the men. But not the tourists who gave away his element of surprise by looking at him. From the wide eyes and gaped mouth of the tourists, the gunmen recognized something happening behind them and turned in time to see Alex a few feet away from the Jeep.

Alex fired a shot in the air.

Brilliant.

That'd hold their attention for a second as they instinctively ducked. The tourists screamed and fell to the ground, distracting the gunmen as well.

Alex was to the car. He jumped into the driver's side of the vehicle. The men ran toward him. With their guns raised. Another good thing. They wouldn't shoot as straight on the run.

The tires spun slowly in the desert sand, but Alex was able to speed away backwards. Driving with one hand with his head down. From memory. Fortunately, there were no obstacles between him and my position.

The white Jeep sped by me like a blur. The men stopped when their guns were empty of bullets.

Perfect.

That's when I emerged from my position. Stood like a phantom I'd seen the protagonist in a movie do a hundred times. The sun was directly overhead, so they could probably only see my form in the bright light.

My gun was pointed at them. The men were far enough away from the tourists that I felt comfortable firing.

I didn't have that advantage for long. They'd retreat back to the bus for cover. Use the humans as shields.

I wasn't about to let them.

I ran toward them. Thank you, Curly. I could fire on the move. The first bullet hit the leader in the head. Right between the eyes. He was the only one with the courage or stupidity to try and stand his ground and fight. He tried to reload his weapon, but was on the ground, before he even got the magazine out of his belt.

The other three had their backs to me. I hit one in the side of the face when he looked back to gauge the threat. The other two, I shot in the back. The greater mass. Aimed for the vital organs.

Within seconds the four men were dead.

Alex came running from behind and stood beside me.

"I was hoping you would save one for me," he said, somewhat out of breath.

"I'm sorry. You should've said something, and I would've."

"Next time."

"That was a good idea you had," he said. "Two in two days. You're on a roll."

We walked toward the bus with our weapons lowered.

"The coast is clear. You're safe now," I said to the frightened tourists in Mandarin.

The driver staggered to his feet. Blood ran down the side of his face and his shirt was stained, but the wound wasn't gushing, so he'd be okay.

Alex flashed him his Mossad credentials. Then tore off a piece of his shirt and handed it to the man to put on the wound.

I spoke to him in Arabic and told him we were there to help.

"I speak English," he said.

"Are you okay?" I asked.

"Thank you. Yes. Bless you. You saved our lives."

"It looked like they were just going to rob you," I said.

"More than that. I heard them talking about hostages. They were going to kill half of us and take the rest across the Egyptian border and ask for a ransom. You are a hero. Thank you again."

"I'm sorry this happened to you," I said sincerely.

"If there is ever anything I can do to thank you, don't hesitate to ask me," the man said.

"Where are you from?" I asked.

"Lebanon."

"Does your company do tours into Syria?"

"Yes. I am Syrian. That's my home. I lead many tours into my country."

"Were you serious about helping me?" I asked.

"Of course. You saved my life. Ask anything short of my first-born son and it's yours. I don't have much money, but what I have is yours."

"There is something you can do for me," I said, feeling a wide grin come upon my face.

14

Syria
Al Masnaa Checkpoint

It felt like one of the most dangerous things I'd ever done.

Akeem told me on several occasions not to worry. He was the Syrian guide who assured me he could get us and the tour bus across the border of Syria by way of Lebanon. Akeem was the one who had led the tour of Asians into Israel that we'd rescued near Masada.

We'd gone to Beirut first to change buses and drop off his tour group. Since that bus had been in Israel, it couldn't be taken into Syria. Anything American or Israeli wasn't allowed across the border.

Which caused me to chuckle nervously. Alex and I were American and worked for Mossad. A hated combination in that part of the world. At any given time, and no matter where we were in Beirut, we were within a thousand yards of dozens of people who would kill us in a second if they knew we were there.

Getting in and out of Beirut hadn't exactly been a walk in the park even though Akeem's company was based there. Riots had erupted in the city and getting around the various roadblocks hadn't been easy. He also had his tourists to consider. He had to get the group of Asians to their hotel safely before he could turn his attention to us and the task at hand.

After Alex and I rescued Akeem and his passengers from the Egyptian terrorists at Masada, Akeem had expressed his undying obligation to do whatever I asked. It seemed like a lot, but he was willing to smuggle Alex and me, along with A-Rad and Bond into Syria. Smuggle wasn't the right word. He intended to drive right up to the Syrian checkpoint, flash his credentials, pay a small bribe, and drive us through the checkpoint with us sitting in the bus in plain sight.

And he wasn't worried about it at all. Unless the soldiers searched the bus and found our stash of weapons. Then we'd be lucky to get out of there alive.

If they didn't search us, we should get into Syria without any trouble. Alex and I had fake Swedish passports and A-Rad and Bond had German passports courtesy of Mossad. Akeem was entering Syria under the guise of leading a four-day tour with us as his customers. Since he led tours into Syria all the time, he knew the ropes and had the proper credentials. That's what we were counting on to get us in.

The itinerary had to be precise for the border patrol soldiers. Every minute accounted for. We'd start in Damascus. Then the tour would go north to Palmyra where we'd visit the Bel Temple and the Valley of Tombs. Day three we'd drive back to the old city of Damascus and visit Azem Palace, Hananiya Church, Straight Street, and the Al Hamidiyeh bazaar.

The guide was required to be with us at all times. We could barely go to the bathroom without him. Syria allowed tourists in, but they had to be under the watchful eye of a Syrian guide at all times.

Under different circumstances, I would've loved to go on that tour. It's too bad such wonderful ancient relics were under the control of despots. This was true in many middle eastern countries. I'd love to see the sights in Iran. Probably never going to happen.

What would really be interesting would be to see the Christian sites in Syria. Damascus in particular was mentioned many times in the Bible. The Apostle Paul had his encounter with Christ on the road to Damascus. Saint Ananias Chapel was said to be where Ananias worshiped.

Ananias was the one God told to meet Paul and lay hands on him so he could regain his sight. The Shrine of John the Baptist was said to hold the actual head of the apostle, although I doubted that was true.

Under different circumstances, I'd like to go to the Christian Quarter and Saint Thomas' Gate and tour the many ruins said to date back to the first century.

As it were, we'd see none of those things. Other than that we'd leave the checkpoint and drive to Damascus. That's when we abandoned the itinerary. We would head north, but not to Palmyra. Instead, toward Aleppo and the northern section of Syria. The most dangerous area. Where the girls were being held.

If everything went well, we'd rescue the girls, file them into the bus, and drive them to a different checkpoint where we would exit Syria under the ruse of a tour leaving Syria going to Lebanon.

In the stash of guns and ammo were ninety-six Swiss passports for each of the girls. Another thing I hoped the authorities didn't find.

The biggest worry was if the soldiers found our weapons which were hidden in the floor of the bus. Akeem said they wouldn't look. Probably, he said. Which wasn't reassuring. If they did, we had little to no recourse other than to fight our way out of the situation. Taken alive wasn't really an option.

If we were taken alive, we'd be subjected to hideous torture for several hours. Then beheaded, which wouldn't come soon enough. We all knew the risk. Even Akeem. He knew why we were going into Syria. I thought he had a right to know. He was willing. Out of obligation to us for saving his life, but also out of a moral obligation. He hated what his country had become. That Syria would provide safe haven for a man like Hoffman to kidnap girls and use them as sex slaves. Akeem had a daughter and couldn't imagine someone doing that to her.

The drive from Beirut to the checkpoint took a little over an hour. Ironically enough, a crescent moon lit the sky. The symbol of Islam for centuries. I wasn't sure if that was a good omen or a bad one.

Akeem had insisted on crossing the border at night. We weren't about to argue with him. It made sense.

The guys used the opportunity to catch some sleep. Curly always said to eat and sleep when you could. You never knew when you'd get another opportunity. I couldn't sleep. Either out of nervousness or because my mind was preoccupied with how to get the girls out of their prison.

Getting through the border might be the easiest part of the mission since we might have to blast our way into the prison and fight our way out, with ninety-six young women to protect.

I could see the lights of the checkpoint ahead as we crossed the border. I was concerned about the fact we only had four people on the bus and expressed that sentiment to Akeem. Wouldn't that be suspicious to the border agents?

He waved his hand in the air dismissively. "I'll tell them business is not good. They know. Most buses are half full or less. Too much war. Until it stops, tourism will not thrive. I remember the days when all our tours were full. Not so for years."

I liked Akeem. He drove a taxi in Damascus for many years. Fled his country during the civil war. Settled in Lebanon and worked for a tour bus company. Eventually purchased the company. Expanded it from two buses to four and a dozen or so employees. Leading tours to Israel, Syria, Jordan, and Turkey.

Akeem had invited us into his home earlier for a dinner his wife made. Manakish was a delightful dish. A round bread from dough she had made that morning. It was shaped in the form of a pizza with a spread of cheese, meat, and za'atar, a blend of spices including sesame seeds, dried herbs, sumac, and salt. The middle eastern alternative to tomato sauce.

The food was served with a cup of tea. We were thankful for the hospitality and shared with her our appreciation. She even packed enough food to last us for four days, and enough for all ninety-six girls for two days. At a great expense to Akeem. We offered to pay him, but he would not accept. He did let us pay for the bottles of water needed for that many girls.

Akeem drove the bus slowly to the checkpoint. Alex and the other guys instinctively woke without Akeem or me having to say anything.

If Akeem was nervous, he didn't show it. He had a huge smile on his face. I was nervous enough for the both of us. The guys acted like we were out for a nighttime scenic tour. Didn't seem the least bit concerned.

Almost bored. Like they weren't going to get too excited until we got to the real action.

When I saw the soldiers carrying assault weapons, I touched my hip even though my gun wasn't there. I almost felt naked without it. Certainly vulnerable. Seeing the weapons caused the guys to perk up some as well. Their bodies stiffened and their shoulders squared. We all tried to change our demeanor to that of tourists.

A few extra heartbeats a minute, had heightened my senses. I took in a deep breath to calm my already frayed nerves. I still hadn't fully recovered from the fiasco on the airplane. Perhaps that's why I was thinking so much about the ninety-six girls. To keep my mind off the four I'd already lost.

Akeem pulled the bus to a stop, motioned for us to stay put, then exited before being ordered to by the soldiers. With our passports and itinerary in hand. I couldn't hear what they were saying, but I could see Akeem talking to them. His hands and arms were highly animated.

No cause for concern. Most middle eastern men were highly expressive in their verbal communication. One soldier had his finger on the trigger, but the other was looking at the passports and Akeem's credentials with his gun slung loosely over his shoulder.

Without warning, a soldier stuck his head in the bus and ordered us out. Akeem had said that might happen, so we were expecting it. We weren't armed, although Curly said we were always armed as long as we had hands, feet, elbows, knees, and even our heads that could all be considered deadly weapons when applied properly.

We'd talked through the plan. In the event of trouble, we'd have to fight our way through it and get back to the bus. Then speed back to Lebanon if possible while someone got the weapons out of the hidden compartment in the floor. The checkpoint was a couple of miles into Syria. Hopefully, we could get out without them catching up to us.

One of the soldiers took an interest in me immediately. He got extremely grabby. I could tell Alex didn't like it. I didn't either. In normal situations, he would've lost a couple of fingers. At best. At worst for him, he'd be eating all his meals out of a straw for six months.

I gave Alex a "don't do anything rash kind of look." I could deal with a little groping if it got us through the checkpoint.

The soldier questioning Akeem took our passports into the guardhouse. Presumably to see if they were in order. This was my first experience with Mossad. I'd gotten through many checkpoints with fake CIA passports, and ones we had created on our own. Alex had a number of people proficient at making us every kind of fake ID imaginable guaranteed to get us through any security anywhere in the world.

I assumed Mossad had the same skill. We'd soon find out.

The man's hands were no longer on me, but he stood next to me looking me up and down. I wanted to wipe the lustful look off his face. Instead, I pretended to be scared of him. That seemed to give him enough satisfaction and he left me alone.

I took my cues from Akeem. When he became concerned, I'd be as well. Actually, I was always concerned in these situations. Hope for the best but prepare for the worst. I wouldn't be comfortable until we were on the road. Although Akeem said that was when things got really dangerous.

Once we got further north, and into areas outside the control of the Syrian regime, we could be stopped anytime by Syrian soldiers or by ISIS. Even Russian soldiers patrolled the area.

Fifteen minutes later, we were on our way.

Alex was still a little riled about the man getting handsy with me.

"You were getting a little friendly with that guard," Bond said. Meant to get even more of a rise out of Alex.

"He didn't even buy me dinner first," I said, making light of it. The last thing I needed was Bond and Alex getting into it.

"I didn't know we were allowed to touch you like that, Jamie," Bond said.

"You're not," I said.

Bond had gotten a little too touchy feely on more than one occasion. Before I met Alex and especially after we started dating. Not as much since we were married. Otherwise, Bond might not be able to walk around on his own power.

"I almost broke his arm," Alex said.

"I don't think I'd let someone touch my wife that way," Bond said.

He had a huge smile on his face, so we'd know he was kidding, although Alex wasn't looking in his direction and clearly wasn't amused.

"He didn't even thank me," I said.

"Way to go Jamie. Take one for the team."

"Shut up, Bond."

"Who's going to make me?"

"You know who."

"Both of you shut up," I said roughly. "I'm the one who had to put up with it."

They both did clam up. A-Rad stayed out of it. He was as protective of me as Alex was. He didn't say anything, but he was probably seething as well. That soldier didn't know how close he came to having his neck broken.

Fortunately, the guys had shown restraint. As did I. Part of what we had to deal with as spies. Nothing like what the girls were dealing with up north. Now that we were past the checkpoint, we needed to focus on that.

Alex must've sensed it because he said, "This is your rodeo, Jamie. How do you want to play it?"

"Do you remember what I did in Belarus?"

"Remind me."

"That's where you rescued those girls who were kidnapped by that Turkish oligarch," A-Rad said.

He wasn't with the CIA at that time, but they'd all heard stories. The girls thought they were signing up to become mail order brides to America. Instead, they were loaded on a bus and taken across the border to Russia where they were pimped out as prostitutes. Held in abandoned monasteries outside of Moscow.

"You got them out by bus," Alex said.

"Without firing a shot," I said.

"How did you do that?" Bond asked.

He was with MI6 at the time and knew nothing about the operation.

"I drove right up to the monasteries and told the soldiers guarding them that I had orders to move the girls."

"And nobody questioned it?"

"Not a one. We ran thirty buses. Rescued fifteen hundred girls. We drove them back to Belarus."

"I'm not so sure that would work in Syria," Bond said.

"Do you prefer to shoot first and ask questions later?" I asked.

"Yeah!" A-Rad said enthused.

He was the radical one. He'd always choose a shootout, to subtle manipulation and spycraft.

"I hate to agree with Bond," Alex said, "but why take the risk? There are only two guards according to satellite images. We can take them out with no trouble."

"I'll do it," A-Rad said.

Saul Geller had given us satellite images and plenty of intelligence. We even had a rough layout of the building. The women weren't heavily guarded. Where were they going to go? They were safer inside that prison than out in the desert roaming around with all the hostiles in the area. If ISIS got their hands on the girls, they'd be in much greater danger and their treatment would be even worse. If that were possible.

It was. At least now, they were sold to rich men. Who treated them as high-end prostitutes. Men who wouldn't dare damage Hoffman's assets. As strange as it sounded, that beat being raped and beaten by a bunch of terrorist desert dwellers who were slightly above a caveman in intelligence and common sense. Below the neanderthal man in morals.

We had our guns out of the compartments.

"Let's try diplomacy first," I said. "What does it hurt? We can always kill them if need be."

"I think you're making a mistake," Bond said.

"So noted."

We made the drive to the Aleppo region without incident. In fact, we barely saw any signs of life. The compound where the girls were being held was out in the middle of nowhere anyway though next to a main road.

The sun was up, and we probably should've slept but everyone was in mission mode now. When guns were in our hands, our insides came to life.

I explained everything to Akeem who was a trooper. He'd driven all night, but barely seemed tired. He had a lot more driving ahead of him.

We stopped a distance away so I could view the compound through binoculars. To confirm our intelligence was solid. The compound did have a fence around it with barbed wire on the top. It had been a makeshift prison at one point for dissenters of the government. There were two main buildings. The girls were presumed to be in the biggest one.

The compound had one gate, manned by two guards. No guardhouse. Just two men hanging out by a vehicle. Clearly bored.

Akeem was told what to do. He drove up to the gate and said to the men in Arabic, "We're here to pick up the girls. We have orders to take them to Jordan."

The soldier opened the gate and waved us through.

I glanced over at Bond and gave him an "I told you so" look.

"That seemed too easy," Bond said.

"I agree," Alex said.

"That's twice in one day you agree with me," Bond said. "That has to be a record."

The gate closed behind us. We drove up to the main building. The door opened and a woman exited carrying an assault weapon although it wasn't pointed at us.

"I'll take it from here," I said.

I exited the bus and walked right up to her. My weapon was in plain sight as well.

"I've been ordered to take the girls to Jordan," I said.

"You're too late. They're already gone."

My heart sunk to the bottom of my chest. That's why it had been too easy to get in. The girls weren't there.

Where were they?

15

We'd come all that way into Syria, put all our lives at risk, including Akeem's, and the girls weren't even there. In about two minutes, I was going to take all of my frustration out on the woman in front of me and end her miserable existence on this earth. Right after she told me where the girls were.

To get that information, I'd either have to beat it out of her, or stay in character long enough to get her to tell me voluntarily. That'd take less time, so I chose that tact. I could always force it out of her later if need be.

First, I needed to put on a show. Make her believe I was part of the BGS organization. I paced around in a circle showing my displeasure.

"This isn't good," I kept saying. "Some heads are going to roll."

Curly said spying was acting. Playing a role. People would believe whatever you wanted them to believe if you were convincing enough.

"Where are the girls?" I said, with as much anger in my voice as I could muster without it being over the top. I'd stopped pacing and was now staring straight into the woman's eyes.

"I came all the way out here and they aren't even here," I said, when she didn't answer right away. "Somebody's going to pay for this screwup. Tell me why it shouldn't be you."

The woman seemed confused. Probably wondering how she'd gotten in this situation.

I got right in her face.

"What do you have to say for yourself? Why did you let the girls leave when I'm supposed to pick them up?"

"Who are you?" she asked nervously. "No one told me you were coming. My orders were to load the girls on a plane for Croatia. That's what I did."

We were getting somewhere. The girls were probably on their way to the same place the four girls were headed before we crashed.

I shook my head violently from side to side.

"No. No. No. No."

I let the words sink in.

"They were supposed to go to Croatia," I said roughly. "But those plans changed. I'm supposed to pick them up and take them to Jordan. I've got a hundred customers expecting those girls on their private planes next week. How is that possible if they're in Croatia? This is unbelievable."

"I know nothing of it."

"When did they leave?" I asked.

"They haven't left yet."

"What?"

Now I was the one confused. The girls were still here? It shot a sense of urgency through me. I reacted like a motorcycle that'd been revved with a flick of the wrist from the handlebars.

I was back in her space again.

"Where are the girls?"

The woman motioned for me to follow her to the side of the building. Off in the distance, I saw a plane. We knew the compound had a landing strip. A makeshift airport. We'd seen it in the satellite images. We hadn't seen the activity around the plane because it was behind a hangar. The door to the plane was still open, but it appeared to be preparing to take off.

No sign of the girls. I presumed they were already on the plane. The only muscle I saw was one lone guard standing in front of the door carrying an assault rifle.

I had to act quickly.

"Call the pilot and tell him not to take off," I said to the woman. "Tell him to wait for me. I'll give him his instructions when I get there."

The woman hesitated.

"I need to talk to my boss," she said meekly.

I'd been coming on strong. She was clearly afraid of me. Alex and the guys were standing off at a distance. Having my back in case the ruse didn't work. The menacing looks on their faces probably added to the woman's discomfort. Their guns were clearly visible. Akeem stood off to the side. Behind the bus so he'd be out of the line of fire should a shootout ensue.

"You talk to your boss," I said sharply. "Call whoever you want. Right after you contact the pilot and tell him not to take off. I don't want that plane to leave the ground. I'm in charge of those girls now."

I could shoot the woman and race over in the bus and considered doing it. But the lady would be more help to me alive than dead. Once the girls were safe, we might even be able to gain intelligence from her about Hoffman's organization.

She complied. A relief. I really wanted to keep the ruse going as long as possible.

The woman pulled a radio off her hip and called for the pilot. I heard her instruct him to wait for her okay before taking off.

An idea came to me. I walked over to where A-Rad, Alex, and Bond were standing.

"The girls are in the plane," I said in a lowered voice.

"We heard," Alex said.

"Change of plans. A-Rad, you're going to fly that plane out of here. With all of us on it."

"What about Syrian radar?" he asked.

"That won't be a problem. They're aware of the plane. I'm sure a flight plan has been filed. They think it's Hoffman's plane. Follow that plan until you're out of Syrian air space. Then we'll turn around and go back to Israel. I'll notify Geller that we're on our way and to give us clearance to land in Tel Aviv."

"That sounds like a good plan," Alex said. "We should get moving, though. I don't like this. The woman is suspicious of you. We need to get out of here as quickly as possible."

I looked over her way. She was on the phone. Presumably to talk to he boss.

"I agree," I said.

I'd soon know if the woman intended to cooperate, or we'd have to use violence to get our way.

I looked over at Akeem.

"Can you drive us over to the plane in the bus?"

"Of course."

That's all he said. He turned abruptly and went back inside the bus to prepare to leave.

The woman called me over.

"I can't let you leave with the plane until I talk to someone," she said. "I talked to my immediate boss, and he doesn't know anything about taking the girls to Jordan."

I let out a huge sigh.

"Do you know who you're dealing with?" I asked.

"No," she said sheepishly. "That's what I'm trying to find out. Who are you?"

"I'm your worst nightmare if you don't cooperate."

"I'm sorry, but I'm in charge of the girls. I have my orders. You can't take them until I have confirmation."

"And how are you going to stop me? I don't answer to you. I take my orders from Herr Hoffman. If you've got a problem with that, then take it up with him."

Her eyes widened when I mentioned Hoffman's name.

"You work for Herr Hoffman?"

"Why do you think I'm here? I'm standing in the middle of Syria. Who do you think put this whole plan together? Me. That's who. I'm responsible for these girls. I've already lost four of them in a plane crash. I'm not going to lose ninety-six more."

Her eyes widened some more. She obviously knew about the crash. That's what I was counting on. I wanted to give her information that only someone within the organization would have.

"That's right. One of our planes crashed into the side of a mountain. We lost four girls and two good pilots. Not to mention three of our clients. How would I know all of that if I'm not who I say I am?"

I moved in closer. So I was speaking in her ear.

I was about to put her to sleep. Depending on the next words that came out of her mouth.

Arguing with her might work in time, but Alex was right. I didn't need to push my luck. We should get out of there as soon as possible. Eventually, she'd talk to the right person and the charade would be up.

That'd be fine as well. I could easily kill her and the two thugs at the front gate. That's what I wanted to do. Then burn the whole place down. My body had a lot of pent-up frustration in it. Ready to explode. Killing a few bad guys might do the trick.

But I had to focus on the big picture. Which was, getting the girls out of Syria safely. That was my primary objective. This woman was the only thing standing in my way at the moment.

Two options came to mind. I could simply wrap my left forearm around her neck and choke her out from behind. That'd create a struggle. I was strong enough to maintain the hold, but the guards at the gate were only a hundred yards away and might see me.

The second option was a vagus nerve strike. It's a short-handed strike to the side of the neck. Difficult to execute, but if done properly, it would immediately knock the woman unconscious for one or two minutes. The vagus nerves ran through the neck and any pressure on it would cause dizziness and lightheadedness when the oxygen was cut off to her brain.

Curly spent hours teaching it to me using a dummy to practice on. For obvious reasons, The vagus strike can also be deadly if enough force is applied.

I didn't want to kill the woman. Not yet anyway. I wanted to take her back to Israel where she could stand trial. I had a great disdain for women involved in sex trafficking. In my mind, they were worse than the men. The fact she was young and naïve wasn't enough to cause me to be willing to go easy on her.

How could a woman do that to another woman?

She knew these girls were sex slaves.

Men were usually the ones in charge, as was the case here, but this woman was facilitating the despicable behavior. It made me so angry, I wanted to slap her to the other side of the compound.

The vagus strike would be quicker. She'd have no time to react. Which was what I wanted. I only had to execute it properly. In a split second. The blow had to be precise. The vagus vein was protected by layers of soft tissue and muscle. It was in the neck area, though, and the muscles around the nerve were not that thick. Not like hitting the abdomen or spine.

But I changed my mind.

If I disabled the woman, the two thugs at the gate would eventually come looking for her. We were within ten minutes of being on that plane. They might be able to call for help before we were out of Syrian airspace. The best thing to do was get out of there without a confrontation and disappear. Make Hoffman wonder what happened.

The woman had no idea how close she had come to me taking her out.

"As soon as our plane leaves, clear out of here," I told her. "The girls won't be coming back."

"I'm supposed to stay at my post."

"Look. Do what you want. I'm telling you to clear out of here. Whoever your boss is, I'm his boss's boss. Do you understand? It doesn't get any higher up than me. Cross me at your own peril. I don't want to make life difficult for you, but I will. From what I've been told, you've done an exceptional job here. If anybody says anything, I'll put in a good word for you and tell your boss that you were following my orders."

"Thank you," she said sincerely. "Are you going to take the girls off the plane and put them on that bus?"

"No. We're going to fly them to Jordan. That'll be easier. But I'd better get going."

I turned and walked back to the bus and the guys followed me. Akeem was already in the driver's seat with the engine started and the bus ready to move. He closed the door behind us and took off in the direction of the airport.

"That went better than I expected," I said.

Alex looked around nervously. Ahead and then behind us. From side to side.

He knew what I knew. We weren't safe, but we were close. This was better. We could be out of Syrian airspace in no time. Save having to drive across Syria and taking the girls across the border.

Akeem had us to the plane within three minutes. He parked a few steps away from the still open door. The engines of the plane were idling and on ready.

The armed guard at the bottom of the steps stepped forward when we got out of the bus. He didn't appear to be looking for a confrontation. His weapon was not pointed in our direction.

"I'll take it from here," I said to him.

He hesitated.

"Beat it," I said. "We'll provide the security for the girls from here on out."

A-Rad pushed past the guard, up the stairs, and headed for the cockpit. To give the pilots instructions. Alex and Bond were nearby in case the guard gave me any trouble.

"Okay," he said and walked away. Back toward where we'd come.

"Come on, Akeem," I said. "You're coming with us. We'll make sure you get back to Lebanon."

"I can't leave my bus," Akeem said.

"It's not safe for you here," I argued. "As soon as they realize the plane has been hijacked, they're going to come looking for us."

"It's my livelihood. I can't afford to lose a bus."

"We'll buy you a new one."

I wasn't sure how. I figured Mossad would be greatly appreciative and would reimburse him. If not, I'd find a way to make sure Akeem was made whole.

"They'll be able to track this bus back to me and my company," Akeem said. "It won't take them long to find me in Beirut. My whole family will be in danger."

He had a point I hadn't thought of.

"I'll be fine," Akeem said. "I'll wait until you are in the air safely and then I'll leave. They won't bother me. I'll get back across the border with no problem. They'll never know it was my bus in Syria."

"Are you sure?" I said.

He nodded. I didn't like it, but Akeem was right. He'd never be safe if the bus was traced back to him.

"I'm sure," he said. "You go. I'll be fine."

"Thank you, my friend," I said. "We couldn't have done it without you."

I almost felt a tear escape the corner of my eye. I wondered if I'd ever see him again. Probably not. What a wonderful man. In my experience, most people in the Middle East were like Akeem. Hard working. Ethical. Friendly. The governments were the ones who were evil and corrupt. The fringe elements, the hard-liners, were the terrorists and the ones who oppressed women.

We had some of those in America. Every country had them.

"You're welcome," Akeem said. "I'm glad I could help."

We embraced and he kissed me on both cheeks. I boarded the plane and felt a sadness as I looked back at him. I said a quick prayer for him, that he'd get home safely.

We closed the door to the plane, and I stuck my head in the cockpit.

"Is everything good here?" I asked.

A-Rad gave me the thumbs up. The pilot was in his seat. A-Rad was in the co-pilot's seat. This plane only had the one pilot. Probably because Hoffman had lost two on the other flight.

"Let's get out of here," I said. "The sooner the better."

I went to the back and addressed the girls. Alex confirmed we had ninety-six girls on the plane. For the first time, I let myself feel some joy. It warmed my heart to see them. Broke it at the same time, when I saw the pain and fear in every one of their eyes.

"We're here to take you home," I said.

A murmuring went through the entire cabin of the aircraft. Their faces were like deer in headlights. Like they were in shock. They didn't believe me. Why would they? I'd seen the look before. Forcing a woman into sex trafficking took the life out of her almost immediately. All hope. Eventually, they accepted their fate along with the will to resist.

It'd take time for them to recover. If they ever really did. All I could do was give them as much reassurance as possible.

They could hear the sincerity and the kindness behind my words. Hopefully, it'd give them comfort. They wouldn't fully believe it until we were on the ground in Israel. I shared the sentiment. I wouldn't feel totally comfortable either until we were out of Syrian airspace.

"Your ordeal is over," I said. "I'm with Mossad. You can trust me."

The plane began to move. It taxied toward the end of the runway. I bent down and looked out the window to get one last look at Akeem.

What I saw sent a panic running through my veins. Jolting me out of the sense of relief I had started to feel.

Akeem was on the road that led to the exit. Vehicles had him surrounded. Men with guns were confronting him.

16

Akeem was in trouble.

A moment of indecision hit me. We were on the plane ready to take off. Already taxiing to the end of the runway. Within a minute or two, we'd be in the air. Within ten to fifteen minutes, we'd be out of Syrian airspace and on the ground in Israel within the hour. Having rescued ninety-six girls.

Fulfilled the mission.

We could turn our focus on the Olympics and stopping the terrorist threat there. This was what I lived for. Rescuing girls. For the longest time, it looked like I wouldn't be able to. We'd snatched victory out of the hands of defeat.

Thanks to Akeem.

We couldn't have done it without him. He said he'd be okay. He was a Syrian, so it made sense to leave him behind with his bus. Through the window I could see him surrounded by vehicles. I didn't know what was happening. Were they only questioning him, or were they onto our plot and intended to kill him?

How could I possibly know?

The more important question. How could I abandon him after everything he'd done for us?

I couldn't.

Once I made the decision in my mind, I immediately went to the cockpit. We were about to take off. Once we were airborne, the decision was made for me. There'd be no turning back.

"A-Rad," I said. "I've got to get off the plane. Stop taxiing. I'm going to open the door. As soon as it's closed, get out of here."

"What are you talking about?" he said. "We're this close to taking off."

"You're still taking off. Just without me."

A-Rad gave me a sideways glare. A "have you lost your mind" kind of look.

"What's going on?" the pilot asked.

I had to come up with an explanation for him or he'd be suspicious.

"One of our planes crashed into a mountain," I said. "Several weeks ago. You probably heard about it. Everyone was killed."

The pilot nodded his head. "I know about that."

"It wasn't an accident. Someone took it down. I believe those same people are coming after this plane."

The pilot looked out the cockpit window and began to fidget.

I pointed in the direction of the bus. A-Rad and the pilot had reached the end of the runway and turned around, so we were facing the airport facility. We could clearly see the bus and the vehicles surrounding it through the cockpit windows.

"That's why we were sent here to protect you," I said. "I'm getting off the plane. To deal with the threat. As soon as I'm off, get this bird in the air, and get away from here safely."

"Do you want me to come with you?" A-Rad asked.

"No. You help fly this plane out of here. Don't wait for me. I'll be fine."

"Will do."

I winked at A-Rad. Then touched his shoulder.

The pilot brought the plane to a complete stop. Alex and Bond were at the cockpit door as soon as I came out.

"Why are we stopping?" Alex said.

"Akeem's in trouble. I think they're on to him. I'm going to get off the plane to help him."

"That's not a good idea," Bond said. "If they're on to Akeem, then they're on to us as well. We have to get out of here."

"You will. As soon as I'm off the plane. A-Rad's going to take off as soon as the door is closed. Get the girls back to Israel. I'm going to help Akeem."

Alex stretched his shoulders and neck like he was trying to relieve the tension. He probably felt the same dilemma I was feeling.

My voice cracked. "I can't leave... Akeem... behind. He's a helpless tour bus driver. He's no match for men and women with assault rifles. I have to help him. After all he's... done for us. I can't leave him."

My eyes watered but no tears escaped.

Bond said nothing more. He knew trying to talk me out of it would be a waste of breath.

I opened the door to the plane and lowered the steps to the ground.

"I'm going with you," Alex said.

I nodded. It's what I expected him to say.

"Okay. Bond," Alex said. "You're in charge of the plane. Get these girls home safely. Close the door behind us. We'll see you back in Tel Aviv."

"You got it, mate," he said.

Alex and I bolted down the steps.

A vehicle was now streaking toward our position.

"Go, Bond," I shouted. Then pointed at the threat.

He quickly closed the door.

I could see A-Rad from the ground. I gave him the thumbs up. The airplane engines roared to life. Alex and I cleared the runway. The sound was deafening as it accelerated quickly down the runway.

Alex and I took off running.

Away from the runway.

The vehicle was getting closer.

We wanted him to see us and chase us instead of the plane. When it got closer, it didn't turn in our direction. Like it was going after the plane. Alex raised his gun and fired a shot. Hitting the vehicle. I knew it hit the SUV, because I saw the flash on the fender and then it came to a stop.

The driver looked around. Trying to determine where the bullet had come from.

He didn't see us. The distraction was enough to divert his attention long enough for the plane to take off. Once it was in the air, I let out a whoop and Alex and I began running again.

Toward the bus. We had at least three football fields between us and where the bus was surrounded.

The woman was behind Akeem and had a gun pointed at his head.

I should've killed her when I had the chance.

I wouldn't make that same mistake again.

We had to hurry. We weren't close enough to get a shot off but were close enough to hear shouting.

"Who are you? Who are those people on the plane? You don't really work for Hoffman do you?"

She'd obviously figured it out.

Two threats. The woman and one of the guards. And the guard in the vehicle who was still out on the runway.

I prayed she'd wait long enough for us to get in range. Most likely she would. She'd want answers. Akeem was no threat to her. He had no weapon.

Akeem had his arms in the air.

Akeem leaned backward so the gun was actually pressed against his head.

What?

How did he know to do that? Having the gun pressed against the head was counterintuitive. It was actually an advantage. You knew where the gun was and you could use it as leverage to roll off, away from it and then take the gun from a threat.

Sudden movement.

Before I could answer my own question.

So fast, I could barely see it. Faster than I could process it.

Akeem twirled his torso to the left. Brought his left arm over the woman's elbow and bent it backward. She cried out in pain. The gun fell out of her hand.

With his right hand, Akeem struck her in the bridge of the nose while he maintained control over her bent arm. In one motion, he swept her feet out from under her, and she fell to the ground. We were close enough now to hear the loud crack of her head on the concrete.

The other guard reacted and raised his gun. My mind told me to shout to Akeem and warn him. Somewhere between the time my mind had the thought until it got to my mouth, Akeem had already pulled a weapon from his belt, fired a shot at the other guard, striking him in the chest, before he could even raise his weapon high enough to fire.

How did Akeem get a weapon?

The guard fell to the ground in a heap.

With one more fluid motion, Akeem took the rifle off the woman and had it pointed at her.

She seemed groggy and disoriented. Her hand moved to her head even though Akeem told her not to move.

Alex and I came to an abrupt stop.

Akeem must've seen the movement, because he turned his gun in our direction.

"Akeem, it's us. Don't shoot."

His eyes widened.

Then he looked up in the sky, at the plane which was barely more than a dot in the sky.

"What are you doing?" he said in obvious frustration. "You're supposed to be on that plane," he said.

"We were. I saw you were in trouble. We came to help."

"I told you I didn't need any help."

"Apparently," Alex said. "Where did you learn those moves?"

He let out a groan.

"I thought I was rid of you," he said. "No offense."

"Who are you Akeem?" I said.

"You shouldn't have come back here."

"Where did you learn to do that?" I asked again.

He didn't answer. Instead, Akeem went inside his bus and came out a few seconds later with duct tape in his hand. He rolled the woman over and searched her. Expertly. Then taped her hands and feet. Rolled her back over and put a piece of tape over her mouth.

Then lifted her up on his shoulder and carried her to the side of the bus where he opened a luggage compartment and deposited her inside. Then closed the compartment and locked it.

While Akeem was doing that, Alex checked to be sure the other guard was dead. He was. Alex relieved the man of his cellphone, ID, and weapon.

The three of us stood on the road in front of the bus staring at each other.

"Are you going to tell me who you are?" I said roughly.

"If I did, I'd have to kill you."

I wished I had a dollar every time I'd heard or used that same line. Akeem was obviously some kind of intelligence agent.

"Who do you work for?" Alex said. "You know we work for Mossad."

We hadn't told him our real names, but he had seen our Mossad credentials which were under aliases.

"I know who you are," Akeem said. "You're Alex Halee and you're Jamie Austen. CIA. Former CIA, I should say. More prodigals now, I hear."

Alex took two steps toward him.

"How do you know that?" Alex said.

If Akeem felt threatened, he didn't show it. "Your reputation is well known. Who doesn't know the great Jamie and Alex?"

I couldn't tell if he was being sarcastic or complimentary. Mocking us or showing us respect.

"You owe us an explanation, Akeem," I said. "We got off that plane to save you."

"I told you not to."

"Yeah well. If I'd known you were CIA, I wouldn't have. You should've told us."

He hadn't said he was CIA, but he didn't deny it, so that was all the confirmation I needed.

"We have a right to know who we're working with."

"I'm on your side," Akeem said. "That's all you need to know."

"That's not enough," I said. "We've saved your life twice. That should count for something."

Although, I was beginning to doubt that. Technically, we didn't save him the second time. With his skills, he might've not needed us back at Masada either.

"Let's search the compound first for any actionable intel," Akeem said. "I'll explain everything on the bus."

"Shouldn't we get out of here?" Alex asked. "That woman was on to us. She probably called for backup."

The driver of the disabled SUV on the runway was running away.

"She did call for backup," Akeem said. "I figure it'll take them a couple hours to get here. At least. By that time, we'll be long gone. I've been itching to get inside this compound for a long time. I'm not leaving here without checking it out. We might learn something about Hoffman there."

I felt a charge of anger run through me.

"So you knew they were holding girls here?" I asked. "And yet you did nothing about it."

Akeem shook his head.

"No. I didn't know that until you came along. I thought the Syrian regime was holding political prisoners here. When I met the two of you, I saw an opportunity to get inside here."

"So, you used us?"

He chuckled. "Used. Helped. It's all in the eye of the beholder."

"We helped you because it was the right thing to do," I said. "Not for any ulterior motive."

"I helped you because you asked me to."

"Because we saved your life. At Masada."

"I had that situation under control."

He let out a wide smile to let us know that wasn't entirely true.

"It didn't look like it from our vantage point," Alex said. "Besides, we didn't know that at the time. We thought we were helping a bunch of tourists."

"You were. And I appreciate it. It was a dicey situation. Who knows how it would've ended if you hadn't come along?"

"I can't believe the CIA let you help us," I said.

"They don't actually know about it. You know what Curly always said."

"You know Curly?"

"Yeah. I was sad to hear about his passing. I did eight weeks at the Farm."

"I thought that was one of Curly's moves," I said, more to Alex than to Akeem.

"Anyway. Better to ask forgiveness" Akeem said.

"Than permission," we all said in unison. Laughing. Easing the tension.

We gathered up the intel inside the building, which wasn't much, then we hit the road.

Akeem was an undercover CIA operative. He'd been in for three years. Recruited by a station chief. Because he was Syrian and spoke the languages. He did work for the bus company. The CIA funded the money to buy the business which was his cover to operate in the area.

The woman wasn't his wife, and he didn't have any kids. She worked for the CIA as well. I wasn't sure how Alex and I didn't pick up on it.

Akeem was good. That and we had a lot on our minds.

"How are you going to get us back into Lebanon?" Alex asked. "Can you get us safely through the checkpoint?"

"I'm not going through the checkpoint," Akeem answered. "I'm going to drop you off at the Sea of Galilee. I'll arrange a boat to take you to Israel."

We drove through Syria to the Susita National Park which bordered the Sea of Galilee. Along the way, Akeem acted as the tour guide. Pointing out various sites along the way. He was born and raised in Damascus. Converted to Christianity as a boy. He left Syria and studied in Greece. That's where he was recruited into the CIA.

He graduated college and returned to Syria to drive a cab after eight weeks with Curly at the Farm. At some point, they hoped to use him to infiltrate ISIS. So far that opportunity hadn't presented itself.

By the time we reached the destination, I had a tremendous admiration for Akeem. Alex and I risked our lives periodically on missions. Akeem's whole life was a mission. He lived and slept next to people who would kill him if they knew he worked for the US government.

As promised, he had a boat for us in a little secluded cove near Susita beach. A tourist boat. That seated a dozen or so people. Wooden. Brown. Made to look like something that might've been used in the days of Jesus.

We said goodbye for a second time.

"Good luck at the Olympics," Akeem said.

"How do you know about that?" Alex asked.

"It's my job to know these things."

That must mean the powers that be in Washington knew about it as well. Nothing I could do about it. It made me wonder what else they knew about my activities.

Once we were on the boat, all the events of the last several days were behind me. Out of my mind. The girls were safe. I didn't have to be in Tel Aviv for two days. I was on the Sea of Galilee. Where Jesus walked on water.

I looked out at the smooth blue water and felt an overwhelming sense of joy and peace come over me. I couldn't believe I was on the Sea of Galilee. I looked out over the waves and pictured Jesus walking on the water. The disciples fished there. That's where Jesus told them to cast their nets on the other side, and their obedience brought in a huge haul.

Jesus spent two thirds of his time in that region.

Alex must've been thinking what I was thinking.

"Let's not go back yet," I said.

"What do you want to do?"

"Everything we can squeeze into two days."

And we did. We saw Capernaum. Where Peter lived. The Mount of Beatitudes where Jesus preached the Sermon on the Mount. The area believed to be where Jesus fed the five thousand. Nazareth. Where Jesus grew up. Mount Carmel, where Elijah called down fire.

And Armageddon. That made Alex happy. The highlight of the trip according to him.

We baptized each other in the Jordan River. The highlight for me. One of the best moments of my entire life.

I came out of the water and felt refreshed. An unspeakable joy. Ready to take on the world.

Which was what we were about to do.

Take on the world at the Olympic games. The athletes of the world. And terrorists. Presumably. If they were there.

When we got back to Mossad headquarters, we were full of energy and life. Expecting to be greeted with all kinds of attaboys and accolades.

Instead, the meeting was dire.

The terrorist threat was expanded. Not only was Hoffman going after Israeli athletes, Mossad had further intelligence. Hoffman was throwing around words like Armageddon. The end of the world. A catastrophic event.

They had no idea what it meant.

It was up to us to stop it.

17

Bavaria, Germany
Olympic Village
Two Weeks to Start of Olympics

"Jamie, I have so much on my plate, I don't think I can eat it all," Alex said to me.

He scooped up a big pile of food on his fork and stuck it in his mouth right after he said it.

"You didn't have to take so much food," I said. "It's a buffet. You can go back for seconds. Or thirds. Fourths, apparently."

Alex twisted his lips to the side while he chewed.

"I meant figuratively."

"I didn't know you knew what figuratively means."

He tilted his head from side to side in a mocking manner.

"I'm serious," he said. "This whole mission has been dicey. Your near death experience on the airplane that crashed. The weirdness in Syria. I have a bad feeling about things here. All the Israeli athletes are in the village now. How are we going to protect them? And find a bomb that may or may not exist?"

"I know what you mean. It's keeping me up at night."

"Not to mention compete in our events," Alex continued. "Our bobsled team is *not* very good right now. We only have two weeks to get respectable."

"Don't worry about that. The main thing is the mission. It's more important than the competition. Nobody expects us to do well. I'm concerned about Hoffman. What is he planning? Mossad is certain Hoffman is going to unleash a catastrophic event at the Olympics. Probably a bomb."

"What else could it be?"

I shrugged.

"I'm thinking he's going to target us individually," I said. "That'd be easier to pull off."

"That won't be so easy either. We've made it to where none of the Israeli athletes are ever in the same place at the same time."

We had discussed it in our Mossad planning mission before we came to Bavaria. Alex suggested the Israeli athletes fly to Germany separately. That way Hoffman didn't have only one aircraft to target.

Everyone arrived without incident. They also lived in separate housing for the same reason.

Alex and I traveled separately as well and had our own quarters. But we could handle ourselves. Although, we weren't allowed to carry guns which made things more difficult. As far as anyone knew, we were athletes. Carrying a weapon would tip them off that we were some kind of operatives. We wouldn't get access to the athlete's village in that instance.

We had weapons in our house and could use them if we needed to.

Alex was right, though. We had made it harder for Hoffman.

Wrong that we wouldn't all be at the same place at the same time. "The opening and closing ceremonies," I said. "We'll all be together then."

We had to walk in and out of the stadium together as a team representing Israel.

"That seems like the most likely time to pull off a major attack," I said.

"How would Hoffman get a bomb into the stadium?" Alex said between bites. "That arena is sealed up tighter than a woman's girdle."

My turn to grimace.

"Where did that come from, Alex?" I said. "What do you know about women's girdles?"

He shrugged.

We seemed to be mimicking each other's actions. I grimaced. He grimaced. I shrugged. He shrugged. That or we were too much alike.

"Have you ever seen me wear a girdle?" I asked.

"Spandex then."

I had on tight fitting training clothes at that moment. It occurred to me that I couldn't hide a gun in them even if I tried.

I decided to ignore the girdle comment. I knew what he meant. The Israeli athletes didn't eat together. They trained separately. Even the bobsled team was only together when they were training or competing.

Every possible precaution had been taken. While we hadn't eliminated the risk, we'd minimized it.

The rules didn't apply to us. We were walking targets. Out in the open most of the time. Alex and I were eating in the Olympic Village right then. Mostly to observe the surroundings. We spent a lot of time roaming around the village looking for potential threats.

For the most part, the other athletes stayed in their residences. They were only let out to go to and from their venue to practice. Their meals were brought to them. Prepared by an Israeli chef at a house rented by Mossad. So there was no opportunity for poisoning.

Alex and I weren't worried about being poisoned since we were eating from the buffet. A number of German athletes were in the main cafeteria. Hoffman wouldn't risk accidentally feeding them contaminated food.

"Targeted attacks," I said. "That's what we have to worry about. It's easier to kill one person at a time than spring a major attack."

"It's up to us to protect them then," Alex said, although his words lacked confidence.

"How do we do that?"

"I don't have a clue. We can't forget that we're a target as well. Hoffman thinks we're Israeli athletes."

The entire contingency was nine athletes including us. Four skaters and three bobsledders plus Alex and me. Alex would protect the bobsledders. It was up to me to find a way to protect the skaters.

I was already working with Geller to coordinate a training schedule, so they weren't all at the venues at the same time. Each had a security guard, but I wasn't sure that was enough.

So I expressed my concern.

"I can't be everywhere at once," I said. "They all have security guards, but they aren't trained like we are to spot the threat before it materializes."

Alex tensed.

He actually stopped chewing the massive amount of food he'd just put in his mouth.

My heart skipped a beat.

What did he see?

I looked around to see what had caught his attention. Adolf Roth was standing at the buffet filling his plate. Roth was the leader of the German bobsled team. He'd been razzing Alex almost nonstop over the last two weeks of training.

I let out a noticeable sigh from the breath I'd been holding.

Alex's bobsled team had the second worst time in the practice runs. Behind the Arubans, which was embarrassing. Something Roth teased Alex about at every opportunity.

I thought it was a small victory that they weren't last.

They'd also managed to make it down the course without crashing and breaking their necks. Alex wasn't a bobsledder. What did he expect?

Roth and the German team were the Olympic and World Champions. They owned the World Records and had the best practice times at these games. They were the heavy favorite to win the gold.

It shouldn't bother Alex, but it did. For two reasons. The guy was smug and mouthy. And Alex didn't like losing.

I tried to explain to Alex that it didn't matter. So what if they weren't that good. Roth had been training for years. Alex for two weeks. How could he expect to compete at a world class level in that short of time? Ever really. Alex didn't have the build for a bobsledder. He was better suited for the things he was good at.

Alex was the foremost computer hacker in the world. Even though he was athletic, he was a master at keystrokes and navigating through and behind firewalls. There literally wasn't a website in the world he couldn't hack.

He was almost as good in the field as an operative. Alex could shoot long range better than me. I was better at hand-to-hand combat and making snap decisions. Alex was slightly better at situations which required endurance. Long periods of time without sleep or something to eat. I was better at driving and spycraft.

We weren't sure who had the bigger ego.

We both thought we were the best and, for years, argued about it incessantly. Not so much recently as we'd made a truce in that area.

At this point, we were trying to stay alive.

Curly said the best would be decided by which one of us was still alive at the end.

My morbid thoughts were interrupted when Roth stopped directly behind Alex. I was proud of my husband for not taking the bait and turning around.

Roth had clearly made a special effort to walk that way. It wasn't the most direct path to his seat.

I could feel a confrontation coming.

"Hello, Trodler," Roth said snidely.

Trodler meant slowpoke in German. It also sounded a lot like toddler in English which riled Alex to his core. He hated when Roth called him that.

Alex almost came out of his seat.

I glared at Alex and avoided eye contact with Roth. I wouldn't give him the satisfaction.

Alex couldn't get in a confrontation with Roth. For several reasons. The main one being that he'd get kicked out of the Olympic games. I didn't want to run this mission without him. More importantly, our cover would be blown when Alex wiped the floor with Roth.

His considerable skills would be on display for a room full of bystanders.

Ten men like Roth couldn't overtake Alex if they had knives on them. Alex already knew that, which needed to be satisfaction enough.

Alex continued to ignore Roth which made me crack a small smile. Roth seemed emboldened. Alex's silence told Roth he was getting under his skin.

"You better hurry up and finish your meal," Roth said in a sarcastic tone. "So you can get on the course now. I'll be there in an hour. If you start now, you might finish the course by the time I get there."

I could almost see steam coming out of the top of Alex's head. His face was flush with anger.

Roth laughed loudly with a high pitched, guttural sound.

Annoying.

I wanted to stand up and slap him to the floor myself.

Then he turned his attention toward me. The couple of times I'd seen him, he'd flirted with me. Probably because he saw Alex and I kiss once when I came to watch Alex practice at the bobsled run. Before most of the other athletes were in town.

No one in the village knew Alex and I were married. We weren't wearing our rings. We were supposed to be Israeli athletes at the games to compete. Anyone could tell we were an item since we were together most of the time and didn't always hide our affection for each other.

Roth moved closer. Every muscle in Alex's body tensed. Ready to act if necessary. Alex had a piece of bread in his hand and gnawed on it. Like a cat getting ready to pounce on a prey.

Roth patted Alex on the back. "I'm kidding. You can't help that a turtle could beat you in a bobsled race."

When Roth touched Alex, that's when I thought he'd crossed the line. To my surprise, Alex kept his seat. He knew the stakes. Alex also played competitive football. He was used to trash talking.

Although Alex didn't run his mouth much in the heat of the battle. He let his ability do the talking. The only time I'd ever heard him trash talk was when he was with the guys. Bond. Colonel. A-Rad. They were a band of brothers who could get away with it when it came to each other.

I knew all of them well. They had each other's back. They could say all they wanted to each other. Let an outsider talk badly about one of their own, and they went ballistic and did whatever it took to defend them.

If they were there right now, Roth would already be lying on the floor. Mossad didn't let any of them come. They wouldn't have been able to come inside the Olympic Village anyway. Germany knew they were CIA operatives. Especially Bond, who'd had many interactions with Germany when he was with MI6.

"Why don't you ditch this guy and come sit with me?" Roth said to me with a lustful smile on his face, I wanted to knock to the other side of the room.

I ignored him. Didn't even make eye contact.

"Don't you want to be with a winner?" he added. "I'll let you wear my gold medal as long as you aren't wearing anything else."

That did it.

I stood up. Alex was across the table from me and managed to lean over and grab my arm. I remained standing with my fists balled.

All kinds of retorts entered my mind, but I ignored them. I did look Roth in the eye and stared him down.

He chuckled, then got the message and continued on to his seat.

Probably seconds before the tray he was carrying was smashed through his face. If Alex didn't do it, I might've.

"I hate that guy," Alex said.

"He's a cad," I said. "I'm sorry I let him get to me."

"I'm going to shut him up on the course."

I fought back a chuckle. "How are you going to do that?"

The Israeli bobsled team's time was almost thirty seconds slower than the worst German time. Alex and his team had zero chance of beating the Germans. Didn't matter how much bravado Alex let out of his mouth, they couldn't possibly improve that much. The competition started in two weeks.

I, on the other hand, was within sixteen seconds of a bronze medal. I was entered into the 15K individual biathlon women's competition. My trainer, Felix Asher, said I might be able to make up that much time if we had another month of training. I was a natural at the event, he said.

We only had two weeks until the opening ceremonies. Asher was meeting with me later that day to show me a new technique in the shooting phase that might help me gain some time. A top ten finish would be more than respectable and better than any Israeli athlete had ever done before.

I actually liked the biathlon. I raced through a course on cross country skis. Then stopped periodically to shoot at targets. Asher explained to me the history of the event. I didn't know what skiing and shooting had to do with each other.

It started in Norway. As military training. Which made sense. Most of the fighting in the cold northern Europe in those days was done on skis. The shooting involved four rounds with five targets per round. Each missed target resulted in a one-minute penalty. So accuracy was paramount.

Something I was good at. Alex was even better. He'd probably do well in the men's biathlon except for the cross-country skiing.

Alex was a big guy. And awkward on skis. He'd never make it down the hills. He might make it up the hills with all the power in his lower body, but he'd slide all over the place coming down.

I didn't care for the skiing part either but had managed to learn the techniques well enough to be respectable.

That morning, I had skied through the course only missing two targets. To do so, I'd taken too much time aiming. That's why I still fell behind the best of the best. Asher said he could help me with that.

For whatever reason, I really wanted to win a medal. Israel had never won a medal in the Winter Olympics. My competitive nature was coming out. I didn't like to lose at anything. Not even on the playground when I was a little girl. If a boy challenged me, I accepted it and usually beat him.

My mind was already thinking of ways to best Roth. I couldn't really think of any, other than that Alex and I had each other and he'd never have me. That made Alex the real winner.

Roth was away from us now, so we resumed the conversation. Although I did most of the talking since Alex's mouth was continually filled with food.

When he finished eating, we left the building and walked back toward our residence so we could get dressed to go to training.

"Are you allowed to go bobsledding after eating that big a meal?" I asked. "Shouldn't you wait thirty minutes?"

"It's not swimming," Alex said.

"I could never get on skis with a full stomach."

I hadn't eaten much.

"Did we make any decisions?" he asked.

"I'm going to keep an eye out for the skaters. You keep your men safe."

The skaters trained in different venues. Which made my job more difficult. Two were figure skaters. Two were speed skaters. I'd have to do the best I could, running back and forth between them.

"We'll both keep thinking about how Hoffman could set off a bomb," Alex said.

"Opening and closing ceremonies," I said. "That's where it'll happen if it's going to."

"That means we have two weeks to figure it out."

I shuddered.

Hoffman had months, maybe years to plan his attack. We only had two weeks to stop it. If we could.

Like Alex said, we had a lot on our plate.

Literally. If not figuratively.

A voice cried out behind us while we were walking, "Trodler."

I took Alex's hand and we kept going. Not bothering to look back.

Roth would eventually get his.

I had a lot on my mind. Keeping the skaters safe. Finding the bomb. And making sure Roth left the Olympic Games wishing he'd never opened his big mouth.

18

One week until opening ceremonies

The biathlon wasn't as easy as it looked.

And it looked hard.

I almost dreaded going to training. By the time I finished the 15k course, my legs felt like rubber. I could barely walk. To this point, I hadn't even pushed myself to the limits like I'd have to when the real competition took place.

I should probably take my own advice and not worry about it. I'd told Alex that we weren't there to win. To keep the focus on the mission. No one in Israel would care if I finished tenth or hundredth. I didn't even need to finish the course. I could feign injury. Equipment malfunction.

Whatever.

The only thing important was to be inside the Olympic Village, which we were. Not that we'd made much progress on the mission front either. So far, there hadn't been any incidents with the athletes, which was a good thing. As Curly always said, prepare for a mission like you have to execute it, but hope like the dickens you don't have to.

Curly never used the word dickens in his life, but in my head, I always substitute his colorful four-letter words for my own.

As far as the search for a bomb, Alex and I were at a dead end. We were skeptical the bomb even existed. There wasn't a way Hoffman could sneak a bomb into the Olympics. Security was too tight. Which meant he had to sneak it in before the security tightened.

Where would he hide it and how could it evade the radiation detectors?

A fifty-mile radius around the Olympic venue protected the area.

Security was tighter than any girdle I'd ever seen. In a few more days, a million spectators would descend on the Olympic venue. Six thousand athletes, two thousand coaches, thirty thousand volunteers and staff were already there.

"This is the safest place on the globe," the director of the International Olympic Committee had said. "If you're inside the perimeter you're safer here than anywhere in the world."

I knew that wasn't true for everyone.

I saw it first hand earlier in the day.

In the eyes of a young Chinese woman. Barely eighteen, if that. Being led through the Olympic Village by the arm. By a huge thug. Burly fellow with tattoos.

Her face said it all. She was being trafficked. Her body sold to some disgusting pig. Several of them no doubt over the coming weeks until the Olympics ended.

Of course, her plight wouldn't end when we all went home. She'd be shipped somewhere else to probably worse conditions.

I followed her through the streets of the village. She was led to a house. I wanted to follow her in and rescue her. How could I? What would I do with her? I couldn't get her out of the village. Security cameras were everywhere. They might've even noticed me following her even though I tried to be inconspicuous.

My stomach was churning. I couldn't help her. I was needed at the skating venue. My mission was to protect the Israeli athletes, not rescue girls from trafficking.

I could probably save her. But then my cover would be blown. Should I save one girl, and then not be there to help the girl figure skaters? What if there really was a bomb? I might be saving tens of thousands of lives if I could help find it.

These were the excruciating decisions that made me want to quit this awful profession I had chosen for myself. Something I decided I'd never do. Despite my complaining to Alex. I wouldn't leave.

Not until I was forced out.

Whatever emotional pain I felt because of my inability to save everyone, those young trafficked girls felt more. By a factor of ten or more. Incalculable and unspeakable. While I still had breath and ability, I'd devote my life to helping these girls.

I couldn't save this one, but there were thousands more out there. Probably several thousand more in the Olympic Village. A report I read back when I worked for the CIA estimated more than forty thousand prostitutes were present at each Olympics. Those were estimates but I didn't doubt them.

As long as I could continue to rescue girls, I'd do so until someone told me I couldn't anymore. Maybe the CIA didn't want me, but Mossad did. I had a standing invitation to work for MI6. Bond had arranged that. Alex and I could go back to freelancing.

That wasn't my current worry. Neither was the young Chinese girl. Nothing I could do about it.

So, I went to the figure skating venue and watched for any sign of trouble. There wasn't any. That part of my job done for the day, I walked into the biathlon venue center and found the conference room where Felix Asher, my trainer, was waiting.

Felix greeted me with a broad smile. I liked him.

He stood and held out his hand. The man was professional in every way. It felt like we were in the trenches together, and had a close enough relationship to hug, but he'd never do it. I'd met his wife and Felix was a stickler for professionalism. Working with female athletes, he insisted on maintaining it.

Something I appreciated in this world of male coaches taking advantage of female athletes. Of course, Felix also knew my reputation. He knew who I was and why we were there. A stray finger would get broken. A hand in the wrong place would be twisted into a mangled mess.

Not that I was worried about it. Felix's picture could be right next to the word gentleman in the dictionary.

I dealt with enough stray fingers and groping hands at night with Alex.

The thought made me almost chuckle. Felix extended his hand motioning for me to take a seat at the conference table.

His laptop was open on the table and appeared to be connected to a television on the wall in front of us.

"There's been a development," Felix said.

"What's up?" I asked.

"Ffion Gwyn has withdrawn from the 7.5-kilometer sprint."

"Okay." I wasn't sure what that meant for me.

Ffion Gwyn was a world-champion. I'd met her out on the courses. She was the most decorated female biathlon athlete of all time. From Norway. She'd won the last three gold medals and had thirteen total. If I remembered correctly.

"She suffered an injury in training yesterday and had to withdraw," Felix said.

"I'm sorry to hear that," I said sincerely.

"Me too. I don't ever want to see an athlete injured. I'd rather lose, than wish for a competitor to go down."

"My sentiments as well. Although, I'm not in the sprint. I'm in the 15K. I wasn't competing against her."

"Right. But I'm an opportunist. You're better suited for the sprint. I didn't enter you in the 7K because you could never beat Ffion."

"Why do you think I'm better suited for the sprint?"

"In the longer 15k, the best skiers excel. As you know, you incur a one-minute time penalty for every missed shot. Because the course is longer, there's more time to overcome a missed shot. Your strength is not cross-country skiing."

"Obviously."

The only reason I was even able to pick it up was because I'd been rollerblading for years. It's my exercise of choice for cardio conditioning. And I enjoy it. The body movements for cross country skiing are similar to roller blading. I'd also skied a lot as a kid.

"Your strength is shooting," Felix added.

Curly had said that as well. That and hand-to-hand combat. I wonder what Curly would think if he could see me now?

"The sprint will be won or lost in the shooting," Felix said. "If you miss a shot, you have to take a penalty loop. That'll cost you about twenty seconds of time. All competitors will miss one or more shots. Ffion excelled at shooting and skiing. She was faster than everyone else and rarely missed a target. The competitors who are left are younger. Inexperienced. You'll have an advantage."

"Are you saying I can win?"

"I'm saying it's possible if you don't miss a shot. That's what it'll take."

"I haven't gone a single practice round without missing one."

"That's because you're overthinking it."

"What do you mean? You keep telling me to concentrate."

"I know. I'm rethinking that strategy. Saul Geller from Mossad said you're the best operative in the world at shooting on the fly."

"I suppose. I see a target and I shoot. I don't stop and think about it."

"Out here, you aim and fire. After taking time to concentrate."

"Nobody's shooting back at you out here," I said. "If I hesitate in the field, I'm dead."

"You still have to shoot quickly in the biathlon, but accuracy is the most important thing."

"That makes sense. In real life, accuracy is important too, but not as much so. A man has a bigger target mass. The margin of error is greater. I can always aim for the chest."

In the biathlon, the target was the size of a silver dollar. I had to shoot from prone and standing positions. The targets were fifty meters away.

In the field, I rarely aimed for the chest. I almost always aimed for a spot above the bridge of the nose. An area smaller than the size of a silver dollar.

I rarely missed.

These were different bullets though. Smaller. Lighter. The bullets were the size of a pellet. A lot smaller than a normal .22 bullet.

"There's another variable," Felix said. "The wind and the weather. How often do you shoot someone in a snowstorm?"

"Not often."

"It's beautiful outside right now. Unseasonably warm. But that's not the forecast. It's supposed to get really cold and windy. Most competitors don't train in those conditions. Even in Norway."

"I don't either," I said. "But I shoot by instinct. Not so much from muscle memory. If that makes sense. I imagine I can hit a target in any conditions. Even wind."

"Have you ever shot several men at once?" Felix asked.

"More times than I can count."

"Which direction do you shoot? Right to left or left to right?"

"Depends on the threats. I take out the biggest threat first. Then take them down in the most logical order."

"Which direction are you most comfortable shooting?"

"Curly told me I was better at shooting from right to left."

"In the biathlon, most people shoot at the targets from left to right. Right to left is counterintuitive."

"You told me to shoot left to right."

"I want you to shoot in the direction you're most comfortable. Try it today at practice. We'll see which direction you are most accurate."

"Sounds like a plan."

I was open to anything.

Over the next two hours, Felix showed me film footage of past Olympic biathlons. Provided running commentary. Pointing out things I wouldn't have seen on my own. Felix showed me several clips of Ffion. I couldn't help but be amazed. She was so smooth.

Felix commented on it.

"This is another advantage I think you have. Geller says you're cool under pressure. Look at Ffion. Notice how she takes the gun off her shoulder."

"It's not rushed."

"Exactly. When you get to a shooting point, your heart will be beating between 180-200 beats per minute. You'll be sprinting from station to station. That's the beauty of the biathlon and what makes it so hard. Most people can't shoot under pressure. Shooting takes calm nerves. Notice how Ffion takes in a breath and steadies herself before she fires."

The footage took me back to my days with Curly. He drilled that into me at the Farm. Calm under pressure. Most people fire wildly in a gunfight. I don't. I have an uncanny ability to aim and fire with a steady hand.

"Hitting a target at fifty meters with a fast-beating heart, with an undersized bullet, is impossible for most people," Felix explained. "Even highly trained snipers."

"I can do it."

"I think you can. But you also have to take into consideration the crowd. You're going to have thousands of people cheering. It can be unnerving in the throes of competition."

"Thousands?"

"The biathlon is the most popular spectator sport at these Olympics. Tickets have been sold out in advance. The crowds will be huge. They'll be screaming. You'll have to keep your focus or you'll miss the target."

"I've never shot anyone with a crowd watching."

"My point exactly. There'll also be millions watching on television."

I let out a groan. "Don't remind me."

This had been a major concern. As a CIA operative, we went to great lengths to keep our identities hidden. We weren't even allowed to have our pictures taken. I was going to be on worldwide television.

If this were the Summer Olympics, I couldn't do it. Fortunately, it's in the wintertime. I intended to wear goggles and have my head and face covered to protect them from the elements. Also, so no one could see my face. Otherwise, my days as an undercover operative would be over.

"I think we're done here," Felix said, as he closed his laptop. "Let's go out on the course and practice."

"I'm excited."

"Me too. I think you're going to be great. I think you have a good shot at finishing in the top ten."

"I want to win a medal."

"Anyone in the field can win, including you. As long as you don't miss a shot. That's what it'll come down to."

"I can do it."

"We'll see."

My rifle was kept in a locker. We went there to check it out. I slung the rifle over my shoulder, and we went outside and put on our skis. I could already feel it getting cooler.

Felix had my skis outside waiting for me. Waxed for competition. He put his on as well. He always went out on the course with me. During the competition, he'd be a spectator like everyone else.

We made our way to the course. It felt strange going to the 7.5K starting line. I was actually relieved. While the sprint was more intense from a cardio standpoint, it was easier for me than the long-sustained endurance required for the 15K.

Felix pointed out the differences in the shorter course. The 7.5K was basically one big oval. The penalty lap was in the center. If I missed a shot, that's where I had to go at the end. If I missed two shots, I did two laps. So on and so forth.

I could see why shooting was key. Too many penalty laps would seriously hinder any opportunity to win.

Felix skied along with me to the first shooting station. Barking out instructions. He was a stickler for details. Like Curly. Giving me helpful hints. Use my arms and poles more. Shorter more efficient strides. Glide across the snow. Rather than dig my edges in. I tended to do that to maintain balance.

That slowed me down according to Felix.

We got to the first shooting station. Standing. Five shots. At tiny targets in the distance.

I tried to visualize how Ffion did it on the video.

He wouldn't let me fire. He wanted me to get proficient at getting the rifle off my back and into position.

"Try it again," Felix said, when he wasn't happy with how I removed the gun from behind my back. "Make it more fluid this time. Every second matters."

I tried it again. And again. Several times.

He grimaced each time like he wasn't happy with me.

"Let me show you," he said.

It reminded me of Curly's voice except for the accent.

I handed Felix the rifle. He handled it skillfully.

The Anschutz 1826 Fortner Rifle.

Ninety seven percent of all biathletes used it. Apparently, it's the most reliable rifle in the cold. Lightweight and dependable. Which was necessary considering I was sprinting with it on my back.

Cold resistant for obvious reasons. One small pinhole for the sight which took some getting used to. Magnification wasn't allowed so I had to rely on the rifle to fire the bullet exactly where I aimed it. It had little to no recoil, so I could focus and fire five times in a row without resetting my body. Without having to regain my balance.

Ten bullets. Two shooting stations. Five targets each. I looked over at the penalty lap and vowed not to ever have to go there.

The rifle also had flap covers. Not all of them did. Mine did. Felix said it kept moisture out of the barrel and off the sight so I could see clearly.

I wondered if I'd get to keep it after the Olympics. As a keepsake. It'd never do in a real gunfight, but it was a conversation piece.

Felix took my rifle in his hand and put it over his back. We were about the same size, so he didn't need to adjust the straps. He showed me how to take it on and off quickly. And get into firing position.

I think I understood after he showed it to me several more times.

He held onto the rifle. He wasn't done teaching.

"You'll shoot between heartbeats," Felix said. "Otherwise, the beat will throw the bullet off course."

I already knew that from Curly, so I was proficient at that. It came naturally to me. In a firefight, my heart was racing. Not as much as most people's. I had the ability to calm it. Then aim and fire.

"Let me show you the best firing position," Felix said.

He faced the target and raised the rifle to his eye. Put his feet apart and steadied his upper body.

"Set your feet the way I taught you," Felix said, with his right eye still in the sight. "Set up a little bit to the left. So you can shoot right to left. Like this."

I felt myself take in a cold breath, then steady my heart which was still elevated from the sprint to the first station.

"Take in a breath," Felix said. "Aim and fire."

He pulled the trigger.

A small explosion startled me.

What was that?

I let out a scream.

Felix dropped the rifle and bent over clutching his face.

What happened?

He let out an agonizing moan and collapsed to the ground.

The rifle had exploded in his face.

What?

My mind tried to process what my eyes were seeing.

I smelled burning flesh. The rifle lay on the ground with smoke coming from it.

Felix was on the ground writhing in pain. Screaming for the burning to stop.

A number of officials were running toward us.

I tried to remove Felix's hands from his face so I could assess the damage. His right finger, the trigger finger, was dangling from his hand. His entire arm was severely burned.

When I could finally move his hands away, what I saw was horrifying. The side of his face was badly burned. His right eye was practically blown from its socket.

The officials pushed me to the side and began to attend to Felix. Someone said to call an ambulance.

I stood back. Stunned.

The realization hit me. The gun was sabotaged.

That could've been me.
Was supposed to be.
I was right.
Hoffman!
He was coming after us.
I had to warn Alex.

19

Seeing my trainer and friend, Felix Asher, writhing in pain on the ground and fighting for his life, sent a number of emotions pulsing through my body at one time. A whirlpool of thoughts.

Find who did it and exact revenge.

Warn Alex and the others.

Call Felix's wife and relay the bad news.

Guilt.

I almost couldn't believe what was happening even though this was what we were at the Olympics to prevent. The rifle had been sabotaged to blow up in my face. It couldn't have been a malfunction. If not for my ironic luck and horrible luck for Felix, I would've been the one lying on the ground with half my face blown off.

Felix was being attended to by the officials on hand and an ambulance was already on the way. It wouldn't take long. Emergency workers were at every venue. There was nothing I could do for him other than pray, so I grabbed my ski poles off the ground and sprinted back to the main building to drop off my skis and supplies in the locker and get my cell phone.

Once I had my phone, I tried to call Alex right away, but he didn't pick up. He was at the bobsled venue preparing for the team's preliminary run. After my training, I had intended to go and watch him.

The preliminaries were part of the main competition and counted toward their times. The Olympics had officially started even though opening ceremonies weren't for two days. Today's run determined the order of competition for the main competition when the medals would be awarded.

Fastest time went last. Worst time started first.

Alex barely slept the night before worrying about being the slowest time. He desperately wanted to avoid being the team with the worst time and having to start first. The German bobsledder, Adolf Roth, would never let him hear the end of it. They would almost certainly finish with the best time and have the prime starting position. An advantage in the real competition, because you knew what time you had to beat to win the gold.

Alex had actually discussed his angst with John Keller, the team leader and driver of the Israeli bobsled. He apologized to John for slowing the team down.

"I'm sorry. It's my fault we're so slow," Alex had said. "You're only as fast as your weakest link. That's me. You've worked so hard to get to this point. You wanted to compete so badly, and I was thrust on you. I've ruined your team. I'm sorry."

The Israeli team that qualified for the Olympics wouldn't have won a medal but wouldn't have finished last either.

John had confessed, "It's not you. It's me. We could go faster. I just haven't been willing to take the risk."

"Don't worry about me," Alex said. "I've been in a lot more dangerous situations than this."

"I'm not doing it for you. I slowed us down for Handy. I thought it wouldn't bother me having him on the team, but it has."

Handy was the brakeman and paralyzed from the waist down. His back was broken in a bobsledding competition, and he was in a wheelchair. Still able to compete, Alex admired Handy's courage for being willing to get back in the sled.

He started inside the bobsled. This slowed the team down. Only having three pushers instead of four. That was the case even before Alex joined the team. The team had always been at a disadvantage to the other competitors.

"What about Handy?" Alex asked. "Why are you slowing down for him?"

"I've been too careful on the curves. If the bobsled crashes again, Handy could die. He can't take another blow to his spine. That's why we aren't going as fast as we could. We're not going to win anyway. Why take the risk? I could never forgive myself if something happened to Handy because of me."

Alex understood the sentiment and let it drop even though it didn't fully assuage the guilt he felt.

He was clearly still bothered by it that morning. Whenever I thought of it, I prayed that they wouldn't finish last. If I were honest, I was glad John wasn't taking any risk. This mission had enough risks as it was. Never more apparent as I watched the ambulance drive away to the Olympic Village hospital carrying Felix's maimed body.

When I couldn't reach Alex, I called Saul Geller. To my shock, he was already aware of the incident and surprised to hear my voice. He thought I'd been the injured one.

"What happened?" he asked.

"Somebody doctored my rifle. Rigged it to explode in my face. Felix was showing me how to improve my time. When he fired..."

My voice trailed off. Even thinking about it caused a groundswell of emotions inside of me. A need to shoot somebody. I could feel the righteous indignation boiling up like a cauldron full of hot oil.

I choked back the tears and regained my voice. "This confirms our worst fears. Hoffman is targeting us. He has somehow infiltrated the Village. We need to warn Alex. I couldn't reach him."

"They're preparing for their preliminary run as we speak," Saul said.

"I'm headed that way."

"No! You need to go to the skating venue. Keisha is there practicing."

"What? She's not supposed to practice until five."

"Her coach wanted her to get some extra work in."

"Why wasn't I told?"

"I tried to call but you were on the course. Get over there now. I'll try and get word to Alex."

I'd had my entire day planned out. I was going to practice for the biathlon. Then watch Alex's race. Then go to the skating venue to watch over Keisha. The other skaters had plans to practice tonight and I'd be there to keep an eye out for threats. Alex intended to go with me.

My day was completely full. Now even more so. I'd have to figure out time to get to the hospital. Which reminded me. It panicked me that Keisha would have a window without my protection.

"Can you call Felix's wife?" I said. Another thing pressing on my mind.

"Yes," Geller said soberly. "I assume Felix is already on his way to the hospital."

"Yes. I'll meet her there. After I check on Keisha. The bobsledding venue is on the way to the hospital from the skating venue, so I'll go there first and warn Alex. I pray to God that Felix doesn't die."

"How bad is it?" Saul asked.

"It looks bad. I'm not going to lie. His eye was on the scope. Within inches of where the bullet exploded. There's probably brain damage."

I shuddered when I thought about it being my face.

When we hung up, I decided to run to the skating venue rather than take a car. A slight snow had begun falling, but the roads weren't slick. I practically sprinted and made it within ten minutes. I flashed my credentials and was let into the main concourse of the arena. I walked directly to the entryway that led down to the seating.

I exhaled a notable sigh of relief when I spotted Keisha on the ice along with a dozen other skaters. Her coach leaned against the side of the rink observing her. Yelling out encouragement and instruction. He saw me and waved.

I quickly scoured the arena for threats. All I saw were a few workers cleaning the aisleways and rows. A few more workers were in the control booth where they were testing the big scoreboard and the music the skaters used for their routines.

Satisfied none of them were a threat, I collapsed into one of the chairs and put my hand to my head and tried to process the unsettling events of the day. Exhaustion wanted to take over, but I fought it back.

I still needed adrenaline rushing through my body. I wouldn't relax until everyone was safely back inside their residences.

Saul texted me that Felix was taken directly into surgery. He was on his way to the hospital and then to the bobsled venue. He'd see me at one of those two places. I had a feeling it was going to be a long night at the hospital.

I could only hope. That meant Felix would still be alive.

No word from Alex after a second try. I sent him a text. He wouldn't get it until after his bobsled run.

For the next thirty minutes, I watched Keisha practice. The sixteen-year-old was as graceful as a swan. Barely eighty pounds soaking wet, she flowed over the ice like a gazelle. Jumping and spinning. Stopping on a dime and starting again. Toe loops. The Lutz. Axels. Double and triples.

I almost smiled. I'd learned a lot about skating over the last two weeks watching her and the other skaters.

Keisha was Israel's most promising young skater. A joy to watch. She wouldn't medal at these Olympics, but they had high hopes for a top twenty finish. Someday, she might be one of the world's top skaters with more experience.

She was in the center of the rink doing what was called a Biellman spin. Where she lifted one leg above her head, held it in place and spun at a high rate of speed. I was dizzy just watching her. The flexibility and balance almost defied the laws of gravity and centrifugal force.

When she came to a stop and threw her hands in the air, a number of the bystanders burst into applause. Me included. Keisha seemed embarrassed. She skated over to her coach who seemed pleased. Then he began giving her animated instructions. She listened intently.

That made me smile a second time. Good coaches were like that. Never satisfied.

It reminded me of Curly, my mentor who died of a heart attack recently. And Felix. Another stickler for details. Fighting for his life at the hospital.

Tears welled up in my eyes and I didn't try to control them. One or more escaped and ran down my cheeks.

I brushed them away and stood to go talk to Keisha and her coach. To warn them to go directly back to the residence. Keisha's assigned security guard was off to the side. Alert. Looking around for threats.

I wouldn't breathe easy until she was out of the arena. The next couple of weeks were going to be nerve racking. We'd duplicate this routine at least a dozen more times with each of the competitors.

Getting Keisha home safely was the priority now. It bothered me that I didn't know what we were dealing with. Were the attacks coordinated or spread out? Would they try to hit us all at once? On the same day. That was my fear.

All we had to do was get Keisha into the car. She didn't walk over. None of the Israeli athletes walked anywhere. Which was a bummer for them. Part of the fun of the Olympics was the experience. Not just the competition. The Israeli athletes were robbed of that by Hoffman.

A maniac. Intent on killing or maiming these young innocent world class athletes. Simply because they were Jews. And for the publicity of it.

My blood was boiling again. I felt my face flush. When I was mad the tears quit flowing. I felt my whole body tense.

Keisha's eyes brightened when she saw me, and she threw her arms around my neck.

"That was beautiful," I said. "You'll have to teach me that last spin."

"I will," she said with a broad smile.

"I'm kidding. I don't think my body will go in that direction."

I was fairly flexible, but not like that.

Keisha seemed oblivious to any impending danger which was a good thing. My heart was racing, and my head was on a swivel. After the pleasantries, I took the security guard to the side. I didn't want to alarm Keisha or her coach.

"There's been an attack," I whispered in his ear.

"I heard," he said. "It came over the radio."

"Good. Then you know to take them directly to the residence."

"That's always been the plan."

"Where's your car?"

"Here in the arena. Downstairs."

"I'll walk down there with you."

The arena had an underground entrance where the athletes could come and go. Cars were able to drive in and drop off the athlete's and coaches at the lockers one level below the main arena.

Most walked over for practice. Only those who needed tighter security used that entrance. The favorites for the gold also usually came in that way with an entourage of coaches, nutritionists, trainers, and media types who followed them.

We walked out of the main skating area and into the lower dungeon as the skaters called it. Keisha and her coach went into the locker to change. The security guard and I waited outside.

When she came out and was ready to go, we continued walking toward the waiting car.

Then I saw him.

A familiar face.

A worker was ahead mopping the floor.

Where have I seen him?

Panic pulsed through me.

At the biathlon venue. He was the man behind the counter at the locker. The one who handed me the rifle.

The one who sabotaged it!

Confirmed when he reached into his bucket of water and pulled out a pipe. About eighteen to twenty inches long.

His jaw clenched.

He started toward Keisha.

I barely had time to react.

The configuration wasn't ideal. Three people were between me and the assailant. He was moving quickly now.

I heard Keisha scream when she saw the man. She instinctively stopped walking and cowered back.

The security guard was at the wrong angle. He hadn't perceived the threat. Only saw the man as one of many workers. I now knew Hoffman's plan. He had somehow gotten this man a job with the Olympics. So he could get close access to the athletes.

The pipe was in the man's right hand. I went to my left instead of the right.

He was close to Keisha.

He reared back. Like he was going to swing at Keisha's knee. I pushed Keisha out of the way and put myself between her and the assailant.

His eyes widened when he saw me and stopped the swing in mid flight.

Then he made a mistake. Reloaded and reared back even further. When swinging a bat or a pipe, you want to make short and quick strokes. He also held the pipe with both hands like a batter swinging at a pitch.

Most people would step back from the threat. Out of the way of the bat. I was trained to step into it. To cut off the angle of the arc of the bat.

I made it in the nick of time. The pipe was at the back of his backswing, and he'd just started forward. From his position, I could tell he intended to swing at my head.

Another mistake. He should've aimed for my body. My midsection. The greatest mass. My head and legs were smaller targets.

Didn't matter. I had the advantage. He didn't know it, but soon would.

I pivoted my body to the right. So I was sideways to him with my back to the pipe. I pushed my left shoulder into his left shoulder. Effectively cutting off the swing. Without his shoulders, his hips couldn't gain the velocity he needed to make the pipe a dangerous weapon.

Our faces were within inches of each other. I brought my left hand up and under his two arms which were stopped in mid motion by my shoulder pressed against his. I wrapped my elbow under his two arms and secured them.

At that point, I could've easily headbutted him. I'd avoided that most of my career. A last resort. Not executed properly, I could do as much damage to me as to him. If he turned his head slightly, I could smash my nose into his skull. Disabling me instead of him.

Instead, I brought my right palm in a short precise motion aiming for slightly below his nose. Not ideal either at that close range because I was about to get showered with soft tissue, bodily fluids, snot mostly, saliva, blood, and shards of broken teeth.

I intended to take all of my frustration out on him. He'd tried to kill me. Felix's face flashed through my mind.

This was for him.

The blow was meant to kill the man.

Then I had the presence of mind to pull back. We could gain intelligence if he were alive. The blow was strong enough to inflict tremendous pain, but not enough to knock him unconscious. I maintained my grip on his two arms so he wouldn't fall to the ground and crack his skull on the concrete floor.

The blow hit its mark and he cried out in pain. The nose was one of the two or three most painful places to take a blow. The shower wasn't as drenching as what I had expected since I softened it.

It did get in my eyes and mouth making me want to gag.

The security guard had recovered and was by my side with his gun drawn. He took the man to the ground, and I bent over spitting the man's bodily fluids out of my mouth and rubbing my eyes with my shirt which were stinging.

I shouted for Keisha and her coach to continue to the car and get in it.

Once I was satisfied that I had all the crud off me, at least to the extent I could manage without running water over my face, I called Saul and told him what had happened.

"I'll have someone there immediately," he said.

I looked around. No one saw me take the man out. I had an idea.

"Don't bother," I said. "I'll take care of it."

Then hung up.

I lifted the assailant from the ground. He was still holding his nose. I wondered if he knew how much worse it could've been.

He was burly, but I controlled him easily enough.

"What are you doing?" the security guard shouted at me.

I looked around. Not seeing anyone, I went to the vehicle and opened the trunk. Searched the man for any weapons. When I didn't find any, I lifted him into the trunk and shut it.

I then faced the security guard.

"He's German. I don't want to turn him over to German authorities. Take Keisha back to her place and then drive the man to Saul's house outside the village. Where we can interrogate him. He has intel. Maybe he knows something."

Thankfully, the security guard didn't argue. I didn't necessarily outrank him, but he knew my position with Mossad.

I waited until they drove away. Then went into the restroom and cleaned the blood and snot off my face and clothes. Gargled with water several times to get the awful taste out of my mouth.

It looked like today was the day for coordinated attacks.

I had to get to Alex.

As soon as possible. All the other athletes were safe in their residences. The bobsled team were the only ones out in the open.

I had to hurry.

20

Under normal circumstances, my heart beats at a steady rate of fifty-eight reps per minute. Felix said it'd jump to 180-200 during the competition, but he didn't know me. I'd found that 110 beats per minute was standard when I was in a tense situation. Even in a gunfight. And it doesn't get any tenser than that.

It'd been nearly ten minutes since I busted the low life in the face to prevent him from hitting Keisha with a pipe. My heart was still racing by my standards, 105 and it showed no intention of slowing.

Too many things had me on edge. The unknown number of assailants in the village. Protecting the Israeli athletes. Concern for Alex and his bobsled team.

Not to mention my biathlon competition was rapidly approaching. And of course, the prospects of a bomb exploding killing tens of thousands of people. It seemed like all of those things were on my broad, but not all-powerful, shoulders.

Truthfully, I didn't handle things as well as I did when I was younger. Back then the stress didn't get to me. I went from one dangerous situation to another, fearlessly and with ease.

A confrontation like the one I'd had a few minutes ago and my heartbeat would've returned to normal by now, back in the good old days when I was young and stupid. Some might say what I was doing now wasn't all that bright.

Somebody had to do it.

Curly said I'd know when it was time to get out and let someone else dodge the bullets. Or lead pipes in this instance. Since now was not my time to hang up my weapon, I had to keep pressing on. Swimming against the current like a salmon trying to evade the grizzly up ahead.

Something had me still at a high level of stress.

It had to be related to Alex. Why was I worried about him? He was more than capable of handling whatever situation was thrown at him. Alex went on dangerous missions all the time.

I never really worried about him before now. I always assumed he'd be okay.

Why did I have this nagging feeling that he wasn't?

My heartbeat sped up when he didn't answer the third call.

I told myself not to worry. So what if he didn't answer? He was in the throes of competition. He had a lot of things on his mind as well. Answering my courtesy wellness call wasn't on the top of his list.

His competition should be over by now, though.

I wasn't sure where they kept their phones while they were competing. He might not even have it on him. Probably didn't.

I walked with a purpose toward the bobsledding venue which was adjacent to the main arena where the opening and closing ceremonies were to be held. I wasn't running because I wanted to keep an eye out for any potential threats along the way. My threat radar was off the charts and my head was on a swivel.

I'd gotten distracted when I saw the young sex trafficked Chinese girl again. Being led to the same house. To do unspeakable things for some low life scumbag. That probably had something to do with why my heartbeat was elevated. Anger for a number of people was burning inside of me like an uncontrolled forest fire.

That and the guilt for letting her pass by me a second time. Within ten feet. I could've reached out and touched her. Killed the thug, forcing her along. It broke my heart that I couldn't help her.

With all the distractions, I decided to stop walking and look on my phone to see if the bobsled preliminary race was finished. Off to the side with my back against a building was a good place to look. No one could sneak up on me.

A website posted all the results from the Olympic games. I found it easily enough. I surfed through it until I found the results of the bobsled preliminary competition.

The race was over.

My heart skipped a beat when I hesitated to touch the results button. Something I was dreading.

What if Alex and his team finished last?

He wouldn't be in a very good mood. He'd be wanting to punch somebody. Especially after he heard about what had happened to Felix and what almost happened to Keisha.

I wondered if he had heard about what happened at the biathlon venue. Was he as concerned about me as I was him? Probably not, since he hadn't called to check on me.

I maneuvered through the website to the results page. It listed each country by order of finish. I scrolled down to the very bottom. No use looking at the winners.

A notable breath I didn't realize I'd been holding escaped my lungs when I didn't see the Israeli flag at the bottom. The results were reported as the number the team placed, the flag next, then the three-letter country code, then the time.

I stared at the last country on the list.

28. The Aruba flag. ARU 3.05.24.

I wanted to let out a cheer. Alex hadn't finished last!

Thank God for small miracles.

To my surprise, I didn't see the Israeli flag in the bottom ten.

What?

How was that possible?

I went back down to the bottom of the list and began to look at each number closely.

Aruba was last. Jamaica was next at 3.03.25. Then Italy. Netherlands. Republic of Korea. Switzerland. I was surprised to see Canada next at number 23.

Alex and his team beat Canada?

How was that possible?

Canada was a cold weather mecca. Known for its winter sports. Canada had a bobsledding course. It snowed ten months out of the year there in some places. Snow in Israel was rarer than a sunny disposition on a rooster.

Maybe I didn't have the right competition. It must be the two-man bobsled I was looking at.

Sure I'd been right, I was surprised when I saw the heading at the top.

4-man Bobsleigh.

Today's date was even below it.

I went all the way to the bottom and worked my way up again. I stopped again when I got to the top ten.

There's no way Alex's team made the top ten.

I checked it closely and didn't see the Israeli score or place in the competition.

Were they disqualified? Did something happen and they didn't complete their run?

The sense of dread returned.

This didn't make any sense.

United States was tenth. 2:57.25

No way!

Alex didn't beat the U.S. team.

I kept scrolling.

Number five. Germany.

I felt an elation and laughed out loud. Then remembered Germany had more than one team.

Norway, third. Germany was number two. That must be Adolf Roth's team. The ones favored to win the gold. They didn't win the preliminaries.

What a shocker?

I blinked my eyes several times when I saw who was in first.

1. The Israeli flag. ISR 2.54.25.

Good thing I was leaning against the side of the building or I would've fallen over.

Germany second. 2.55.63.

Not only did Alex's team beat Germany, but by a full second!

My eyes had to be playing tricks on me.

We won!

I looked at it several times to be sure. Every time, the results were the same. The Israeli bobsled team won the preliminary competition. Beat the Germans and that smug Adolf Roth by a mile in the bobsledding world.

My heart was racing now. I couldn't wait to see Alex and find out how they did it. No wonder he hadn't called me back. They were celebrating.

I tried to call him. Still no answer. I put the phone in my pocket and took off running, throwing caution to the wind. Barely watching for threats. From a distance away, I could see the huge leaderboard inside the bobsledding venue. It confirmed what I already knew but didn't believe.

ISR was at the top of the leaderboard.

Saul Geller was coming out of the venue as I was going in. I practically ran him over. His head was down and his eyebrows and forehead were furrowed in deep concern. He didn't notice me either.

Likely because of everything that had happened with Felix and Keisha. He'd be thrilled that Alex's team won the preliminaries, but Geller was an intelligence man. Constantly worried about terrorism threats. He probably couldn't care less about a sports competition.

I knew the feeling. Hard to celebrate victories when you didn't know what terror lurked around the corner. If it hadn't been Alex in the race, I wouldn't have cared either.

"Have you seen Alex?" I asked Saul.

He looked up and our eyes met. "Alex is at the hospital, Jamie," he said in a serious tone.

"Oh. So he heard about Felix?"

"No. That's not what I mean. He's in the hospital. He was taken there by ambulance nearly an hour ago."

My stomach did a couple of somersaults and smashed against my pulsing heart rate which was now beating so hard I could feel it in my chest and hear it in my ears.

What did he mean?

"What happened?"

Saul pointed toward the bobsled track. The entrance was at the finish line. The course was elevated and started high up on the mountain and snaked down to the finish. Built so that spectators could see the finish line and the huge scoreboard even outside the arena and for hundreds of yards in every direction.

I looked toward where Saul pointed.

What I saw sent a horror through me. The Israeli team's bobsled was being lifted by a crane. It hung in the air. The front end was a mangled mess.

I let out a shriek.

"What happened?" I cried out.

Saul answered, "I don't know all the details other than that the brake failed, and the bobsled crashed into the wall at the end of the course. Alex and all the men were taken to the hospital."

"What's their condition?" I asked.

"I don't know."

"I have to go there."

"I'm headed that way now. Hop in."

I hadn't noticed it before, but a car was idling at the entrance. Saul motioned to it and I followed him and got in the back seat. He instructed the driver to take us to the hospital.

After the car started moving, I said bitterly and with angry emphasis, "The brake failing is no accident."

"Nope," Saul said.

He stared out the window. Saul wasn't a warm man. All business. A man of few words. His calloused personality came from the years in the terrorism trenches. He'd suffered personal loss more times than he could document. I had as well and knew how he felt. But that was the nature of counter terrorism. Constant losses. As many wins as defeats.

For me, my husband was injured, and I had no idea what condition he was in. For Saul, one of his operatives was in the hospital which was bad, but a common occurrence.

I was stunned.

I couldn't imagine Alex plummeting down the mountain and hitting the wall at ninety miles an hour. It must've been horrifying for those few seconds before impact.

Could he survive it?

"They were sabotaged," I said sharply.

"My first thought as well. I'm having the vehicle inspected by experts. We'll find out who's behind it."

"I already know who. Hoffman."

Saul nodded.

"Alex and his team finished first in the race," I said, as if that made any difference by this point.

"I saw that."

Saul's words were measured. He barely responded to my comments. He was clearly deep in thought. My mind was racing as well. I had a hundred questions. Saul clearly had none of my answers.

I couldn't quit talking. "My rifle. Keisha. The bobsled. It can't all be a coincidence."

"Nope."

The driver dodged the cars and pedestrians and seemed to be trying to get us to the hospital with a sense of urgency.

"What about the goon I took down at the arena?" I asked. "Where's he?"

"He's in custody. He's at a safe house in the mountains."

Smuggling something out of the village was easier than bringing something in. Every vehicle was thoroughly searched when entering the checkpoints. Nobody really cared what was taken out of the village. They wouldn't even bother checking the trunk.

I assumed Saul had someone there skilled at interrogation. If not, I'd convince him to give me five minutes with the scum of the earth.

"Thanks for taking him down," Saul said, in a rare show of warmth. "My country is very appreciative. You saved Keisha's life."

"That's why I'm here."

"Also, thanks for not killing him, Jamie."

"I thought he might have some useful information."

"Let's hope so."

"The events of the day make me think there might really be a bomb."

"I'm working under that assumption as well. Although, we have nothing to back it up. Other than a lot of chatter. I'm not optimistic that the man you caught today will have any information about the bomb. He can link the assaults on Felix and the bobsled team back to Hoffman. I presume. We'll see."

"When are you going to act against Hoffman?"

Saul continued to stare out the window of the car and didn't answer. His way of saying, *Above my paygrade. Need to know basis. Mind my own business.*

I'd used those same lines dozens of times on others. Saul saved me the indignity of speaking one of those lines to me. Putting me in my place.

The truth was, he probably didn't know. They hadn't formulated a plan yet. If they had, they might not have approval from the higher ups to execute it. Even if they had approval, missions like that took time to develop. A team could already be training somewhere in secret. I'd never know until after the fact.

The car pulled to a stop in front of the emergency room. I was out the car door almost before it stopped. I raced inside to the information desk. Trying to regain my composure.

"I'm looking for the members of the Israeli bobsled team," I said. "I understand they were brought here earlier."

"Yes, Ma'am," the lady said. She stared at a computer screen, typing something.

"I'm the girlfriend of one of the team members," I added, when she didn't respond fast enough for my liking.

I had to be careful. I still had a cover to maintain. I was an athlete. Here to check on my boyfriend. Not a Mossad agent. I couldn't throw any diplomatic weight around.

Saul came up behind me and flashed his credentials.

"Through those double doors and down to the end of the hall," the woman said.

Asking her about Alex's condition was a waste of time. I'd know soon.

Once inside the double doors, I heard shouting at the end of the hall.

Alex's voice.

He's alive!

21

Alex was alive but yelling at someone. His voice filled the entire emergency room. I practically ran down the hall toward the din.

The emergency room had dozens of sections separated by curtains. Some closed. Some open. Most had a person in the bed. Dozens of doctors and nurses scurried around the long hallway. They seemed to be overwhelmed.

The shouting came from the last area on the right. The curtains were slightly open and I was through them in a flash.

Alex sat on the edge of the bed. He had a neck brace in his hand and was waving it in the air. A doctor and nurse tried to grab it and take it from him. He wasn't letting them.

Alex smiled when he saw me. "Hi honey. Tell these people I don't need a neck brace."

It became clearer what was happening. Alex was being a difficult patient. I'd seen this rodeo before.

"I'm his wife," I said, forgetting my cover as his girlfriend. "What's going on?"

The doctor turned toward me.

"You need to talk some sense into your husband," the smallish doctor said. Alex was showing restraint. He could squash the man under his thumb.

"Trust me," I said. "I've been trying to do that for many years now."

Alex made a mocking face at me. Then winced in pain.

I examined him with my eyes. I didn't notice any cuts or bruises. He was clearly himself, personality wise. As obstinate as ever.

Like I was one to talk. These roles had been reversed more than once. I'd been the one resistant to the instructions of doctors more often than Alex.

"What's the problem?" I asked.

I repositioned myself next to my husband so I stood between him and the doctor. I put my hand on his knee in a gesture meant to let him know I'd handle the situation.

"Is my husband okay?" I asked.

"No. He suffered a concussion and a whiplash. He needs to wear that neck brace."

"I'm fine," Alex said. "I want out of here, so I can check on the other members of my team."

"You're not fine," the doctor said. "The MRI confirmed the concussion and bruising to your neck and spine. Ma'am, we need to keep your husband overnight for observation."

"I'm going home," Alex said roughly.

"May I speak to my husband alone?" I asked.

The doctor let out a sigh. "Fine by me. I have other patients. I'll be back later to admit your husband to the hospital."

He turned and left the room and the nurse followed. Alex started to say something but my lips were on his so fast, it prevented him from speaking.

He let out a yelp. I'd pressed too hard against him.

"I was worried about you," I said. Smothering his cheeks and lips with softer kisses.

"I'm fine."

"You obviously do need that brace," I said. "Are you okay?"

"I'm fine."

His speech was slightly slurred. A sure sign of a concussion. He started to stand, but then got dizzy. Another sign.

"Hold on, Alex," I said. "Don't try to get up. The doctor's right. You're not yourself."

"I've had worse concussions."

That was true. We'd both had our share of injuries in the line of duty.

"I've got to check on John and Matthew," Alex said. "They were hurt pretty badly. They took the brunt of things. I was in the back."

I suddenly remembered the team member in the wheelchair.

"What about Handy?"

"He wasn't hurt at all. He was sandwiched between me and Saul. So we protected him. Thank goodness. He just had the breath knocked out of him."

Alex took in a labored breath. I wondered if he had cracked ribs as well.

He continued. "John was in the front. We smashed into the wall going nearly a hundred miles an hour. The three of us in the back pushed against John. He was crushed against the front of the bobsled."

"Is he alive?"

"I don't know. He was unconscious. I heard the EMT's say he probably has severe internal injuries."

"What about Matthew?"

"He was awake and moving his arms. He couldn't move his legs."

I let out my own deep sigh. Thankful that Alex was okay, but now I had John and Matthew to worry about along with Felix.

I hadn't even had time to process all the ramifications. The bobsled team was obviously out of the competition. I didn't have a rifle. My competition was up in the air. How could I go on without Felix?

Hoffman was winning this dangerous game of chess. Now that I knew Alex was okay, I didn't try to hold back my anger or disdain for Hoffman and his band of thugs. I had no idea how many of them were still out there.

With Alex out of commission for a few days, it'd be up to me to stop them.

"I saw your bobsled," I said. "It looked like it ran into the back of a semi-truck."

"Our bobsled was tampered with," Alex said. "We didn't have any brakes or steering."

I was glad to see Alex still able to function with critical thinking and didn't have any memory loss.

"You're right. I think it was sabotaged. So was my rifle."

I told Alex all about Felix. He hadn't heard.

Then I told him about Keisha.

"These were coordinated attacks," I said.

"Hoffman," Alex replied angrily. The hand not holding the brace balled into a fist.

"Tell me what happened to you on that bobsled course," I said. "Did you see anyone suspicious hanging around there?"

"I think I saw the German in the crowd."

"What German?"

"The one we saw in Jerusalem. Remember. Wolf was his name. The one following us."

I'd almost forgotten about him. Out of sight, out of my mind. I hadn't even contemplated him following us to the Olympics.

I should've.

"Are you sure you saw him?" I asked.

The concussion might be affecting Alex's memory. He might remember seeing him in Israel and confused it for here.

"No. I'm not sure. It was brief. I saw him in the crowd, then he was gone. I think it was him anyway."

If Alex thought he saw him, then I had to go under the assumption he did.

"Did you see anyone else around your sled?"

"Bobsled," Alex corrected.

"Bobsled. Tell me what happened."

"Everything was going smoothly until the first curve. We got off to a good start. I think it was our fastest one yet. Everything went perfectly. Probably from the adrenaline flowing. This was the real thing. The time counted. It was exhilarating."

He paused to let that sink in. Either that or the concussion was affecting his ability to think and he had to gather his thoughts together.

"That's when I knew something was wrong," Alex said. "The steering wasn't working. We were out of control. Somehow John was able to keep us on a line, otherwise, we would've flown off the course and we'd all be dead."

I gingerly put my arm around him. Talking about it probably wasn't helping. We could discuss it later. He'd have plenty of opportunities to relive it for me.

"Where does it hurt?" I asked.

I looked deep in his eyes. I could see the signs of a concussion. Difficulty focusing. Slowed eye movements. Slight pupil dilation, although that wasn't always a reliable symptom. Muscle weakness. I took his hand and squeezed it. He squeezed back. His grip wasn't as strong as usual.

"I'm okay," Alex said. "I was lucky. I can't believe this happened. I'm going to find out who did it and kill them."

I knew Alex. If he knew who had sabotaged the bobsled, he'd already have left the hospital looking for him. Concussion and all.

I wanted to change the subject. Alex did it for me.

"How did we finish?" he asked. "What was our time?"

"You won."

"What?"

"You had the fastest time."

"Quit lying to me."

"I'm not lying. You won. Germany finished second. You beat them by a full minute. No wait. A full second."

"We won? I don't believe you."

I pulled my phone out of my pocket. It didn't take long to pull up the results.

Alex's mouth flew open, and his eyes widened when he saw them. To the extent they could, considering the pain in his neck.

"Well, I'll be a monkey's uncle. I knew we were going fast. I didn't know we were going that fast."

"I guess since you didn't have a brake, you had nothing to slow you down."

Alex shook his head from side to side, but grimaced when he did so. He put his hand to his neck.

"Take it easy," I said.

Alex explained.

"That's not how a bobsled works. You can't use the brake until you cross the finish line. We'd be disqualified if we did. You slow things down by steering into the curves. By using drag and friction. John didn't have steering, or it was limited, so he didn't have any way to slow us down. That must be why we went so fast. Imagine that."

"That makes sense."

"I can't believe we won. Somebody sabotaged our bobsled and it made us go fast enough to win. How ironic."

A momentary smile came on his face. Mine too. If Alex was using the word ironic in a sentence, then he was going to be okay.

"I guess you showed Roth who the trodler is," I said in a mocking voice.

I saw Alex grimace.

Not from the pain in his neck. He was probably thinking the same thing I was thinking. It's nice to win, but all that matters was that his mates were okay. I needed to find out. For both of our peace of mind.

We were perilously close to another tragedy like the 1972 Olympics. That's what Alex and I were there to prevent. So far, we weren't doing a good job of it.

"Humor the doctor and put the neck brace on," I said to Alex sternly.

"No. I ain't no invalid."

Alex was an intelligent man, but sometimes he talked like a hick. Especially when he didn't want to do something.

"You can take it off once we're out of the hospital."

"All right."

He started to put it on.

I added. "I'm the boss of you for the next few days. Get used to doing what I say."

Alex glared at me, but then put the white brace around his neck. It looked uncomfortable.

He probably should wear it for a while. Knowing him he wouldn't. If I could get him to wear it while we were in the hospital, I'd consider it a victory. Hopefully, the doctor could give him some pain medicine to knock him out. I agreed with the doctor. Alex needed to stay overnight. For observation.

While I didn't think the concussion was that serious, it could get worse over the next few hours. It wasn't life threatening but could be painful. The nurses could keep him sedated and give me time to think without having to take care of him.

I needed a game plan. God only knew how many threats were out there. Now I had the German to occupy my mind. I'd been impressed by his skills in Israel. I hadn't really been using evasive tactics while at the Olympics. He might've been following me the whole time and I didn't even know it.

"I'm going to talk to the doctor," I said. "I'll find out how your friends are doing."

I also wanted to find out the real nature of Alex's injuries. Did he have a fracture or a neck bruise? If only a bruise, it'd be hard to keep Alex down. Even with a fracture, he'd want to join me in the fight. I wanted to make sure he wasn't risking further injury.

Alex attempted a nod, but all he could do was move his body forward. The white neck brace restricted his movements.

"Keep that brace on," I said. "I'll be right back. Be nice to the nurses."

I left the room with mixed emotions. Thrilled that Alex was okay. Now concerned, for not only Felix, but John and Matthew as well.

I was also as angry as a junkyard dog. Alex might be injured but I wasn't.

Hoffman had played his hand.

My turn to play mine.

First, I had to talk to the doctor. I found him in one of the treatment areas. When he finished with a patient, I got his attention.

"Thank you for taking care of my husband," I said.

"You're welcome."

"Can you tell me the extent of his injuries? I have some medical training as well. I can help him if I know what I'm dealing with. The concussion seems mild."

"It is. The damage to his neck and spine are more concerning. I'd like to keep his neck immobilized for a few days until the swelling goes down."

"Is the damage to his neck a fracture or bruising?"

"Bruise to the spinal column."

"Any muscles or ligaments torn?"

"The MRI didn't show any."

"Any herniated disks?"

"No. Your husband told me he used to play football. His neck is thicker than most. It's used to absorbing contact. He was in the back, so the ones in front took most of the force of the blow. He's still lucky he didn't break his neck. The helmet probably saved him."

"Yes. My husband is a tough man."

"He said he's never had a concussion before."

I knew that wasn't true but wasn't going to share that information. The doctor didn't seem that concerned. I didn't want to give him any reason to be more concerned than he was. It was reasonable for Alex to stay the night for observation.

"He did say that the hardest he'd ever been hit was by his wife," the doctor said with a grin.

I chuckled, but ignored the comment.

"Can you give him some painkillers that will put him out for the night?" I asked.

"I tried, but he wouldn't take them."

"Let me deal with that. My husband is kind of stubborn when it comes to doctors and medicine."

"I noticed."

"Thanks again."

"I'll have the nurse bring his medicine and we'll get him into a room."

"Do you know how the other members of the bobsled team are doing?"

"No. You can check up front."

"I'll do that."

The doctor went one way, and I went the other. Toward the front desk. When I got to the double doors, I could see into the lobby. What I saw stopped me in my tracks.

The German!

No doubt about it. He was talking to the lady at the front desk.

I instinctively reached for my gun. Which wasn't on my hip. I felt naked without it. This whole three weeks I'd been walking around without it.

I could take the man with my bare hands, but that wasn't wise.

The nurse pointed toward the double doors. The German looked in my direction. I ducked down.

Did he see me?

Was he there to kill Alex? Was he there for surveillance purposes? No. If he were, he would've remained outside the hospital and watched the entrances.

Did the German sabotage the bobsled? Was he there to finish the job?

I pushed myself against the wall expecting him to walk through the double doors. I wasn't going to wait around to see. I walked briskly back to Alex's location. The nurse was there with the pain medication. Alex was resisting taking it.

"I'll take those," I said. "I'll see that he takes them."

"I don't need it."

I ignored Alex and took the pills from her hands.

"Take the neck brace off," I said, after she left the area.

I needed him to walk quickly. The brace would slow him down. We were getting out of there. I couldn't protect Alex at the hospital. We had to go to our residence where I had weapons and could see the German coming.

"Put it on, take it off," Alex said jokingly. "Make up your mind."

I took it off for him. Then I stuck the pills in my pocket. I looked around for anything sharp to carry in my hand. I found a pair of scissors.

"Can you walk?" I said to Alex.

"I think so. What's wrong?"

"Nothing's wrong. You're right. You don't need to stay the night. I'm taking you home."

"Now you're talking."

If I told Alex about the German, he'd be in the lobby in a flash. I wouldn't be able to stop him. I had to keep up the ruse and get him out of the hospital without being seen. I wanted to kill the German, but on my own terms.

Alex stood, then wobbled.

"You're okay. Take my shoulder."

He put his arm over me, and I walked him slowly out of the area. Steadied him, until he got his balance. Alex was a big man. I couldn't carry him out.

Outside the curtains, I remembered a wheelchair. I made sure he could stand on his own.

"Sit in this," I said to Alex after retrieving it.

"I want to walk out."

"You know the regulations. They won't let you. Sit down in the wheelchair. Right now."

I didn't have time to argue with him. He gave me a face but did.

I saw the relief on his face when he was seated. The concussion was still affecting him. When we got back to the house, I'd put the pain pills in his drink. He'd never know about them. Then he could sleep through the night and give me time to think about a plan.

I opened a door that said employees only. It led to a staircase. I presumed it led to the outside. I glanced back in time to see the German come through the double doors at the other end of the hall.

He didn't see us. Or at least I don't think he did.

Alex complained when I had to bounce the wheelchair down the stairs, jolting him.

Couldn't be helped. I told him to keep quiet.

The door at the top of the staircase creaked opened.

The German!

It had to be.

We were almost to the bottom of the stairs. I opened the exit door half expecting an alarm to sound even though there was no sign. It did lead outside. The cold air hit us at once. Alex shivered. He wasn't dressed for it. His coat was back in the emergency room. I didn't think to grab it.

The German wasn't stupid. He'd see Alex's coat and know we left. He probably saw me enter the emergency room entrance.

I wheeled Alex around the corner of the building and waited. I might have to deal with the German now whether I wanted to or not.

I heard the door open. The same one we'd just come out of.

I put my back to the wall and steadied my breathing. Clutched the scissors in my left hand. The one nearest the corner. Closest to where the German would appear.

"Quiet," I whispered to Alex. "Don't say anything."

"What are we doing?"

"I'm sneaking you out of the hospital. The doctor said you had to stay the night. I'm taking you home. Be quiet. I don't want anyone to hear us."

I felt the presence.

My body tensed.

I was ready to act. All my senses were alive.

Snow was falling. I took that into consideration if I had to fight the German. My shoes weren't ideal. They'd be slippery. I made calculations in my mind as to the man's size and weight. Level of fighting experience. He wouldn't have any weapons like a gun or knife. Couldn't get those through security.

That wasn't true. Hoffman was resourceful. I couldn't assume anything.

When the door opened and I heard it shut again, I let out a sigh.

Was it a trap? To make me think he left.

After a few seconds, I looked around the corner and he was gone.

I quickly wheeled Alex away from the hospital. Through a series of sidewalks until we were safely away. When I felt like the coast was clear, I took out my phone and called Saul and told him about the threat.

He arranged a car to meet us several blocks away.

I got Alex home, spiked his drink, and put him to bed.

Waited for Saul to call me.

Six hours later, he still hadn't called.

I had so many questions.

22

3:00 a.m.

In the spy world, imposter syndrome was a real malady. It usually reared its ugly head in the middle of a sleepless night.

Like tonight.

I sat in a chair in the living room of our residence in the Olympic Village waiting for Saul Geller to arrive and give me news on John, Matthew, and Felix. The only thing I knew was that they were all in critical condition. John and Felix were in surgery. Matthew was touch and go, with severe injuries to his spine and neck.

It didn't matter how many mission successes I'd had in my past, the failures were foremost on my mind. It felt like this mission with Mossad was one of our biggest failures to date. I'd rescued ninety-six girls from sex trafficking but lost four. I saved Keisha but couldn't save Felix.

Or protect Alex for that matter.

He was sound asleep in the other room. I'd given him enough sleep medicine to knock a horse out for a day. Alex would probably be up and around before sunrise, knowing him. I hoped not. Sleep was the best thing for him. Rest allowed the swelling in his brain to subside and would keep his neck immobilized.

Alex's physical injuries would heal over time. The emotional wounds never seemed to heal. No matter how much time passed.

Curly always said not to even try to make sense of it. Don't deal with your emotions. Bury them instead. Push them deep into the recesses of the cavern of denial. Block them off in a wall somewhere behind your heart. Then pick yourself up and go do it again.

"You're not Jesus," Curly had said to me on more than one occasion. "You can't save everybody."

No more apparent than right now. I could've left the Biathlon Village and gone straight to the bobsledding venue and warned Alex about the threat. Before he went on his preliminary run. Had I done so, maybe he would've never suffered his injuries. John and Matthew wouldn't be in the hospital. They wouldn't be out of the competition for good.

But then Keisha would be dead or permanently lamed. I wouldn't have been there to stop the man from striking her with the lead pipe.

Such was the life of an operative.

That's how the imposter syndrome really applied to us.

One time, years ago when I first got in the business, I looked up the word imposter after I heard others in the CIA using it. It meant a fake. Someone who pretended to be someone they weren't.

Why did they call us imposters? It didn't make sense back then. Curly mentioned it. Warned about it. Other operatives talked about it.

I didn't understand it then. I did now.

I wasn't a fake. I really was a spy. I did save people. I'd saved thousands of them. To be in this business, you had to have a certain bravado to you. A confidence. An air of invincibility. Alex and I had it in spades.

No one could kill us. We'd kill them first. No threat was too big for us to take on. Case in point. The Olympic Games. There were twenty-one hundred armed guards within a few miles of me. Two billion dollars had been spent on security by the Olympic Committee. Every nation in the world had measures in place.

Why did I feel like it was my responsibility to find the bomb? That I will have been the one who failed if the bomb went off and I hadn't stopped it.

That's where I was an imposter. I really believed I could do it. No. That I *should* do it.

If there were a bomb, Alex and I should find it. So what if I stopped the threat on Keisha? That's what I was supposed to do. That's my job. Of course, I stopped it.

Most of the time, I did succeed. I could never play baseball. If you failed to get a hit three out of ten times, you were in the Hall of Fame. If I stopped three out of ten threats, I'd want to crawl into the nearest hole and die. If I only rescued three out of ten girls, I'd consider myself one of the worst operatives in the history of the world.

My percentages were way better than that. That should be satisfaction enough.

It wasn't.

There were always bad guys out there to kill. Men like Hoffman. With resources. Alex said Alabama was better than them when they played in the National Championship game. Sometimes, the other teams win.

I couldn't accept that when the toll was human lives. I wanted to always win. In fact, I wanted to leave the house right that moment and hunt down the German and end his miserable existence.

Go find the bomb myself. Search every nook and cranny until I found it. I'm supposed to be smarter than Hoffman. Tougher minded. More skilled. His goons were no match for me.

That's why I was an imposter. A fake. I couldn't succeed every time, even though I thought I could. Just because I thought I should.

That was the problem. I had set expectations for myself that were impossible to meet.

Curly understood it. Probably not when he was my age. His reputation was well known. He was like me in his younger years. Ready to take on the world. At some point, he got knocked down enough times that he understood that he couldn't save everybody which was why he told me what he'd learned the hard way.

Curly eventually quit when it got too hard. Went into training. Then made us feel like we were invincible.

How many times did Curly tell me I was the best operative in the world? That there weren't five guys out there who could beat me up in a fight. His exact words were, "If you can't beat up any five guys in the world regardless of their ability, then I haven't done my job."

He'd created this monster. This killing machine.

But I wasn't invincible. Or all powerful. I was made of flesh and blood. A bullet would kill me. A speeding bobsled with no brakes will crash into the wall. The laws of gravity superseded Alex's self-confidence in his abilities.

It didn't make us imposters, just human.

I made a decision.

Right then. In the wee hours of the morning.

I'm going to save that Chinese girl.

The one sex trafficked. It seemed like she was taken to the same house every day. I might not be able to find the bomb, but I could save her. Curly said the best thing to do when you were in the midst of a pity party was to get outside your own mind and do something.

Alex could help me. When he was better. He could hack into the Olympic security cameras and disable them at the house long enough for me to get the girl out of there. If we could get Keisha's assailant out of the village in the trunk of the car, I could smuggle the girl out in the trunk as well.

That thought made me feel better. This was who I am. Rescuing girls from sex trafficking. I needed to get back to that.

Finding bombs wasn't my expertise. I didn't even know where to start.

"Stay in your lane," Brad, my handler at the CIA, used to say.

As if on cue, my phone rang.

I thought it had to be Saul. It wasn't. The caller ID told me it was a blast from the past. Someone I hadn't talked to in months.

Brad.

His familiar voice was on the other line. Why was I not surprised? He had an uncanny ability to call me during these times. He'd raised my spirits when I was in the dumps more times than I could count.

"Your ears must be burning," I said without so much as a greeting.

"Hello, Jamie."

"Hello, Brad. It's three in the morning."

"I figured you'd be awake."

"I was just thinking about you."

"Do you always think about me in the middle of the night when you're lying next to Alex?"

"He's in the other room."

"How is he?" His tone was serious, meaning he already knew about Alex's injuries.

Not much happened in the world that Brad didn't know about. His reach always amazed me. I shouldn't be surprised that he already knew about the bobsledding incident in Bavaria. Although, it didn't take any high level of intelligence. It was probably international news.

"Alex was lucky. The blow was to his head," I said jokingly.

"He's fine then. We both know how hard-headed he is. It'd take a lot to do any real damage to that bull head of his."

It felt like old times.

Curly said the best thing to do when I felt this way was laugh about yourself. That's how we kept our sanity.

"He has a mild concussion," I said, putting the joking aside. "His neck'll be sore for a few days."

"How's the mission going?"

"It sucks."

"I hear you're in the biathlon."

"Yep. Although, I'm not sure I belong there."

"I'm sorry about what happened to Felix."

I should've been shocked that he knew but wasn't.

"You should be working for me," Brad added.

"You fired me, remember."

"They made me. I didn't want to."

"Why are you calling, Brad?"

When we were first fired, I was angry. After awhile, I thought it was for the best. Now I realized, I still had some unresolved anger. Not surprisingly. Curly taught us to never resolve emotions. To just bury them.

I wasn't trying to be rude. Brad was the no nonsense guy. Never one for chitchat. He had a reason for calling me and was putting off getting to it. For whatever reason.

"I can't call to see how my friends are doing?" he said.

"Not at three in the morning. What do you want?"

"You sound like Alex."

"He's rubbing off on me."

"Marriage will do that to you. Don't say I didn't warn you."

"If it weren't for you, Alex and I wouldn't be together," I said. "Do I have to remind you that you sent him on the cruise to spy on me? Then to Belarus to nursemaid me. You're the reason we're together."

"I suppose."

"Thank you, by the way. It's the best thing you ever did for me."

"The two of you were meant for each other. If I hadn't brought you together, the universe would've. Somehow. You are the only two people in the world who could stand each other."

"I'll take that as a compliment."

"That's how it was meant."

"God brought us together."

"Right. A match made in heaven."

"I think so."

"So, I was doing the Lord's work."

"You still haven't told me why you're calling me."

He hesitated.

"Have you heard?" he asked.

"Heard what?"

"Randy has been nominated for Director of the CIA. To replace Fuller."

"No. I hadn't heard that. Talk about a fast track."

Randy Coldclaw was the son of former CIA Director, Amy Coldclaw. She was the director when I first started in the business. Her son worked for AJAX for a period of time. Helped Curly in Costa Rica. At the time, he was so wet behind the ears, he needed to wear a diaper on his head.

Now he was going to be the director of the largest intelligence agency in the world. Alex and Curly wanted to wash him out. I went to bat for him and practically forced them to work with him.

Randy grew up fast working with Curly. Eventually, Curly even vouched for him. That had as much weight as his name. Maybe more so.

"I'm happy for him," I said sincerely. I had always liked Randy. Saw his potential. Apart from Curly and Alex, Amy Coldclaw was my favorite person in the spy business. I'd fall on a grenade for her. Back when she was still alive.

I'm glad I got one thing right. Amy would be proud.

I was feeling sorry for myself again. Brad would have to talk me off that ledge.

"Guess who's going to be Assistant Director?" Brad said.

"I thought you didn't want an administrator's position."

"Things change."

"That's the truth. If you don't like the spy business, wait until tomorrow. Things will be different."

"Yes, things do change. Which is why I'm calling?"

"I thought you were concerned about Alex."

"No. I mean, yes. I've kept up with the two of you since you left the agency. A sad day for all of us."

"Don't patronize me."

Even though Brad wasn't the reason we were fired, Alex and I had an underlying ill will for the agency. We'd been done wrong. Brad knew that as well as anyone. I'd fall on a grenade for Amy Coldclaw. Brad would fall on one for Alex and me. I needed to cut him a break. I was coming across as bitter and rude.

"What's up Brad?"

"Randy wants to bring AJAX back."

"I figured you were calling to offer us a job. I didn't think you'd go that far."

"I'm serious. Business as usual. Everything goes back to the way it was. Things haven't been the same around here without you."

"I don't know how they can go back to the way they were."

"They will. You'll answer to me. I'll answer to Randy. You'll have the yacht back. The plane. All your paintings are in a warehouse somewhere. You'll have your cover back. You love art. You'll handle sex trafficking. Alex cyber security. It'll be like you never left."

"What about all the problems with the IRS?"

"Don't hide any bank accounts. Declare all your income. That way, everything's above board."

"Alex and I got used to being on our own. Why would we want to go back to answering to you?"

"I'm not that bad to work with. You'll have that freedom again. I won't micromanage you. You know that."

"Why would Randy want to open up that can of worms again?"

"Because our numbers are way down. We rescued fourteen girls this year. Can you believe that? You rescued fourteen girls in a couple of hours. We need you back."

"I do miss it."

"Talk to Alex about it."

"I don't think he's going to want to do it. Like I said, the whole thing with Fuller left a bad taste in his mouth."

"Fuller's in jail."

"What about when the next Fuller comes along? Randy is only CIA director until the next administration comes in."

"Maybe. Maybe not. Some directors are there for a long time. We'll cross that bridge when we come to it."

"Like I said, I'll talk to Alex."

"Let me know. You can start as soon as you're done in Bavaria."

"Thanks for calling. I mean that."

"There's one other thing that might persuade Alex."

"What's that?"

"Pok is back to his old ways."

I let out a huge moan. If there were anything that'd influence Alex, that'd be it.

"He's using your billions to fund his operations," Brad said.

That thought made me angry. Alex would go ballistic.

"That son of a biscuit eater," I said. "Alex's head will explode when he finds out."

"Then wait until he's over his concussion."

That made me laugh, easing the tension somewhat.

The malaise was gone. It felt like we had a purpose again. I'd try and convince Alex to do it if he resisted.

"Alex needs to hunt Pok down and kill him once and for all," Brad said.

"We had a chance."

I related to Brad about how Alex found Pok. He had his rifle sights on him. Pok had a wife and child. Alex didn't want to kill him in front of his kid. So he let him live. We both knew it was a mistake at the time.

"Apparently, Pok has developed some new technology," Brad said. "He's wreaking havoc in the financial world with his hacking operations. His reach is bigger than ever."

"I'll be sure and tell Alex. He'll want to know that for sure."

"Take good care of Alex, will you?"

"You know it."

I saw headlights pull into the driveway. Probably Saul.

"I've got to go."

"Think about it."

"I will."

I hung up the phone. Stunned. Not sure what to think about this sudden turn of events. Before Brad called, I was thinking about how I wanted to get back to rescuing girls. Not necessarily back to AJAX. Although, those were the best of times, before Fuller came along.

Can you really go backwards in time? Would things really go back to the way they used to be?

I don't know why they couldn't. I did love art. I'd love to be back on the yacht. To work with A-Rad, Bond, and maybe Colonel again.

The thought energized me. A burst of joy pulsed through my veins.

Until I saw Saul's face when he walked through the door.

I didn't bother standing.

He sat across from me.

"I'm afraid I have bad news."

"Which one of them died?" I asked.

"All three of them."

The malaise was back. The chasm as deep as a trench in the bottom of the ocean.

I couldn't believe it.

Imposter.

Why did I think this was my fault?

That I could've saved them.

No. Should've saved them.

23

Saul Geller, Director of Mossad, had given me the worst possible news. Unimaginable. John and Matthew, members of the bobsled team, had died of their injuries sustained when the bobsled was sabotaged and smashed into a wall at the end of the course. Felix survived the six-hour surgery but went into cardiac arrest in the recovery room and they couldn't save him.

I'd seen a lot of death over the years. This hit me hard.

How did I tell Alex?

I wouldn't. Not now.

Not until he recovered from his concussion. That'd take three or four days. I'd need to keep him sedated because he'd want to go kill someone the moment he knew. The grief would stunt his recovery. Best he not know for a couple of days.

We didn't know who was behind it anyway. The results weren't back yet from the examination of the bobsled even though I knew it was sabotaged.

Saul agreed that I should wait until Alex was better. He was sitting in the living room of our residence. What he said next shocked me to my core.

"What do we do now?" I had asked.

"We're shutting down the whole operation," Saul said.

"Everything?"

"We're pulling all of our athletes out of their events."

"That seems a little drastic. They've trained so hard to get here. I think we can protect them now that we know what we're dealing with."

"Already done," he said matter-of-factly. "They're on a plane back to Israel. Along with the bodies of the three men. I'm leaving in a few hours. I thought you deserved to hear it from me since I brought you into this mission."

"I can't believe it. I'm stunned."

"As soon as Alex is well enough to travel, I'll arrange for your transportation anywhere you want to go."

"He'll want to stay."

"That's up to you. There's nothing for you to do here. The mission is over. I don't even have the authority to ask you to buy a toothbrush."

"What about the bomb?"

"We don't even know there is a bomb."

"What if there is?"

"Not our problem. The International Olympic Committee can handle it. They aren't concerned. Why should we be? We'll be thousands of miles away."

"I'm concerned. I can feel it. Hoffman didn't run this big a mission to kill a few Israeli citizens. He'll want to make a bigger splash in the media."

"If he did, he'll be disappointed. The official line from the Olympic Committee is that the bobsled incident was an accident. So was Felix's death. The rifle malfunctioned. The brakes on the bobsled failed. No mention of sabotage to the media."

"That's a lie."

Saul only nodded.

I scratched my head in bewilderment. I couldn't think of a good argument to stay. He was right. We should cut our losses and get out of there. A sense of failure came over me like a tidal wave. I wasn't used to giving up in the middle of a mission. Alex and I never did, even though we should've on more than one occasion.

"So there's nothing we can do?" I asked, more of a comment than anything.

"You've done all you can."

"I'm sorry we failed you."

Tears had welled up in my eyes. If Saul saw them, he didn't say anything. It was the middle of the night, and I only had a dim light on. I didn't want to give a sniper on the outside a good look at a target. We were sitting away from the windows for that reason.

"You didn't fail me," Saul said. "It's not your fault. It's mine. I was in charge of the mission. You did everything you could do."

"Why does it feel like I didn't?"

"I'm serious, Jamie. I'm grateful for everything. You rescued the ninety-six girls. Keisha would be dead if not for you. Once we realized the threat, we never should've brought you here. We should've stayed away."

"Hoffman wins. How will Israel ever compete in the Olympics again? There will always be terrorists out there wanting to kill you."

"That's not the reason we're leaving. To be honest. I'm concerned there is a bomb. I want my people away from here. You need to leave as well. The sooner the better."

"Hoffman wants to kill Jews. He won't stop, just because you leave."

"We're used to it. Our tiny country is surrounded by a dozen despots who have vowed to wipe us off the face of the earth. We've survived as a people for several thousand years. Hoffman will never succeed in destroying us. God will protect us."

My mouth flew open when I realized something.

"What about the biathlon?" I asked.

"What about it?"

"I want to compete. Felix thinks I can win a medal."

"Felix isn't here to help you."

The comment shot a pang through my heart. Before I knew Felix was dead, I'd summoned up the "win one for the coach" sentiment inside of me. Not that I needed motivation. But I was resolved to do everything in my power to win that medal. For Israel. For myself. For Felix.

"I want to at least try," I said with my voice struggling to get out the words without cracking.

"I won't be here to help you. You'll be on your own."

"I've always mostly been on my own. Alex and I are used to it."

"It's going to be dangerous."

"I know."

"If you're caught, my government will deny that you were acting on behalf of Mossad."

"I expect that."

"I can't order you to leave."

"What about the house and credentials? Can we use them?"

"Of course."

"I'm not sure what we'll do. I'll talk to Alex when he wakes up."

"I have to go. I suggest you do the same as soon as you can."

With those words, the conversation ended. Saul stood to his feet, reached out his hand, which I shook. Then he kissed me on both of my cheeks and left. Presumably to catch his plane.

Leaving me to pick up the pieces.

He was right. I needed to get Alex out of there.

In the morning.

After we rescued the Chinese girl. We'd drive her out of the village to a safe place. I could no longer count on Mossad to help with the rescue. *Save The Girls* would help me. They were a Christian organization involved in sex trafficking. I'd been working with them for years.

Back when Alex and I were running AJAX and had billions of dollars at our disposal, we funneled tens of millions of dollars to them. I'd recently learned they'd made cutbacks to their operations. Almost certainly because our funding was cut off.

Another reason to accept Brad's offer. With AJAX operational, we'd have the money to help them again. Run all kinds of operations worldwide. Under the guise of an art distribution company.

I was excited. The disheartening news aside. Nothing I could do about that now other than get Alex healthy and live to fight another day. That's the problem with this kind of war. The threats and bad guys were everywhere. We leave one battlefield and go directly to another.

Alex wouldn't be happy. He'd say the fight wasn't finished here. The German was around and needed to be dealt with. He'd agree that the competition was over. That I shouldn't compete in the biathlon. That's not why we were there to begin with. I couldn't think of a single argument as to why I should subject myself to that risk. And embarrassment. I'd probably finish last.

We could leave as winners. The bobsled team won the preliminary heat. That could never be taken from them.

Although, it came at a great cost.

We had to move on from that. Now that we no longer had any obligations to Mossad, we were free to operate in whatever way we saw fit. Hunt the German on our own terms. Or not. Alex may agree that it's not worth the effort or scrutiny. Running a mission in the midst of all this security wouldn't be easy. Especially since we were no longer competing as athletes.

I slumped down in my chair. I didn't need to figure it all out in the next few minutes. I was exhausted and needed sleep. Curly said to sleep when you can. You never know when you'll get another chance.

My gun was on the table next to me. I'd sleep out in the living room so I wouldn't run the risk of waking Alex. It wouldn't bother me if he slept the next day. It'd do him good and give me time to develop an exit plan. I'd talk to Brad again and tell him I was on board if Alex was.

I fell asleep quickly and slept later than I'd intended. A knock on the door woke me from a deep slumber. I looked at the clock when my eyes focused. It was after nine o'clock in the morning.

Another knocking sound. A slight rap. Sounded like a woman's knock.

I instinctively reached for my gun. Thought about not answering it. What if it was a threat?

The German probably wouldn't knock on the door. He'd be at a severe disadvantage. I'd be able to see him through a window. All I had to do was fire two bullets through the door and he'd be dead.

I couldn't imagine who it could be.

No sign that Alex had stirred, but I didn't have time to check. Another knock came. Louder this time.

With the gun behind my back, I walked over and looked out the keyhole on the door.

A woman stood on the doorstep. With a heavy coat and hat on. Her head bent down making it hard for me to see who it was.

I opened the door slowly and peeked around it. It felt like I still had goop in my eyes. No telling what my hair looked like or what my breath smelled like.

The woman smiled warmly. She looked familiar. It took me a second to process who she was.

"Ms. Gwyn," I said. "I'm surprised to see you here."

"Call me Ffion, please."

"What are you doing here?"

"May I come in?"

Was it a trap? I scoured the road behind her. Searching for any threats. I was being paranoid. Why would the most famous Olympic woman athlete of all time be a threat to me?

"Of course," I said. "I didn't mean to be rude."

I closed the door quickly when she entered after I stuck my head out long enough to glance around for any threats. The cold air shocked my senses, so I was fully awake.

"I'm sorry to barge in like this, Esther," she said. "I was wondering if we could talk for a few minutes."

"Sure."

I invited her to sit with my free hand. The gun was still behind my back held by my other hand. I sat down on the couch across from her and discretely stuffed the gun behind one of the cushions.

"Esther, I'm so very sorry to hear about Felix," she said, leaning forward in her chair.

Why did she call me Esther?

Then I remembered. That's the name I was competing under. The alias Mossad had given to me. I had a passport in that name. I might need it to get out of the country.

It took me a second to get back into my cover.

"It's a real tragedy," I answered. Nodding.

I noticed her eyes welling up with tears.

"Did you know Felix?" I asked.

She raised her head and chuckled nervously. "Everyone knows Felix. He was one of a kind. Did you know he used to coach me? When I was barely a teenager."

"I didn't know. I know he thought very highly of you. Said you're the best biathlete who ever lived."

She waved her hand dismissively.

"That's a thing of the past now. I'm retired."

"I was sorry to hear about your injury."

She chuckled nervously. "I strained some rib muscles. Stupid actually. I'm so clumsy walking on ice. Imagine that. Put skis on me and I can go forever without falling. Ask me to walk around the village on a slick sidewalk and I'll end up on my rear end more times than not."

I respectfully chuckled along with her. I could relate.

"That's how I am on the skis," I said. "Clumsy."

A second wave of the hand.

"Don't sell yourself short. I've seen you practicing."

"You have?"

"You're a natural."

I felt myself blush at the compliment.

"I guess I'm pretty good at shooting. Skiing, not so much."

"I think you can be better."

"It doesn't matter. I'm withdrawing from the competition."

Her mouth flew open and eyes widened.

"Heavens no. You can't withdraw. You have a chance to win."

"That's what Felix said. But he's no longer here to help me. I can't do it without him. I'm not sure I could even do it with him."

My turn to tear up.

"That's why I'm here. I want to help you."

"I'm sorry. But my husband and I are leaving today."

Right before I went to sleep, I decided the safest thing to do was to get Alex out of the village as soon as possible. And on a plane to somewhere safe. After I found the Chinese girl and rescued her. Which I intended to do today sometime.

I hadn't anticipated this interruption. If you'd told me a surprise was coming, it would've taken me ten thousand guesses to come up with this one.

I was honored that Ffion had come to see me. I appreciated the sentiment. She really was a lovely lady. Beautiful and kind. Along with being talented.

Under different circumstances, I'd love the chance to pick her brain. I'd always been intrigued by someone who was the best in the world at something.

Ffion spoke with exaggerated hand motions. "You can't leave," she said with emphasis. "You have a chance to win a medal. As you know, Israel has never won a medal in the Winter Olympics."

"Not to sound rude, but why do you care? Aren't you from Norway?"

"I was born in Tel Aviv."

"I didn't know that."

"I have dual citizenship. My Mother and Father are Jews."

"How did you end up in Norway?"

"My parents took us on a vacation to Europe one winter. I put on a pair of skis and was hooked. A few months later, my parents found Felix and he started training me. Said I was a prodigy. He encouraged me to go to Norway and join a biathlon training program. I didn't know such a thing existed."

"It's a small world."

"My parents would only let me go if Felix went with me. We went there for four weeks the next winter. I was thirteen and hooked. My parents moved there so I could train full time. We became citizens and I entered my first Olympics and competed under the Norwegian flag. The rest is history."

"You should write a book."

"Most people don't know I'm Jewish. If they did, I'd be a target like you. Esther, may I be frank?"

"Always."

"I don't think your rifle exploded by accident."

"I don't either."

"Rifles don't explode like that unless they've been tampered with."

"I agree. And it should've been me. Felix was only holding the rifle because he was showing me something. Somebody was trying to kill me. Not him."

"I understand why you want to leave. I'd be afraid, too."

"I'm not afraid. I don't want to embarrass myself. I have no chance to win without Felix. I probably didn't have a chance anyway."

"I think you do. You're the best shooter I've ever seen. Better than me."

"Oh well."

"Your technique is lacking. I can help you with that."

"The competition is in ten days."

"We'd better get to work."

"What do you mean?"

"I mean, that I'm going to be your coach."

"Are you allowed? I mean, what will your team and country say?"

"I'll coach you behind the scenes. No one will need to know. You're not the first young athlete I've mentored who wasn't from Norway."

"I don't have a rifle."

"You can use mine."

"This might be dangerous for you. Whoever tried to kill me is still out there."

"I'm not afraid."

"You're a remarkable woman. I don't know if I've ever met anyone quite like you."

"I could say the same thing."

"Let me think about it."

"If you want to do it, meet me at the biathlon training center at one. Right after lunch. I'll have the rifle with me."

"One o'clock. I think I might do it."

"I hope you do."

I stood to my feet. She did as well, and we faced each other. We were about the same height. I was trimmer. Her legs were wider and more muscular.

"By the way, never let the rifle out of your sight," she said.

"I learned that lesson the hard way. They told me I had to check it into the lockers. That's where it was tampered with. I even know who did it."

"You can keep the rifle with you as long as it's not loaded."

"I wish I'd known that sooner. I have a lot to learn."

"I'm here to help you."

"Thank you."

"It's my pleasure."

As fast as she appeared at my doorstep, she was gone.

I met her at one o'clock. Alex had awakened enough to drink more water and go to the bathroom. The water had medicine in it and he went back to sleep. I figured he'd sleep through the rest of the day.

I hadn't made my final decision. I wanted to see how the training went.

* * *

The training went well. Ffion was amazing. She taught me the things Felix was trying to teach me before he was killed. She showed me how to prepare my equipment. The best technique to improve my speed in the cross country. Limited movements. Don't get in too big a hurry.

Definitely shoot from right to left. I'm better that way.

I taught her a few things about slowing down the heart rate. Shooting while controlling your breath. Things Curly taught me that she couldn't possibly know. Since her targets were small. Mine were human beings.

By the end of the three-hour marathon session, I was convinced.

I was competing in the biathlon.

And I was in it to win it.

Two days later

I felt guilty. Like I had Munchausen Syndrome. I kept spiking Alex's drink with pain medication, so he'd sleep.

It gave me time to train and him time to heal. Eventually, I'd have to let him wake up.

Maybe tomorrow.

Before the opening ceremonies. I needed his help.

24

Becker Biathlon Center
Ten Days Later

In a matter of minutes, I'd be standing at the starting line of the Biathlon competition in the International Olympics Games. Who would've ever thought that possible? I barely believed it myself.

My whole body was shaking. I wouldn't be more nervous if I was about to charge a compound full of Russian KGB agents armed with assault rifles.

The stadium was electric. Adding to the adrenaline pumping through my veins. I'd never seen anything quite like it except on television. Real life was much different. Nothing like being the center of attention. On the biggest stage in the world.

The competition was at night and the massive lights brought in to illuminate the course cast eerie shadows throughout the huge complex. Felix's predictions of inclement weather hadn't come to pass. The conditions were blistery cold, but no wind. Perfect for a biathlon competition.

The scene around me was chaotic. The crowd roared as each contestant left the starting line and was even louder as contestants crossed the finish line which were right next to each other.

Reporters from all over the world were crammed into the staging area. Hundreds of cameras would be pointed at me when I got to the starting line.

Not ideal for an undercover CIA operative. I adjusted my cap so it came down lower on my forehead. I wanted to raise the wool scarf to cover my nose and mouth and hide my face completely, but I wouldn't be able to breathe.

Alex and Ffion had left me a few minutes before to go to an area where coaches could observe their athletes. Technically, Ffion could follow me on the course yelling instructions, but she didn't want to be that conspicuous. Openly rooting for someone competing against her Norwegian teammates.

Alex was back to his old self, but wasn't proficient enough walking on the ice to even think about following me. It took several days, but he now showed no physical effects from the injuries he received in the bobsled run.

With Alex, you never knew how he was dealing with the emotional effects. He hid those from me. Curly drilled into us to let those things go and focus only on the things we could control. That's what I was doing now.

Ffion and Alex both thought I could win the gold medal. I only wanted to finish without embarrassing myself.

The last ten days had been a whirlwind. We'd been working diligently on two fronts. Searching for the German and the potential bomb, and preparing me for this moment. Alex hacked into the security cameras and spent most of his time scanning the footage trying to find the German. He installed some face recognition software and caught the man on camera several times. For the most part, the German was good at keeping his face off the camera.

I focused on my training. Ten hours a day. Every day. Unless we were sleeping, Ffion and I were either on the course or in the classroom. She was with me constantly. More obsessed with me winning the gold than I was.

She was as demanding as Curly. Her attention to detail was even beyond his. I could see why she'd won three straight Olympic gold medals. She left nothing to chance. We went over every inch of the course. Looked for the trouble spots. She showed me where to take risks and when to slow down.

Constantly working on technique. If I did the least little thing wrong, she stopped me, and made me do it again and again until I got it right.

"Two tenths of a second could be the difference between winning and losing," she had said. "Trust me. You don't want to live the rest of your life coming that close to a medal in the Olympics only to fall short by several tenths of a second."

Her input was invaluable. I improved my time daily. My confidence grew. Listening to her constant input, I had actual moments when I believed I could win.

Her pep talks were inspiring. She had a rule. Sixty percent encouragement. If she said something critical, she had to say something positive. At the end of the day, the positives had to be greater proportionately than the negatives.

Today, all she spoke were positive words. She didn't want a negative thought in my head.

"You can win this," she said. "Stick to the plan. This is your moment. Block out the unimportant. Remember what I taught you."

That would be the impossible part. She'd taught me so much.

As I waited to hear my name calling me to the starting line, her many instructions were battling in my head for attention.

"Shooting is the key. One missed shot and you're likely on the podium," she said. "No missed shots and you'll win."

In practice, I hit every target at least fifty percent of the time. Some days more. It'd be harder in the throes of the competition. With the crowd cheering.

Alex helped me with that. He was a standout college quarterback for Stanford University. Played in the national championship game against Alabama. A hundred thousand people were in the stands that day and millions watched on television.

"Block them out. Don't even pay attention to the crowd," Alex had said.

He wouldn't let me talk about winning the gold.

"Don't think about the fourth quarter. One play at a time. One shot at a time. Don't think about the finish line until you have it in your sights. The podium will take care of itself."

Good advice. I needed to keep my focus on the task at hand. Each laborious step on the ski.

My heart raced. That's the first thing I needed to correct.

Ffion had been adamant. "Before the race starts, get your heartbeat down. Most contestants can't do it. That's what separates the good from the great. Most people come to the starting line and their heart is racing at 180-200 beats a minute. Because of all the nervousness and excitement."

I understood. My senses were in overload. I'd never experienced this before. The cheering crowd. The cameras. The other coaches were shouting instructions all around me.

Being a spy was a lonely existence. There were no crowds. No one was cheering for you. Killing terrorists wasn't a spectator's sport. No one was around to see me when I faced down terrorists. No experts would be commentating on the way I held my gun or how I fired my shots.

In this instance, every cross-country ski step would be analyzed. Every shot was documented for years to come. I'd never felt pressure like this before.

I checked. My heartbeat was already at 120. Extremely high for me.

I took the steps necessary to bring it down. Breathe deeply. Close my eyes. Block out the distractions.

Ffion explained why it was so important.

"Those contestants who start out at 180 beats per minute have no shot," she said. "As soon as they're on the course and start sprinting, their heart rates jump up to 210 or so. By the time they get to the first shooting station, there's no way they can accurately shoot a gun."

One twenty for me was the equivalent of one eighty for most other people.

Ten minutes later, I had my heart rate down to seventy-three. Not as low as I wanted but good considering the circumstances.

I was next in line. The horn sounded and the contestant ahead of me was off. My name was called by a race volunteer. The racers went off in thirty second intervals.

I skied over to my position. A large tent on the snow. I got into the starter's stance and stared down the long straightaway. My eyes focused on the woman in front of me.

Ffion showed me the proper starting position. We practiced it a thousand times. At least it felt like it.

I took in a cold breath. It felt refreshing and energizing.

Remember your instructions.

Ffion had detailed them for each segment of the race. First segment was from the starting line to the first curve.

"Don't start out too fast," she had said. "Pace yourself. Get your skis under you. Try to relax and get into a rhythm. When you approach the first curve, don't get too close to the boundary on the left. Your ski can get caught in the rope and you can go tumbling down."

The horn sounded.

My instinct propelled me forward like a bullet shot out of a gun.

I pushed off with my poles.

I felt strong.

The first steps were powerful and smooth. It might've been my best start ever.

It felt exhilarating. I couldn't believe it.

I was racing in the Olympics!

The crowd cheered. So loud I couldn't block it out.

Deafening.

They were cheering for me!

The lights were blinding. A slight snowy mist formed on my goggles.

"Don't worry about that," Ffion had said. "The fog will clear off within a few meters."

It did.

"Don't lose momentum on the first curve!" I heard Ffion yelling the instructions in my head.

It's like she was right there.

This course was difficult according to Ffion. The first curve led into an incline. I could lose valuable time if I slowed down too much at the curve. It'd take a lot of effort to recover the momentum.

As I neared the curve I accelerated. Pushed off with my right ski to make the left-hand turn. Careful not to get too close to the edge.

My right foot slid on the ice.

Oh no!

I could feel myself losing my balance.

I don't remember doing it, but I compensated and regained my stride. We'd practiced it so much it had become second nature to me.

A relief washed over me. Ffion had prepared me for that situation. The first few times I had overcompensated. Once I fell over. I was thankful she had taught me how to get out of that situation.

It gave me a burst of confidence. I could do this. I was prepared.

Having dodged that potential problem, I settled into a steady rhythm like she told me to do.

I was almost having fun.

Almost.

I couldn't grow overconfident.

My margin of error was razor thin.

Ffion explained. "Emilie Schenck is the favorite now that I'm out of the competition. She's from Germany. She's a great skier and a great shooter. She's a better skier than you, but you're a better shooter. I think she'll miss at least one shot. We can hope she misses two."

"You're about thirty seconds slower than her on the course. That means you'll have to hit every shot to beat her if she only misses one shot. If she misses two, you can still miss one and win."

Emilie had already raced. Put on the board her best time ever according to Ffion. She only missed one shot. Which meant she had to take a penalty lap which cost her around twenty seconds. The pro German crowd had spurred her on.

That meant I couldn't miss a shot.

I was skiing fast. So fast, I'd almost caught the Finnish girl who'd started in front of me.

I came to the first shooting station right behind her. The standing position. By the time I made it to the station, the rifle was already off my back. One fluid motion.

Ffion would be proud. Was proud. She was no doubt watching it on a television screen.

I took a quick glance at the clock. I was seven seconds ahead of my best practice time.

I got into position and made sure my rifle was in working order.

"Always check it before firing," Ffion said. "The scope can get knocked out of position from the jostling on your back."

I made a couple of adjustments. Looked at the targets through the sights.

I slowed my heartbeat which I estimated at slightly above a hundred.

Perfect.

Felix had taught me to shoot from right to left and to shoot quickly. From instinct. Ffion had taken the same approach but slowed me down some. Still shooting with feel but not as wildly.

I let out five quick breaths. One for each shot. Blew them out.

First shot.

The black target turned white.

A hit!

Whew!

I'd had nightmares about that first shot. I dreamed I missed all five targets. Hitting one made me realize I could actually do it in a competition.

Four more to go.

"One shot at a time," I heard Alex screaming at me. It almost seemed like he was right there as well.

The next four targets turned white as I shot with precision. Confidently. I heard a roar go up from the crowd in the distance.

Was that for me?

Ffion said at this point, the announcers would be confused. Wondering where I'd come from. I wouldn't be expected to be a contender for a medal. Not very many athletes hit all five targets at the first station.

They'd be shocked. Talking about an upset.

I pushed that out of my mind.

I quickly put the rifle on my back, lowered my goggles and was off. A glance at the clock informed me that I was now fourteen seconds ahead of my fastest time.

With a perfect shooting round behind me.

Emilie had missed a target at the first station. Technically, I was ahead of her.

Don't think about it.

I visualized the next part of the course.

The hardest part was coming up. A series of undulations. Up and down. Sudden accelerations. Sharp turns. Surprisingly enough, the downhill gave me more trouble. The proper technique was to get into a tuck position. I have long legs. Ffion taught me to remain more upright. That caused more drag against the wind but gave me more stability.

I preferred stability to speed.

I was too careful in that part of the course. I could feel it. I'd lost time. I didn't take many risks.

"Better to lose time than risk falling," Ffion had said. Felix said the same thing.

Thinking about Felix gave me added motivation. I wanted to win for him. So, his death wouldn't be in vain.

I was right. At the next checkpoint, I'd lost time.

I was five seconds faster than my best time but slower than Emilie at that point. Not considering the penalty. I did the quick calculations in my head. Emilie was likely a second or two ahead of me even with the penalty. Assuming I hit all my targets at the next station. I'd have to make up the time somewhere.

"Don't try to make it up all at once," I heard Ffion say. "You'll actually lose time. You'll start to labor and exert too much energy."

I could feel it. My legs were burning. My lungs sucked in breaths at a quicker rate now as I was exerting more energy.

Pounding the skis. Planting the poles in the ground with more force.

Ffion warned me this would happen. I'd hit a wall. No matter how hard I trained, there'd be a point in the race when I'd feel exhaustion come over me. Since I'd never faced that before in these circumstances, it'd make or break me.

"Sheer determination must take over," Ffion said.

"Losers quit when they get tired," Curly said. "You don't quit until you win."

"Fatigue makes cowards out of all of us," Alex said. A quote from a famous football coach.

My legs didn't want to move. The poles felt like they weighed a hundred pounds each. I had a hill before me. The last one before the prone shooting station. I could feel the medal slipping out of my grasp.

"You can do anything, but not everything," I heard an unrecognizable voice in my head.

Not Ffion or Alex. Certainly not Curly. He made me feel invincible.

Imposter syndrome.

What was I doing?

How stupid was I to think I could actually compete in the Olympics?

I'd been skiing many times growing up. I loved it. But I wasn't a world class athlete.

What a farce this was. A joke. An embarrassment. I'm a CIA operative, not a biathlete. Those women trained for years. I'd been training for a month.

Stay in your lane, Curly said.

Right.

I was so far outside my lane I couldn't even see it. I was a trained killer. Not a cross country skier. I shot people not targets.

Stupid.

What was I thinking?

"Stay in your lane," a woman's voice said.

Not Curly. Ffion.

That reminded me.

Take the outside lane on the last hill, she had said.

I had drifted too far inside. The inside was smoother. All the athletes took it. But it was also steeper around the curve. They lost momentum. The outside lane was slicker. More dangerous.

"The end is the time to take more risks," Ffion had said. "The outside lane will slingshot you down the hill."

I wasn't good at going downhill. The times I tried it I was going too fast.

A moment of indecision hit me.

"Do you want to win?" Ffion shouted in my ear.

"Go big or go home!" Alex said.

"Kill or be killed," Curly shouted at me.

The biggest risk is not taking any risks, Felix's still quiet voice whispered in my ear.

I maneuvered to the outside. The indecision gone.

The ice was slick. It took all the muscles in my legs to keep the skis from sliding out from under me and me doing the splits right in the middle of the course.

I topped the hill.

With momentum.

"Use your poles!" Ffion said. "To push yourself off the hill."

I dug my poles in the snow. And pushed off with all my strength.

I almost lost my balance as my right ski lifted in the air and I leaned back to regain it.

Somehow, I managed to stay upright.

I got into a tuck. Tighter than I did in practice. Throwing all caution to the wind. The wind whooshed around me.

I was barreling down the hill to the second shooting station.

I had to slow down. I was going so fast. I was in danger of overshooting the station.

I didn't even look at my time.

It is what it is.

I got down in the prone position.

Steadied my breath.

Checked my rifle.

Hit the first target.

And the second and third.

Took in a deep breath and concentrated.

Hit the fourth target.

Only one to go.

Then I saw him.

The fourth station was at the back of the course. Abutting a forest. A cluster of trees was behind the targets. The lights from the shooting range cast eerie shadows into the trees.

No doubt about it.

The German was in that grove of trees. With a rifle pointed at me.

25

The German had his rifle aimed at me. I had mine on him. I had the advantage. He didn't know it. He wouldn't shoot me while I was lying down. He'd wait until I stood to my feet.

I could shoot him from my position. He didn't know I knew he was there.

Why hadn't I already shot him?

In a life-or-death situation, not making a decision could be worse than making the wrong one. If I didn't shoot him, I was a sitting duck. I had to presume he was proficient as a sniper. He didn't have to be that good to hit me from that distance.

On the other hand, could I hit him with my .22 caliber bullet? From the same distance. My bullet was smaller. Lighter. Not designed to kill a man. Designed for target practice. I had to take into consideration the wind. The angle. He was slightly above me.

All my training on this rifle was hitting a target fifty meters away.

I could hit him if I aimed for center mass. His chest.

What if I was wrong? Miscalculated. Took the shot and missed. I'd be dead.

The race.

What about it?

I could win.

A debate suddenly raged in my head.

I'd hit nine of nine targets. Ffion said if I hit all ten, I'd likely win the gold medal.

The shot at the German would count as a miss. I'd probably lose the biathlon. I was so close to a medal I could taste it.

The whole debate was stupid. What difference did it make? I was going to lose either way. If I shot the German, I'd have to take a penalty lap. If I didn't, he'd shoot me as soon as I stood up.

The few extra seconds I was taking to make a decision had probably taken me out of the medal round anyway. Even if I hit the target.

It was a no brainer. How could I even consider not shooting the target?

What if I shot the target, then fired a second shot at him? In rapid fire. Would anyone notice?

I'd be disqualified. They counted the number of the bullets in the rifle at the beginning of the race and at the end. For that very reason. A competitor could cheat and shoot twice at a target.

The debate continued, costing me valuable time.

Israel has never won a medal. I could make history.
Who cares about a medal?

I didn't realize how much I did.

Shoot the German.

The decision was made. It was my only choice. I moved the rifle scope slightly to the right. He was in my sights. Now that the decision was made, the anger inside of me exploded. I knew I was doing the right thing. I'd been wanting to kill this German since Alex and I were in Jerusalem.

Now that he was costing me a medal, I really wanted to kill him.

I'd take great satisfaction in watching him die through the scope.

I breathed in. Like I was aiming for the target.

Then it dawned on me. A chest shot wouldn't kill him. The bullet was too small. It'd wound him, but he'd still get a shot off.

The head was the only option. The kill shot. This small a bullet would rattle around in his brain. Bounce from one side of the skull to the other. His brain would be mush in a matter of seconds.

That made the shot more difficult by a factor of four or more. 150 meters I estimated. Shooting uphill. Wind blowing slightly.

My odds weren't good. More than likely, the wind would blow the bullet off course.

I had to try.

I let out a breath.

Steady.

A muzzle flash startled me. The German's head exploded right before my eyes.

Not from my bullet. It wouldn't do that kind of damage.

What happened?

I took my eye off the scope and looked deep into the forest and strained to see a shadowy figure kneeling over the German. Checking for a pulse.

I blinked twice to make sure I was seeing clearly.

Akeem.

The CIA agent from Syria. What was he doing here?

Brad obviously sent him to watch over me. To protect his assets. Knowing Brad, he had assumed Alex and I would come back to the CIA. How could we turn down that opportunity? Our mission was dangerous. He sent Akeem to linger in the background in case we ran into a threat we couldn't handle.

I'd thank him later.

I was losing valuable time. The commentators were probably going crazy wondering what in the world I was doing.

Out of the corner of my eye, I saw Akeem drag the German away. Deep into the woods. Brad probably had a cleaner team nearby to clean up the mess and dispose of the body.

Focus Jamie.

One shot. Possibly for a medal.

I fired. I don't even remember aiming. Shooting from instinct. Like someone had just pulled a gun on me and I had to kill him quickly.

The black target turned white.

I hit it!

A perfect ten for ten. Ffion said that was rare.

Did I take too long?

I stood to my feet and looked over at the clock. I hadn't lost as much time as I thought. In the heat of a gunfight, time slowed down. I'd only lost twelve seconds. Since I didn't have to make a penalty lap at the end, I could race for the finish.

My skis were moving now. The rifle was on my back. I don't remember putting it there.

My jaw was clenched. I relaxed it. Every ounce of energy needed to go to my arms and legs. The skis and the poles.

"The last two meters are the most important," Ffion had said. "Give it all you have."

Alex was in my head now. "At the National Championship game, our coach told us to leave it all on the football field. You can live with losing if you give it everything you have."

"Winning isn't everything, but wanting to win is," Felix said above the other voices. "Winning a medal will make you a hero."

"Do you want to be a hero?" Curly chimed in one day at the Farm. "Heroism is having the courage to die for something."

It all came into perspective at that moment. My purpose in life. Not to win a medal at the Olympics. To save lives. Rescue girls.

God. Family. Country.

I dug deep. I would give it all I had. Today. Tomorrow. For the rest of my life. As long as I had breath.

I intended to push myself to the limits of my ability. Today and always.

My legs were churning. My arms thrust the poles into the ground, and I pushed off the hardened snow with all my might. With the intensity of an earth mover.

With new resolve.

I didn't care if I won or lost. My purpose in life was Alex and the girls. The ones who still needed rescuing.

The face of the Chinese girl was in front of me. Like she was on the course. I was going to rescue her.

We would take that job with Brad. Return to the CIA. That gave us the most resources to rescue girls. That's what mattered in life. Alex could have his cyber lab back. He needed to deal with Pok once and for all.

Tomorrow.

I'd worry about it then.

Today, I'd focus on the race. I wanted to win. I was so close.

The course had one long uphill before I got to the home stretch. Almost unfair, according to Ffion, considering it was at the end of the race, when the competitors legs felt like rubber. Like mine did now. It took every ounce of resolve to make my legs take one more step across the snow.

My breathing became labored. Did I save enough for the end? I had to quickly get my breath back. I needed the oxygen.

I pounded the skis and poles. Every muscle in my body ached. My legs screamed for me to stop the torture. My lungs burned which was strange considering how cold my breaths were.

The wind had picked up and was in my face. I willed myself to the top of the hill. Got into a tuck on the downhill. A welcomed respite on my legs although they were shaky. My skis were bouncing. I needed other muscles in my legs to hold them in place. Muscles I hadn't used up until now.

At the bottom of the hill was a curve. I had to slow down for it. Then regain momentum and sprint to the finish line.

How did I do that? I didn't have the strength. I felt like I'd already expended every ounce of energy.

"Don't worry about it," Ffion had said. "As soon as you're on the home stretch, you'll find energy you didn't know you had."

What I'd found was peace. A purpose. Alex and I had been floundering somewhat since AJAX was stolen from us. Like Brad said, their numbers were way down. So were ours. It broke my heart. Every number was a girl. Stuck in slavery because I couldn't help her.

The world needed Alex and his skills. Pok had stolen more than our money. He'd taken all our resources. Fuller had stolen our position with the CIA. We could get it all back. Things would return to how they were. I'd start saving girls again. Obsessed with it. Like I used to be.

That thought propelled me forward. I rounded the curve. It seemed like a blur. I was on the home stretch. The finish line was a football field away. Next to where I had started a few minutes before.

It seemed like yesterday.

I pushed harder. Faster. With every ounce of my being.

Ffion was right. I don't know where it came from, but I felt a rush. A second wind. Maybe a third or fourth by that point.

The crowd cheered. The lights were bright. I saw Alex and Ffion at the finish line screaming at me. Hands raised. Jumping up and down. Spurring me on.

I must be close to the medal.

"You don't want to be the person who finishes fourth at the Olympics," Ffion had said. "It'll haunt you the rest of your life."

Did I have more in me? I might already be out of the running for the medal. Part of me wanted to slow down. Catch my breath. I felt like I was dying.

Instead, I pushed harder. My heart had to be beating 180 to 200 beats per minute. I'd never taxed my body to this extent.

Every last ounce of strength went into every step.

I neared the finish line. I was spent.

My balance shifted. I could feel the skis coming out from under me.

I wanted to scream, but had no air in my lungs.

I fell forward. Instinctively reached out my hands with the poles to catch myself. I was ten feet from the finish line. Was I going to fall flat on my face? Before I even reached the finish line.

I lunged. I was airborne now.

I landed face first in the snow. My skis bounced awkwardly behind me and came off my feet keeping me from injuring my knees and ankles.

Did I make it across the line? Only one part of my body had to touch and I will have completed the race.

I was unable to breathe. It felt like I had an elephant sitting on my back.

I pushed myself up to my knees. Desperately searching for air.

This must be what a heart attack felt like.

Alex and Ffion helped me to my feet. I bent over with my hands on my knees. Still trying to breathe.

I didn't know if I won or lost.

It didn't matter.

I had won either way.

* * *

Later that night

Alex sat at his computer in our residence in the Olympic Village. I'd taken a long hot bath to soak my sore and aching muscles.

I came up behind him. He looked to be deep in the middle of something. Olympic Village security cameras were on his computer screen. He had hacked into them several days before. Looking for the German.

The German was no longer a problem, so I wasn't sure what he was doing.

I put my hands on his shoulders and began rubbing them.

"You realize that you have to treat me differently since I'm an Olympic gold medal winner," I said to him jokingly.

He chuckled.

"Fat chance of that. You still put your pants on one leg at a time like the rest of us."

"Actually, I'm not wearing any pants." I said it in my most sultry voice.

Alex swiveled around in the chair faster than a tilt-a-whirl at an amusement park. His eyes were as big as snowflakes.

"You're such a liar," he said roughly.

"Why do you say that? I'm not wearing pants."

"What are those?"

"Pajamas."

"Pajama pants!"

"Pants are what you wear outside."

"Anything that covers your legs are pants as far as I'm concerned."

He turned back around and focused on the computer screen again. When I got out of the hot bath, I was cold. I put on a pair of thick wool pajamas that covered almost every square inch of my body. The only thing showing were my hands and face. My head and feet were covered.

I turned Alex's chair back around and sat on his lap.

"I'll wear my gold medal to bed sometime," I said. "Won't that be fun."

"Tonight?"

After a chuckle, I patted him on the shoulder. "No way. Not tonight. My entire body feels like it's been hit by a semi-truck."

"Tomorrow, then."

"Check back with me in a week."

"A week!"

"Make it two."

Alex grimaced at me.

"I'm just kidding."

I patted him on the chest. Affectionately. Although, I had a feeling I'd barely be able to walk tomorrow. It might be a week before my body could absorb any more punishment.

The thought made me laugh. But I kept it to myself. Alex wouldn't think it was funny calling sex with him punishment.

"The best thing for you to do tomorrow is to go for a long run," Alex said. "Or get on a set of skis again. Get the muscles moving. I always did that the day after a rough game."

He was right. It always amazed me how real athletes recovered from grueling competitions. We'd met a former biker who rode in the Tour de France. He was in the Olympic Village competing for his country in one of the events. The Tour was one of most grueling and difficult endurance feats in the world. He related that on their rest days, they rode seventy-five to a hundred miles.

For the reason Alex said. To keep their bodies from actually resting. It's hard to get the body going again at that level if it starts to shut down and relax.

I hoped I recovered quickly. There were bigger things to consider. How to rescue the Chinese girl for one. My complete focus could be turned to that now that the competition was over with. With the German dead, we wouldn't have to always be looking over our shoulders either.

"Do you know what you call a monkey who wins a gold medal at the Olympics?" Alex said with a wide grin on his face.

I let out a moan. Alex had a corny joke for every occasion. I think he looked them up on the internet when I wasn't around, so he could spring them on me.

"What?"

He was going to tell me anyway. I might as well humor him.

"A Chimpion."

"That's funny."

"A chimpion. Like champion. Do you get it?"

"I got it."

"You know a Knight still trumps a gold medalist," Alex said.

"It does not!"

"Yes it does."

Alex was knighted by the Queen of England. We were on our honeymoon in London and came across a terrorist plot to kill the Queen. Alex saved the day by flying the bomb out of London where it exploded in a desolate area. Where no one would get hurt. Alex almost died that day. The Queen was so appreciative, she knighted Alex, giving him England's highest civilian honor.

He'd been hard to live with for several months. He tried to get Bond and A-Rad to call him Sir Alex. That didn't go over so well.

"Nope," I said. "Gold medalist is above a Knight."

"How do you figure?"

"Knights are exclusive to England. The Olympics are world-wide. Every country participates. I'm the world champion. Nothing trumps that."

Alex stuck out his lower lip like I'd won the argument.

His tone turned serious.

"I'm proud of you," he said. "I'm serious. What you did was incredible."

"I couldn't have done it without you."

I planted a big kiss on his lips. It warmed my heart to be close to him.

Sitting on his lap was getting uncomfortable on my aching bones, so I stood to my feet and let out a loud moan when my muscles rebelled. I stood up like an old lady. Slightly hunched over.

The bed was calling me, but I wanted to talk to Alex about something.

"I've been thinking about it," I said. "We should take Brad's offer."

"I agree. It's the best thing to do. It'll be good to have our old jobs back. We'll do things differently this time."

"We'll call him tomorrow."

He nodded.

I leaned over and gave Alex another kiss even though I wasn't sure I'd be able to straighten again.

"What are you doing?" I asked.

"I'm looking at surveillance footage."

The images were still on his computer screen.

"What are you looking for?"

"That house in the village. You know. The one where they take the Chinese girl every day."

"I've been thinking about that, too."

"So have I. I'm not sure it's a good idea to storm that house. Even if I can get the security cameras turned off. I can see the headline, *Gold Medal Winner Arrested for Murder*. Your reputation will be ruined."

"I don't think we should rescue her there either."

"What did you have in mind?"

"They have to be keeping her somewhere. They bring her to that house during the day. They take her somewhere at night. I'm guessing outside the village. They wouldn't be running an operation like this with only one girl. I bet my gold medal there are more girls. If we find the house, we might find more girls to rescue."

"That sounds like a good idea. Tomorrow, we'll go to the house and do some surveillance. If he shows up with the girl, we'll follow him and see where he takes her."

I let out a sigh. I hoped my body would recover enough to go on a mission tomorrow. It had to be.

"What about the bomb?" I asked.

Alex shrugged.

"I've been thinking about that, too," I said. "When you pulled up security footage looking for the German, did you see him interact with anyone? I doubt he was acting alone."

He shook his head. "I didn't really notice."

"I think we should look again and see if he was with anyone. For our own peace of mind."

"I've got them saved."

I pulled up a chair. Alex's fingers started banging keystrokes on the keyboard. We scrolled through each one.

"Right there!" I said. "Who's that?"

The image was blurry but the man on the screen was definitely the German. He was talking to someone. The man he was talking to had his back to the screen.

"Let me zoom in," Alex said.

"He needs to turn around so we can see his face."

Alex put the feed in slow motion so we could study it carefully. The conversation appeared animated.

The man the German was talking to turned slightly.

Alex let out a gasp.

"Is that who I think it is?" he said.

He rewound the footage and played it again. Alex turned to me with his mouth still gaped open.

"It's definitely him," I said.

Adolf Roth. The German bobsledder. The one who made fun of Alex and his bobsled team. We hadn't seen him around for days. His team won the gold. He'd disappeared. Alex had wanted to razz him about beating them in the prelims.

"Why was Adolf Roth talking to the German?" Alex asked.

"Only one reason. He works for Hoffman too."

Epilogue

There was a bomb. Hidden in the bobsled. In some kind of new enclosure that allowed it to escape detection by the radiation sensors. Hoffman's intention had been to set it off at the closing ceremonies.

The bobsled course was constructed next to the arena. The starting line could be seen from inside the stadium. Adolf Roth and the German bobsled team were to make a run during the closing ceremonies wearing a camera on his helmet which would be shown on the big screen.

Roth intended to explode the dirty bomb shortly after they started. Tens of thousands of spectators would've been killed. When we saw Roth meeting with the German on the security cameras, we called Saul Geller who notified the security with the Olympic Committee and the plot was thwarted.

Roth was arrested and interrogated. He admitted to the plot. A suicide mission. Turned out he was one of Hoffman's zealots. Had been strategically trained over the years in the bobsled for that purpose.

With the bomb threat resolved, Alex and I focused on our own mission. We rescued twelve girls at a house outside the Olympic village. We drove them to the border of Switzerland and handed them off to the *Save The Girls* group who took them to a safe place.

Our work was done, so we decided to take a vacation to Lake Lucerne in Switzerland, with plans to go across the border to Lake Como in Italy. Some place where I wouldn't be recognized.

Saul Geller wanted us to come to Israel where I was a national hero. The people wanted to organize a parade. He wanted me to make appearances on television. Sign autographs.

Not going to happen.

"How do I explain it to the Jewish people?" he asked. "Where is their champion?"

That was their problem. No one had counted on me winning a medal. I had to get as low profile I could for awhile. Until people forgot about me. When I was on the gold medal stand, my face was visible for the whole world to see.

Saul had been in touch with Brad. They were trying to figure out what they were going to do about Esther.

Should she die in a tragic plane accident? A ski accident? Brad wanted to have a fake funeral for her. Saul wanted her to remain alive. She was a boost to the national pride of the country.

Esther didn't exist, I reminded Saul. It was my cover. Something had to be done. I couldn't come back to Israel for obvious reasons. I couldn't walk down the street without getting mobbed.

Smarter minds than me were working on it.

In the meantime, Alex and I stayed in places where I wouldn't be recognized. We had decided to accept Brad's offer. With all the excitement, we hadn't had a chance to call him and tell him.

On the way to Italy, we decided to do so.

He answered on the first ring. I didn't bother telling him who it was. He already knew.

"How is the most famous skier in the world?" he asked sarcastically.

"Yeah. Sorry about that."

"How was Lucerne?"

I didn't even ask how he knew we were there.

"Good," I said. "A little boring for us. We're not much for resting. Alex is here."

"Hi, Brad," Alex said.

"Hi Alex. Are you driving an SUV?"

"As a matter of fact I am."

"I figured. You'd need something bigger. With more head room. To contain Jamie's head."

"Ha. Ha," I said. "Very funny. I'm the same humble person I've always been."

That got a laugh out of both Alex and Brad. The banter actually surprised me. Brad was normally all business. He rarely joked around. He must be mellowing as he was getting older like all of us.

"We decided to accept your offer," Alex said. "If it's still open."

"It's not."

"What?" I blurted out in total surprise.

Alex pulled the car off to the side of the road.

"What do you mean?" Alex said. "The offer is not open anymore."

"We're ready to come back," I said.

"What did you expect, Jamie?" Brad asked. "Your face was seen by more than three billion people. Why did you have to win?"

"I wasn't supposed to win. I kind of got carried away."

"What were you thinking? You didn't go to Bavaria to win a medal. You were supposed to stop a terrorist attack."

"Which we did," I said.

"And you managed to become the most recognized person in the world. How are you supposed to run an undercover operation as a CIA operative?"

"In a couple of months all that will die down. I'll go back to being Jamie Steele. Owner of AJAX."

"I wish it were that easy."

"Sex traffickers don't watch the Olympics," I argued.

"How are you going to get in and out of those countries?"

"That could be my cover. Olympic athlete."

"That'll draw too much attention to the operation."

"I'll say I look like her if someone asks."

"Won't work. Too risky."

"She can dye her hair," Alex said.

"Alex! I love my hair."

"I'm trying to be helpful."

"Nobody even knows I have blonde hair," I said. "It was hidden under the cap."

"Sorry Jamie," Brad said.

"That's it. Just like that. You're abandoning us again. Like you did the first time."

"It's not my fault."

"What are we supposed to do?"

I could feel the tears welling up in my eyes. Before we decided, I was fine freelancing again. Now that we were willing to go back, I felt like a woman without a country. I was more welcomed in Israel than in my own country.

"If it's any consolation, we can still work with you, Alex," Brad said. "Nobody knows who you are. No offense intended."

I could feel the anger welling up inside of me. They wanted Alex but not me.

"What does that mean?" Alex asked.

I glared at him. It sounded like he was considering it.

"You can start AJAX up again," Brad said. "And the cyber lab. We'll give you back the yacht and the plane. It'll be business as usual on the cyber warfare front. We need you to take down Pok."

Brad was smart. He was making it impossible for me to stand in the way. Alex had been excited about going back as well. Especially about renewing his war with Pok.

"What am I supposed to do?" I said. "Twiddle my thumbs. Stand by my man."

"I have a job for you," Brad said.

Not what I had expected to hear. "You do? Why didn't you say so?"

"You're not going to like it."

"What is it?"

"I want you to take over Curly's job."

"You've got to be kidding me."

"I'm serious. I want you to train the next Jamie Austen."

"I'm not babysitting a bunch of snotty nose recruits who don't know their heads from their back sides."

"I need you to train a recruit I hired."

"Who?"

"A young girl."

"How young?"

"She's nineteen."

"Noooo way. I tried that with Bae. I don't have the patience."

It dawned on me. My mouth flew open.

"Don't tell me you hired Bae?" I said with exasperation.

"I did not."

"Thank goodness. I love Bae, but she's too impulsive. She doesn't listen to instruction. I'd rather have ten root canals than try to teach her anything."

"Where is Bae?" Brad asked.

"Last I heard, she finished college and is traveling around like that character in the book, Reeder Rich. Looking for bad guys."

"I didn't hire Bae."

"Who is it then?" I asked.

"Kale."

"I'm supposed to train a vegetable?"

"Her name is Kathie Lee Miller. She goes by Kale. She's as good as you. Maybe better."

"Then she doesn't need training."

"She doesn't know what you know. She doesn't have your experience. I need you to give it to her."

"Where will I train her?"

"At the Farm."

I moved my head from side to side in a lame attempt to release some tension. "Let us think about it."

"I need an answer right away," Brad said. "We need to go after Pok and I want to get this girl in the field as soon as possible."

"We'll do it," Alex blurted out before I could respond.

I glared at him.

He shrugged.

"Excellent," Brad said. "I'll see you Monday morning. First thing."

The line went dead. Before I could say anything.

So much for best laid plans. So much for our vacation at Lake Como.

"What were you thinking Alex?"

"I was thinking we get our lives back. The yacht and plane and the cyberlab. We don't have to start over."

"You get to start over. Without me."

"You'll be able to run missions on the side. You'll have to train that Kale girl out in the field. Like Curly did. I think you'll be a good trainer."

"Will I still be able to kill someone?"

"I promise."

"Kale, what kind of name is that?"

"I don't know."

"I don't even like kale."

"You'll be great."

"That Kale girl is going to rue the day she met me."

Not The End

Thank you for purchasing this novel from best-selling author, Terry Toler. As an additional thank you, Terry wants to give you a free gift.

Sign up for:
Updates
New Releases
Announcements
At terrytoler.com

We'll send you a copy of *The Book Club*, a Cliff Hangers mystery, free of charge.

READ MORE BOOKS FROM TERRY TOLER

Jamie Austen Thrillers

Read all the Jamie Austen Thrillers. They must be good. They've been number one on Amazon in ten different countries. Click on the link below.

THE JAMIE AUSTEN THRILLERS (12 book series) Kindle Edition (amazon.com)

https://amzn.to/3vmPUy7

Cliff Hangers Mystery Series

Who wants to read a good mystery? We've got you covered! Read the Cliff Hangers where homicide detective, Cliff Ford, solves crimes in Chicago, with help from his wife Julia. These books have everything Terry Toler is known for. Page turning suspense, a hint of romance, and an ending you won't see coming.

The Cliff Hangers Mystery Series (4 book series)
Kindle Edition (amazon.com)
https://amzn.to/36WX3go

About Terry

Terry Toler is an Amazon international # 1 best-selling and award-winning author. He writes clean fiction with a message and life-changing nonfiction. He's a public speaker, entrepreneur, and has authored more than forty books.

Sign up for his newsletter where you'll get free stuff, exclusive content, and news of releases and promotions. He can be followed at terrytoler.com.

If you like his books, please take a few minutes to leave a review on Amazon. We really appreciate it. It helps draw more readers to his books. Thanks!

Made in the USA
Las Vegas, NV
22 September 2025